T0150013

GODS
AND
FATHERS

GODS
AND
FATHERS

JAMES LEPORE

THE
STORY PLANT

The Story Plant
The Aronica-Miller Publishing Project, LLC
P.O. Box 4331
Stamford, CT 06907

Jacket design by Barbara Aronica Buck

Print ISBN-13: 978-1-61188-029-8
E-book ISBN-13: 978-1-61188-030-4

Visit our website at www.thestoryplant.com

For information, address The Story Plant.

First Story Plant Printing: February 2012

Printed in The United States of America

Also by James LePore

A World I Never Made
Blood of My Brother
Sons and Princes
Anyone Can Die

Acknowledgments

I am grateful to Greg Ziemak, as always, for reading and commenting, to Bill Evans for supporting me emotionally for many years, to Tom Connelly and Greg Barber, for keeping the fire of friendship going, to Peter Dalton, for his faith in me, and to John Egan, for his loyalty, his generosity of spirit, and his stories, one or two of which may have found their way into this novel. These are BC guys who, like it or not, are stuck with me.

Thank you, also, to my police consultants, Bob Mahon and Frank Sharpe, not only for their expertise, but for their service. We take our police for granted, but there is no way we could work and play and raise our families without them doing what they do.

My deepest gratitude extends again to my friend and editor, Lou Aronica. I struggled with this novel. If it's any good, it's because of him.

To my wife Karen.

To every man upon this earth
Death cometh soon or late.
And how can man die better
Than facing fearful odds,
For the ashes of his fathers,
And the temples of his Gods.

Horatius, Thomas Babington Macaulay

Prologue

Manhattan, April 4, 1993, 3PM

Matt DeMarco, six foot tall and a trim one-hundred and eighty pounds, his gray, light-weight suit and navy blue tie simple and conservative, stood erect and brushed a hand across his forehead, his fingertips lightly touching his short, thick, black hair as he did. His chiseled face and dark, keenly observant eyes were still marked with the quiet but lethal pride of the Marine Corps ten years after his discharge. He had packed a lot into those ten years, finishing college and sprinting through law school. Not to mention a marriage—now on the rocks—and a six-year-old son. This moment was a culmination of sorts, his first summation in his first murder trial for the Manhattan District Attorney's office, after six years of toiling in the vineyards of misdemeanors and lesser felonies.

He looked at the jury, sweeping his hooded, hawk-like eyes slowly from left to right along the front row, and then right to left along the back, stopping long enough to make eye contact with each one, the first time since his opening statement that he'd looked directly at any of them. He had worked on his summation for two days, but he did not know until this moment how he was going to begin. All sixteen faces were grim, determined, all sixteen pairs of eyes locked on his. Seeing this, he made his decision.

Turning away, he walked over to the defense table and looked squarely at Wael Hakimi. Wael, nineteen, his eyes burning with hatred, stared back. In his peripheral vision, DeMarco could see young Hakimi's lawyer, Kendall Jones, glance up at him, squinting, a suspicious look in his slitted eyes, his full lips slightly open, as if he were about to speak, or gathering himself to pounce.

"Taqiyya," Matt said, in a stage whisper, keeping his eyes locked on Wael's. The young man raised his shoulders and leaned back slightly in his chair, as if he were getting ready to howl. Their eyes, unblinking, stayed locked. Matt stepped closer. When he was a foot away from the edge of the polished wooden table, he leaned even closer, and said it again, a little louder: "Taqiyya."

Jones bolted upright. "Objection! Objection! He is trying to intimidate my client. I move for a mistrial." Jones, at six-four, his burnished skin very dark, nearly black, was an imposing figure at all times, but especially when he rose to his full height to thunder his objections. His physical presence and his bellowing Jamaican accent were, Matt knew, his best weapons in a limited arsenal.

"Sit down, Mr. Jones," said the judge, Joel Coen, peering at the defense lawyer over his reading glasses. The silver-haired jurist, with twenty years as a prosecutor and twenty as a criminal court judge under his belt, had been a model of neutrality throughout the two week trial, but there was no question in anyone's mind that he was tired of Jones' theatrics. "This is fair comment," Coen continued. "There has been quite a bit of testimony about this word, this concept."

"Your honor," said Jones, stretching his frame to its fullest and leaning toward the judge, who sat some twenty feet away, within leaping distance, "Mr. DeMarco was staring at my client with contempt in his eyes. He was only inches away. This is an outrage!"

"You summed up for over two hours, Mr. Jones. There

were no objections from Mr. DeMarco. This is closing argument. Sit down. And by the way, for the record, Mr. DeMarco was standing several feet away from the defendant, and his tone of voice was not intimidating in any way."

DeMarco had walked to the far side of his table while this colloquy was taking place, positioning himself so that he had Jones, Judge Coen and the jury in his field of vision. He waited while the scowling Jones settled his tall, angular body slowly, theatrical disgust in every movement, into his chair. Then the ex-Marine turned prosecutor walked slowly to the front of the jury box, swept the panel's taut faces one more time, and said the word again: "*Taqiyya,*" this time in a normal voice, but spitting the word out, like the bad taste that it was.

"You heard the defendant talk about it on the stand," he continued: "*Permission given by the Koran to lie to infidels, if it advances the cause of Islam.* Mr. Jones objected. He didn't want you to know about this strange principle. I'm sure you understand why, after hearing the defendant testify.

"And then there's *namus,*" Matt continued. "The quaint cultural tradition that permits Muslims to murder their wives or daughters or sisters if they have dishonored the family, for example by dating an American man, or, in this case, *boy.* The defendant's own medical expert, Dr. Zakharia, told you all about *namus*, and how it drove Mr. Rahim temporarily insane. *Allegedly* temporarily insane."

"Objection!" shouted Jones, rising again, "I demand a side bar!"

"Are you *requesting* a side bar, Mr. Jones?" Coen asked, his voice calm.

"Yes and yes again!"

"Excuse the jury," Coen said, nodding to his court clerk. "Stay where you are, counsel."

"You are a Jew," Jones said, when the jury was gone. Jones paused, the scowl still on his face, the whites of his large eyes seeming to expand as he waited—*for effect*, DeMarco, who had returned to stand behind his counsel table, said to himself. *He thinks he's back in Los Angeles, talking to a post–Watts jury. Unbelievable.* The murmur from the gallery—filled mostly with reporters, but also with a sprinkling of Muslims from around the five boroughs of New York—came abruptly to a halt, as all eyes turned toward the bench.

"I'm listening, Mr. Jones," said Coen.

"As such, given the events of February 26 at the World Trade Center," Jones said, "you are in a conspiracy to deny my client a fair trial, to convict him unjustly."

"In a conspiracy with whom?"

"With Mr. DeMarco, with Mr. Healy, with the Chief Justice."

"Anyone else?"

"The Governor."

"I am holding you in contempt, Mr. Jones," Coen said. "I will set the fine after the trial. I will also ask my court clerk to prepare a formal contempt complaint. You will be notified."

"You yourself are in contempt. Of justice."

"I am going to bring the jury back," Coen said, ignoring this last comment from Jones. "Mr. DeMarco will resume his summation. You are free to object at any time. How the jury will react to your objections, I do not know. They may like them. Then again, they may not. I will rule on each one as and when it is made. Please be seated."

Matt DeMarco had also killed someone in a fit of passion: his Drill Instructor at Parris Island in 1979. The DI—Johnny Taylor by name—a large Southerner with a foul mouth and a propensity to spew spittle when he screamed, which was most of the time, had ridden everyone hard, but Matt especially so. Eighteen and very raw, thrown out of high school for breaking a classmate's nose—twice—Matt had prepared for boot camp by memorizing Basic Drill and Ceremony, Marine

Corps Rank, the Eleven General Orders for a Sentry and the entire Marines' Hymn. The more he knew, the more Taylor hated him. *Dago, greaseball, guinea, wop,* Matt heard these words all day, every day. Often the DI's large red face was an inch away, his breath awful, his spit spray disgusting.

One day they marched ten miles through a swamp to a desolate training area. His platoon formed a circle around Taylor, who picked one out and then another to demonstrate lock and hold skills, used to neutralize an enemy, or kill him, in close quarters. When it came to Matt's turn, the DI, a tall muscular man of around thirty-five, added a few sharp elbows to his ribs before disengaging, causing Matt to bend over and gasp in pain. *Dago pussy,* Taylor said, himself bending over to put his face as close as possible to Matt's, the saliva flying. Matt, six-two, a hundred and eighty-five wiry pounds, cat-like when cornered, an ancient mix of Italian and Arabian blood running through his veins, took a deep breath, stood quickly, stepped behind the DI, locked his left forearm under his throat, and, covering Taylor's mouth with his right hand, paused for a split second to let the spray-spitter contemplate his short future. Then he yanked Taylor's head back hard, severing his cervical spine, killing him instantly.

Matt had been hoping for three weeks that he would not snap, knowing that when he did, it would be full out and in no way controllable. But he was lucky. The other platoons in his company had spread out in the swamp to train. No one except his own platoon, reduced from forty-four to twenty-six trainees because of Taylor's insanity, had seen the incident. And if they had, how would they know it wasn't a lock-and-hold exercise gone wrong, a tragic accident? That was Matt's story, and all twenty-six members of his platoon backed him up. Many of them, sweating, thirsty, exhausted, actually thought it *was* an accident. Matt was confined to quarters for three weeks while everyone involved was interviewed. All stood tall.

Matt got a break. The Marine Corps was suspicious, but there was no hard evidence, and his father had been a Marine, had served in the 3rd Marine Division's Amphibious Corps in World War II, had landed on Iwo Jima on February 19, 1945, and received the Navy Cross for his valor there. Matt had to start basic training over again, but there was no court martial, nothing on his record. He was watched and screamed at, but never pushed beyond his limit again. He came to believe that he had done the Corps a favor by eliminating a sadist in its midst. For reasons that he surmised, but could never confirm, after specialty training in South Carolina, he spent the rest of his four year enlistment doing shore patrol, first in San Diego, and then in Naples. His commanding officer in San Diego suggested he take up boxing, which he did with a vengeance, winning the 1980 and 1981 Armed Forces Middleweight Championship at Naval Base Ventura County before moving on to Italy.

Matt did not, however, see a kindred spirit in young Wael Hakimi, who had stabbed his fifteen-year-old sister Aleah to death in their Lower Manhattan apartment while she was talking with her boyfriend on the phone. The boyfriend had testified. *Wael*, the girl had said, *Wael*... What did her voice sound like? Matt had asked. *Terrified*. What did you do? *I called 911*. Why? *She was afraid of Wael. He had threatened her before.* The responding officers had found Rahim, covered with her blood, trying to stuff his sister's body into the building's incinerator.

No, Matt had no sympathy for Wael, whose concept of honor was to kill his sister, then lie about it, to tell the jury that he had no memory of the evening in question. *They were watching television and the next thing he knew he was in a squad car.* Sure, Wael, of course.

Matt could have recited the alphabet for his summation and sat down. There was no way the kid was going to be acquitted. And he wasn't. When the verdict came back, Matt nodded his thanks to the jury, and watched as Wael was cuffed and led away. In the wide marble-floored hall outside the courtroom, his voice echoing off of the domed ceiling, Matt spoke briefly to reporters and then left, heading for Manny's, a local bar popular with lawyers and judges and high-ranking cops.

Outside the courthouse, across the street in Foley Square, television cameramen and reporters were gathered in front of Kendall Jones, who had bolted after the verdict to continue the trial in the media. Matt stepped across and stopped on a patch of grass some thirty feet to the right of this crowd.

"There is no justice for minorities in America," Jones was saying, still in that booming voice, still scowling, "especially now, especially for Muslims. Wael Hakimi is the victim in this case..." Matt tuned him out, and was about to leave when he noticed a stocky, powerful-looking man, swarthy, with a five-o'clock shadow, in his late thirties or early forties, standing in the small crowd of passers-by that had gathered behind Jones, looking at him — at Matt. Then Matt remembered that on the day the trial began two weeks ago, Wael had turned several times to look at someone in the back of the courtroom, a dark complected man with a bluish-black shadow of a beard, a man, Matt remembered thinking to himself, who needed to shave twice a day. A man who had, as far as Matt knew, not appeared again. Was this him?

Before Matt could answer his own question, his boss, Jon Healy, the Manhattan District Attorney, appeared at his side.

"Fuck this bullshit," Healy said. "Let's have a drink."

"I was on my way to Manny's."

Healy, only five years Matt's senior, a tall handsome Irishman with a red face, a thick head of wavy, dark brown hair and sharp, all-seeing blue eyes, nodded. "I'm buying," he said. Matt watched the stocky man for a second or two as he walked toward the far end of the square, then turned to join his boss.

"I just spoke to Coen," Healy said. "He wants me to file a criminal contempt complaint against Jones."

"Good."

"I told him no."

"Why?"

"It'll just give him another soap box. And I'd lose."

"I guess Coen didn't like the 'You are a Jew' comment."

"Correct."

Manny's was only a block away, on Broadway. The two lawyers, carrying their suit jackets over their shoulders, both tall — one a savvy politician from a rich, well-connected family, the other, forced out of high school for assault, his connections all wrong, a street fighter who had just tried, and won, his first murder case — cast long shadows on the sidewalk ahead of them as they walked in the last bright light of a beautiful spring day. Near the bar's entrance, Healy took hold of Matt's forearm to stop his forward motion. "Wait," he said, "how are things at home?"

"I left."

"When?"

"Sunday."

"Where are you staying?"

"My dad's on City Island."

"How's he doing?"

"Two weeks."

"I'm sorry, Matt."

Healy let go of Matt's arm, and they remained silent for the time it took a small group of judge's law clerks, men and women not too much younger than Matt, to pass and enter Manny's. One or two nodded diffidently at Matt and congratulated him, the rising star in the Manhattan DA's powerful universe. One of the law clerks was a tall, striking blonde who looked straight ahead as they passed.

"What's going on there?" Healy asked, nodding toward the blonde as she stepped off the sidewalk, her stockinged legs long and graceful, into Manny's.

"I can see her openly now," Matt replied.

"How did Debra take it?"

"Not well."

"Did you tell her about your friend?"

"She knew."

"And your boy?"

"He'll be okay."

Matt sized up his boss, who he knew was doing the same to him. Healy's offer, made subtly over the last two weeks, in the elegant code used by all good politicians, was simple. Win *The People v. Hakimi*—the first honor-killing case ever in Manhattan—*and you'll get all the top murder cases. You're a very tough kid and can take the heat. You'll be a star. I'll get re-elected.* Simple. *Until I don't need you any more* was of course never said, never even hinted at. But Matt heard it nevertheless.

"Let's go in," Healy said.

"No, I changed my mind."

"Why?"

"My father. I should get back."

"Okay, but you deserve one drink. That was a huge win today."

"A first year law student could have won that case."

"I meant politically."

"So I'm your star A.D.A. now?" he said. "Your gladiator?"

"Yes."

"You don't want me getting depressed."

"Right."

"Are you my Caligula?"

"Always with the ancient Romans," Healy said. "They're dead. And they were crazy."

"Not all of them."

"You have a trust problem."

"Politicians scare me."

"Caligula was a tyrant, not a politician."

"His palace guard killed him. He thought they were his friends."

"Have *you* ever killed anybody, Matt?"

"Not without a good reason," Matt said, smiling, deciding to let Healy think he was taking this question as a joke, though he knew it wasn't. *So he knows,* Matt thought. *So be it. I was cleared, honorably discharged. I've got other things to worry about.*

His father, the toughest guy he would ever meet, the ex-jarhead who had survived, unscathed, at the age of twenty, five Pacific island invasions, would be dead in two weeks of lung cancer, the only enemy he couldn't beat. His marriage of seven years had ended bitterly. His six-year-old son seemed distant, already taking his mother's side. Could that be possible? Or was he just paranoid, guilty? And then there was the young blonde law clerk he was seeing. There was something different about her now. Her ambition seemed to be showing for the first time, like an old-fashioned slip beneath the hem of a skirt. Or had he missed it before? Yes, lots of other things to worry about, but these did not include the size of his heart or the fight in him. These, he knew, would not fail him, no matter what the future held.

1.

When he saw the silver BMW parked in front of the garage, and the lights on in his house as he turned into the driveway, Matt DeMarco knew that his son, Michael, a graduate student in Boston, was home, and that his weekend would be ruined. When Michael was a boy, Matt, chafing under the rigid visitation schedule imposed by his bitter ex-wife, had yearned for spontaneity in his relationship with his son. Now he dreaded it.

He took a deep breath of the cold night air as he turned the key in the front door, letting it out slowly as he entered and hung his winter coat in the hall closet. The television was on in the living room, where the remains of a half-eaten pizza sat congealing on the coffee table. In the kitchen he put his briefcase on a counter and splashed some scotch over ice. He could hear the thud-thud-thud of a lopsided load in the washing machine in the adjacent laundry room, and, over that, the angry cadences of rap music coming from upstairs. Back in the living room, he flicked off the television and then headed to his bedroom at the back of the house, shaking his head as he went, trying to ignore the pizza, the misuse of the washing machine, and his son's nasty music.

In the bedroom, a small sanctuary with a sitting area facing a fireplace and a study tucked into a corner, he placed his drink on his dresser and changed into khakis and an old sweater. As he turned to pick up his scotch, his eye was drawn to the nearby gleaming gold frame of a color photograph of him and his son taken on the day of Michael's graduation from high school in Manhattan. He picked it up and stared at it.

They were standing side by side at the ornate front door of the Parnell International School on Central Park West. Michael's thick head of hair was a deep, lustrous brownish-black, like Matt's, but unlike Matt's it contained streaks of light brown, as if sand had been mixed with ebony, the result of his mother's northern Italian genes. Other than those sandy streaks, they could, from not too great a distance, be taken for twins. They were both the same lithe and graceful six-foot in height; they both had the same wiry, hard muscled bodies, and both had the same deep-set raven-black eyes above high, wide cheekbones and full lips. Their dusky complexions, aquiline noses, and hooded, piercing gazes spoke of a bloodline that had spawned desert nomads and medieval warriors, its feral nature never quite yielding to the civilizing influences of Europe and America. That nature, Matt knew, thinking of the scene he had made in court that afternoon, was never far beneath the surface. Of all the facts of his life, it was the hardest and most durable, almost completely resistant to the softening forces of time and experience, like a rocky outcrop still sharp and jagged, and lethal, though the sea's waves had broken over it for centuries.

Matt focused on the photograph again, on the two DeMarco men as they stood next to each other on that day six years ago. He had chosen this picture because he and his son were together and smiling, a rarity. But of course it had been a mistake, wishful thinking. They were not really together, and the smiles were not real smiles. Matt's was forced, and you could tell, if you looked hard enough, that, lurking beneath his son's was a smirk. A smirk that had evolved into a more or less permanent sneer as the years passed and the barren ground between them became impassable.

Next to this picture was one of Matt and his father, taken at Rose Hill on the day Matt graduated from law school in 1986. Seven years later Matt, Sr., who had raised Matt alone in the Gunhill Road neighborhood of the Bronx before buying a small house on City Island, was dead from lung cancer. Like his son and grandson, Matteo DeMarco, Sr., was dark and charismatically handsome, one of the cigarettes that killed him dangling from his half-smiling lips. It was the money that his father left him that had enabled Matt to buy his Pound Ridge house and still keep his small apartment in Manhattan. The guy was a worker, and a fighter, Matt thought, the same half-smile crossing his face for a second, remembering the daily early morning calisthenics and the weekly shooting lessons that were as much a part of his childhood as spelling and math.

The ringing of his cell phone broke Matt's brief reverie. He returned the picture of himself and his son to its place on the dresser, and looked at his phone's screen. The call was from Jon Healy. He thought for a moment, then decided to let it go to voice mail. As he made his way through the living room, Matt was surprised to see Michael in the entry foyer talking to two young men. He had not heard the front doorbell ring, which was not surprising since the rap music, or whatever it was, was still blaring. He was about to turn toward the kitchen, to avoid an introduction, but something about the two men, presumably friends of Michael's, made him change his mind. They did not look like the pseudo-hip, superficial young men, with their spiked hair, polished fingernails and meticulous, form-fitting clothes that his son usually gravitated toward.

These two were a bit older, perhaps in their late-twenties. Both wore jeans, expensive leather jackets and the bulky type of shoes that looked like if they kicked you, could do some damage. Both were swarthy, with several days' growth of black beard. The taller one was balding, his dark eyes heavy-lidded. The shorter one had a crooked nose and a head of thick, black, wiry hair. They seemed civilized enough as they chatted with Michael, smiling at something he was saying, standing casually

with their hands in their jacket pockets. But there was a hard-
ness about them, in their eyes and in their bearing—intensity
that he knew his unworldly son, eager to be cool, would either
be oblivious of or think fascinating—that Matt did not like.

Neither of them looked at Matt as he entered the foyer.
Michael ignored him too for a couple of long and uncomfort-
able seconds, then turned to greet him.

"Hi," he said. "I didn't know you were home."

"My briefcase is on the kitchen counter."

"I didn't see it."

"I didn't know you were coming. Is your mother away?"

"They're in St. Moritz."

Sometimes Matt's ex-wife, Debra, and her husband, Basil,
let Michael use their Park Avenue apartment when they were
away, and he was in town to see his girlfriend, Yasmine, who
was a senior at Columbia. Sometimes—for reasons Matt
could not quite understand—they didn't, which is when
Michael condescended to visit him, if you could call it that, at
his place in Pound Ridge, the heavily wooded, extremely quiet
enclave fifty miles due north of New York City.

"And you are?" Matt said to the taller of Michael's friends.

"This is Adnan," Michael said, "and Ali. They work for
Basil. We're going out."

Matt stood motionless, looking first Adnan and then Ali
in the eye, waiting for one of them to put a hand out, but neither did. Instead each nodded slightly and made half-hearted
attempts at smiles. Fake smiles.

"Where are you going?" Matt asked. He was curious
because he knew of no place in the area that was hip enough
for the likes of Michael and his new friends.

Michael rolled his eyes at this question, then, shrugging
his shoulders, said, "Greenwich, we're not sure." Turning to his
two friends, he said, "come on up."

"Wait," Matt said, before any of them could move.

"What?" Michael said, the irritation in his voice sharp
and unmistakable.

"You need to move your car," said Matt, his voice measured, under control. "It's blocking the garage and it's starting to snow."

Matt met Michael's glare with one of his own, tired of these small battles but unable to stop engaging in them, even though the war had been lost long ago.

"Sure, Dad, no problem," Michael said, feigning agreeability, but making little effort to hide his real feeling, which Matt could see was closer to disgust than mere irritation. *Because I asked him to move his car.*

Matt watched as the three went up to the second floor, which contained Michael's room and a second bedroom that used to function as Matt's office. He waited, pondering these two new, and different, friends of his son's, until he heard the door to Michael's room click shut. Then he retrieved the pizza and brought it into the kitchen, where he picked up his brief-case. Back in his study he returned Jon Healy's call—without listening to the message—but the D.A. did not answer.

He turned on his computer and, sipping the remains of his scotch, turned his mind away from Michael and onto work, something that had not been so easy to do when his troubles with his son first began, but that—for better or worse he could not be sure—had gotten easier over the years.

He was trying a case in which an illegal Mexican immigrant had been charged with the rape and murder, by stabbing, of a young black prostitute in a courtyard of the Lillian Wald housing project on Manhattan's Lower East Side. The NYPD had installed an extensive video surveillance system in and around the Wald Homes in 1997. Despite relentless vandalism, the camera in the courtyard of 12 Avenue D still worked ten years later, and the thirty-year-old defendant, Mauro Morales, had been caught on tape. Mauro offered an alibi defense through his grandmother. *They were watching American Idol in her apartment in East Harlem. The tape was grainy. That wasn't her grandson. He would never do such a thing.*

The problem for Mauro was that DNA taken from sperm found in the girl's vagina matched his. Also, the jacket that the attacker was wearing on the tape, with a picture of John Lennon painted on the back clearly visible, was found in Mauro's girlfriend's place in Brooklyn. Fabric samples found at the scene matched this very jacket.

The problem for Matt was that the judge trying the case, Pete Sullivan, had taken it upon himself to harshly cross-examine the grandmother, his tone of voice increasingly sarcastic and incredulous with each new question. Matt had gone easy on her. She was lying to help her grandson. The jury would see that, might even respect it. Also, it never paid to beat up old ladies in front of juries. They all had grandmothers. They might get mad enough to give your defendant a pass.

In the middle of Sullivan's questioning, Matt knocked a glass carafe of water onto the floor, shattering it. Everyone was startled. The bailiff cut herself cleaning up the shards. The jury was excused. While they were out, Matt politely asked Sullivan to apologize to the witness and to tell the jury to disregard his unnecessary intrusion into the case. *That's what a competent judge who had temporarily lost his mind would do,* Matt had said. Sullivan went berserk and had probably called Healy. And now Healy was calling him.

Matt searched through Westlaw, the legal search engine, for a case that would help him, but none of them did. When judges lent their authority in this way to a prosecution, the convictions that inevitably followed were just as inevitably overturned by appellate courts. *A fair trial,* one court said, *difficult as that concept might be of precise definition, definitely does not include the court acting as a second prosecutor.* He e-mailed this opinion — as it happened, from the New York Court of Appeals, New York's highest court — to Healy to lay the groundwork for his explanation of his stunt in court today. If Healy supported him, he might actually get Sullivan to say and do the right thing, which was Matt's only hope of successfully defending his conviction at the next level. But Healy wouldn't, Matt was all but certain. He was a publicity whore who lived for conviction headlines. Appellate reversals meant nothing to him. The case could always be tried again.

He reached for his cell phone to call Healy again, but before he could start dialing, the music from Michael's room suddenly invaded his bedroom, its volume so high that it would make talking impossible. Trying to control his anger, Matt made it to his son's room where the noise was so loud the door was shaking. Matt knocked as hard as he could but got no response. He was about to kick the door in, his frustration building with every *motherfucker* coming over Michael's fancy speakers, when, simultaneously, Adnan emerged from the hall bathroom, zipping his fly, and the music stopped.

"The door is not locked," Michael's friend said, smiling his faux smile, deigning to look directly at Matt through his lowered eyelids, still in his leather coat.

Matt said nothing. *What is it with this kid*, he thought, *why is he so cocky?*

"What do you do, Adnan?" Matt said. He had waited a few seconds, his eyes locked on the young Arab's, before speaking.

"What do I do?"

"Yes, for a living."

It was Adnan's turn to pause, his face serious now, the smile gone.

"This is a question I am not used to answering," he said, finally.

"Do you think it disrespectful?" Matt asked.

"Not the question," Adnan replied. "The tone."

"Ah, the *tone*," Matt said. *It was meant to be disrespectful, as you are to me in my house.* But before he could speak these words, Michael's door opened and he and Ali came out of his room.

"Dad," Michael said. "What's up?"

"The music, Michael."

"The volume control got stuck."

"The volume control got stuck?"

"Yes."

Matt shook his head, then, nodding in Adnan's direction, said, "Your friend won't tell me what he does for a living."

"What?"

"He thinks I disrespected him."

"They were just leaving," Michael said, shaking his head again. More disgust.

"Good. What about you?"

"I'm staying in."

Staying in, Matt thought. That's a new one. Before he could assimilate this, Adnan said, "Yes, we go." Gesturing to Ali to follow, he turned and went quickly down the stairs. Michael, following them, grabbed his coat from the hall closet, and walked with his two Arab friends out to their car.

Matt watched through the mullioned windows of the front door as Michael, Adnan and Ali shook hands and did some kind of ghetto chest hug before the two Arabs got in their car, a black Mercedes sedan, which was parked at the curb, and drove off through the now steadily falling snow.

Matt was still in the foyer, standing at the foot of the stairs, when Michael returned. He watched his son as he took off his coat, carefully brushed the snow from it, and hung it in the closet.

"Who were those guys?" Matt asked, when this coat removal ritual, which took too much time to be anything but affected nonchalance, was finished, and Michael had no choice but to turn toward him.

"I told you, they do odd jobs for Basil," Michael answered, facing his father, standing slightly slouched, slightly bored. "We hang out sometimes."

"I thought you were going out?"

"You scared them away."

"Why can't you stay at your mother's when they're away?"

"I told you, Basil's worried about security."

Though this statement was challengeable on several levels, Matt let it pass. The marriage six years ago of Debra DeMarco, nee Rusillo, and Basil al-Hassan, a rich and handsome Syrian businessman, had marked the beginning of the end of Matt's long and tortured fight for a place in his son's heart. Armed with the ultimate weapon—her new husband's money—Debra had made quick work of destroying the last vestiges of Matt's hopes. A penthouse on Park Avenue, a beach house in East Hampton, a flat in Paris, a "cottage" in Bermuda, clothes and cars virtually on demand, Matt had no way of competing with all this, and no way of expressing his anger—until tonight.

"What about Mina?" Matt asked.

"What about her?"

"Why aren't you seeing her?"

"She's studying."

"Studying?"

"Yes, studying. You keep repeating what I say. She's a student. Students study."

This statement was delivered dismissively, not sarcastically. *You're stupid, Dad. I'm tired of you. Why am I bothering with you?* is what Matt heard, and it occurred to him, with a clarity that shocked him after all these muddled and painful years of effort and rejection, effort and rejection, *ad nauseum*, that he could not hurt Michael, that his own son was indifferent to him, and this was a blow, and strangely a release.

"Well, your friends are assholes, and you are too, Michael. You're an arrogant, shallow asshole. Where you came from, I don't know. But not from me."

"That could be. Maybe Mom had an affair—like you did—and I'm not your son. Do I care? No, I don't. Can I go upstairs now? I'll leave in the morning."

In the kitchen, Matt poured himself another scotch. He took the pizza out of the refrigerator and sat down to eat it, surprised to find that he actually had an appetite. Until tonight, despite the bad cards he had drawn, he had never stopped trying to break through to his son. It's over, he said to himself, *over and done*. He's not your son. He's Debra's son, Basil's son. You lost him a long time ago.

He finished the pizza and was wrapping the garbage to take out in the morning when the doorbell rang. He looked out the kitchen window and saw that it was snowing heavily.

Those idiots, he thought, they're probably stuck someplace. No choice but to let them in. But when he swung open the front door, it wasn't Adnan and Ali, but his friends Jack McCann and Clarke Goode, homicide detectives who he had worked with for many years, standing facing him. He could see their unmarked car at the curb, and behind it, blocking his driveway, a Pound Ridge patrol car, its engine running and headlights on, two uniformed officers in the front seat. McCann, a florid Irishman whose blue eyes were usually lit by some inner secret joke, looked grim, and Goode, a gnarled black man who never failed to greet Matt with a big smile, was not smiling. Far from it.

"Come in. What's up?" Matt said. Then, nodding toward the street where the patrol car sat: "What's with the uniforms?"

The two detectives stepped into the foyer.

"Take your coats off," Matt said. He could see they were dressed for work, sport jackets and ties on under their trench coats.

"Matt..." McCann said.

"Talk, Jack," Matt said. "Is somebody dead?"

"Is Michael home?" Goode asked. He had not taken off his coat, and neither had McCann.

"That's his car out there," Matt said. "You know that."

"Where is he?"

"He's upstairs."

Matt looked from McCann to Goode, then back to McCann; looked in the eyes of each, and did not like what he saw. "What about Michael?" he asked.

"We're here to arrest him," McCann replied.

"For what?" *Drugs*, Matt thought, *good, let the kid get a taste of the pain he's always inflicting on others. Him and his two Arab suppliers.*

"For murder, Matt," Goode said. "His girlfriend was shot dead today in her apartment. Yasmine Hayek. I'm going upstairs." Goode, burly and very strong, headed toward the nearby staircase. Matt stepped quickly in front of the detective, blocking his way. "No you're not," he said.

Matt knew Goode's story: raised on the streets, a Desert Storm veteran, a decorated patrolman. But Matt's other nature, the one that killed Johnny Taylor, announced itself with a whoosh of blood that swelled his brain and turned the low thrum that always murmured, sleeping lightly, somewhere in Matt's psyche, to a too-familiar wild drum beat. He stood there, waiting for Goode, now a predator in his house, to try to force his way past him. Because then it would have to be over Matt's dead, or unconscious, body. *Murder,* Goode had said. *Murder.* The word echoed in his head, the dry, metallic taste of fight night once again in his mouth. *I'll kill this cocksucker,* he thought, *I'll kill him if he tries to get past me. It'll be easy.*

Goode did not blink, but after a long two seconds, in which each man's eyes remained locked on the other's, he did step back. Reaching into his inside coat pocket he pulled out some papers, the kind with the old fashioned light blue backers that the State of New York uses for service of legal papers on its citizens, and handed them to Matt.

"There's a search warrant there, too," said McCann, stepping between his two friends. "Come on, Matt." The detective put his hand, gently, on Matt's bicep. "We asked for this detail. You're a friend. It's bad shit. Very bad. Come on. I need a drink."

"I'm going up with you," Matt said, still looking at Clarke Goode, but the drum beat getting softer, the monster retreating to its cave. He doesn't know how lucky he is, he thought. Me too.

"You can't, Matt," Goode said. "You're lucky Healy let us be the ones to do this."

"We had to fight him," McCann said. "Come on, I need a drink."

His heart rate slowing, his head clearing, Matt allowed himself to be led into the kitchen by McCann, where the Irishman, who had been there many times, poured them each out three fingers of bourbon neat. Matt drank his down in one gulp, then picked up the warrants: *Murder...probable cause...Michael DeMarco...Yasmine Hayek...the entire premises and a late model BMW automobile...computer and/or computer hard drive...*

"Pete Sullivan," Matt said, seeing the signature on the warrants. "When did you bring these to him?"

"About an hour ago."

"Where was he?"

"At Manny's, where else?"

"He hates my guts."

"He's a jerkoff," McCann replied. "But the warrants are good."

Matt knew what this meant, but remained silent, staring at his detective friend, making sure he had heard right.

"I can't believe it," he said, finally, shaking his head. "The kid's a..." Matt paused, thinking of what he had called his son, to his face, just a few minutes ago, but not willing to utter the word to McCann. "He's a snob, Jack," he said. "A wise guy, a momma's boy, but he's no killer. Drugs, I could see, but not murder. I know this kid. Talk to me. What do you have?"

"His prints, of course," McCann replied. "The surveillance tape, the doorman, e-mails."

"What kind of e-mails?"

"Arguments."

"Lover's quarrels? Come on, Jack."

"Your son can get pretty nasty."

Matt let this pass. He had no choice. It was true.

"What about a weapon?" he asked.

"Here it is," said Clarke Goode, stepping into the kitchen and holding up a Ziploc bag with a nine-millimeter pistol and detached silencer in it. Michael stood next to him, his face drained of its usual color, but his eyes haughty. His hands were cuffed behind his back.

"That's not mine," Michael said.

"It was in the bottom drawer of his dresser," said Goode. In his other hand he was holding another Ziploc evidence bag, a large one, with Michael's Blackberry and laptop in it.

Matt looked directly in his son's eyes. He saw no fear in them, just the same contempt for inferiors—that would of course include McCann and Goode — that was his default attitude when dealing with people outside his circle of wealth and privilege.

"Is this a joke, Dad?" Michael said. "Did you put these two idiots up to this?"

"Don't say another word, Michael," Matt said, his voice clear and sharp. "Not one word. Here — in the car — at the station. Nowhere. I'll be down with a lawyer very shortly. Not one more word."

"He has to put his coat on, Clarke," Matt said, turning to the black detective.

"You're right," Goode replied, taking the handcuff key out of his pocket and leading Michael by the arm to the hall closet.

"What else?" Matt asked McCann, when Goode was out of the room, wanting to get as much information as he could before the detectives left.

"The bullets were nine millimeter."

"She's been autopsied already?"

"No..."

"What?"

"Two went through her neck into her desk."

"So he hides the gun in his dresser? Come on, Jack."

"It's not my case, Matt," McCann replied.

"Whose is it?"

"Bobby Davila caught it. Him and Nick Loh. Talk to them. I've said enough already."

"Bobby? He can't keep it either."

"I know, it'll go to Homicide South."

"Let's go, Jack," said Clarke Goode. "The kid's in the car." He was standing in the kitchen doorway, snow melting on his short thick hair. Then to Matt: "We're taking him to the two-o, on 82nd Street."

"Do me a favor," Matt said.

"What?"

"Tell the front desk I'm right behind you."

2.

Manhattan, Friday, January 30, 2009, 11:30 PM

"Jade? Matt DeMarco."

"Matt...It's..."

"I know, it's late. Listen, my son's been arrested."

"Michael?"

"Yes."

"Where?"

"They're taking him to the 20th Precinct right now."

"For what?"

"Murder."

"Murder? Are you sure?"

"Jack McCann and Clarke Goode just took him from the house."

"Is it their case? It can't be."

"No, it's Bob Davila's and Nick Loh's."

"Did they have a search warrant?"

"Yes."

Jade Lee leaned over to peak through the half-closed blinds of the window next to her bed. Heavy snow. Eighth Avenue, ten stories below, a valley of white.

"I'll get dressed," she said, looking at her watch. She had been asleep when the phone rang, heavily asleep, but was now fully awake. Matt DeMarco's voice and the word *murder* had done the trick.

"Thank you," Matt said. "I'll meet you there."

"Don't," Jade replied. "Let me call you."

"Why?"

"The press, Matt. You're famous." *Plus, you're a hot head,* Jade thought. *We don't need any scenes.*

"I'm coming, Jade."

"I have a friend at The Post. She says their police photographer has a high connection in the NYPD. What if a photographer shows up?"

"Call your friend. You spin it first."

Jade, standing now, holding the phone to her ear with one hand, swinging open her closet door with the other, pondered this.

"No," she said, finally, selecting and pulling out a pair of bootleg jeans and a dark green cashmere turtleneck sweater. "I don't trust her."

"I'm coming."

"OK, don't say I didn't warn you."

"Thanks. We'll talk about a fee when I get there."

"Matt."

"Yes?"

"He won't get bailed. You know that."

"I'll call Healy."

"He'll be remanded. Then the bail will be a couple of mil. Can you handle that?"

Jade laid the jeans and sweater on her bed, thinking *they'll do*, waiting for Matt to answer.

"No," he said, finally. "I can't."

"Don't call Healy. There's nothing he can do," Jade said. "You realize how bad it would look if he did?"

"Christ, Jade, the Tombs, Rikers. Can you bring a *habeas* petition with you?"

"Yes, but you know what the appellate division does."

"Bail has to be set."

"It will be, after he's indicted. This is murder, the top charge. Everyone will go by the book."

"It's bullshit."

"You're sure of that?"

"Yes."

"Didn't his mom marry a rich guy?"

"Yes, she did."

"How rich?"

"Hundreds of millions."

"There's your bail money. Call her. She has to know anyway."

"I will. I'll meet you at the precinct."

"Did you tell Michael to say nothing?"

"I did."

"I'm on my way."

Jade hung up the phone and looked around her small bedroom. The gray wool suit she had worn to court that day was strewn across a nearby armchair. Jay Leno was on her television screen, the sound muted, saying something to a guest she didn't recognize who was bent over at the waist laughing hysterically. Attuned to the sounds of her apartment, she listened for anything untoward, but heard nothing. Her seventeen-year-old son, Antonio, a senior in high school, was out with his friends. Her heart rate spiked at the thought of the things he could be doing in the city that never sleeps. He had a one A.M. curfew. She'd have to leave him a note.

Matt DeMarco had spent a night in this room five years ago. One night. After dating for four weeks, they had made love once, and then, two days later, over coffee at a diner near Foley Square, she had broken up with him. The look on Matt's face that morning as they faced each other across a tacky Formica table—surprise and then nothing, the curtains in his eyes, invisible but unmistakable, abruptly drawn—came back to her now. On the surface they had remained friends, polite, respectful friends. Jade had less experience of men than people might think. She knew what the term soul mate meant, for example, but only in theory. One thing she did know from experience, though, was that surfaces meant nothing. Thinking of her son and of his father in California, she regretted, now that she could use one, that Matt was not a real friend, that she had pulled the cord to draw those heavy curtains over his eyes five years ago.

Dressing quickly, Jade put these thoughts out of her mind. There was no way to keep Michael DeMarco out of the Manhattan Detention Complex — the holding pen for the mixture of unfortunates and low-lifes scraped daily off the city's streets, known as the Tombs because of its basement labyrinth of cells. It didn't matter who you were — a star athlete, a Wall Street con artist, a politician caught with his pants down — if you were arrested in Manhattan you went to the Tombs for booking and arraignment. If you were unlucky enough to be arrested on a weekend and couldn't make bail, or were remanded to custody without bail, as Michael DeMarco would be, you'd be spending two or even three nights in a holding pen filled with drunks and junkies and their various bodily emissions. She had met Michael once. He would not fit in.

Before leaving she called the 20th Precinct and told the duty officer that she had been retained by Michael DeMarco, that no one was to speak to him or ask him any questions until she got there.

When she got out of the cab at the precinct house she got lucky. Bobby Davila was standing under the small portico at the front entrance talking on his cell phone, his breath steaming as he spoke and nodded his head. She could make out his sharp features and goatee clearly in the cone of light from the fixture above his head. He was snapping his phone shut and putting it in his coat pocket as she approached through the steadily falling snow.

"Just the man I was looking for," she said.

"It's my body you want, I can tell."

Jade ignored this remark. Half Chinese, half African-American, tall, her skin a pale translucent amber, her nomad's eyes set above pronounced, angular cheekbones, she was used to being hit on by cops. A defense attorney with the Legal Aid Society for twelve years, recently out on her own, she took on-the-make cops as an occupational hazard, so hazardous that she had married and divorced two of them in the last ten years. Davila had taken an unsuccessful run at her years ago, when he was a beat cop. He was still trying, although they both knew his heart wasn't in it.

"No, Bobby, Matt DeMarco called me," she said.

"Oh, that," the detective said, the smile gone from his face. "That was Jack McCann on the phone. They're stuck on the Hutch. That drawbridge went up and they can't get it down."

"How long will they be?"

"A while. McCann will call me when they get close."

"Good, we can talk. Let's go someplace. You can buy me a drink."

"Joe Delaney's is right up the block."

The bar, one long, dimly lit room with a pool table on a raised platform at the back, a juke box and cozy booths along the wall, was not crowded, the snow having driven people home. They took a booth and ordered drinks, a Coke for Jade, a Jameson straight for Davila.

"I imagine McCann and Goode are anxious to drop the kid off to you and Nick," Jade said, while they were waiting for their drinks. She had hung her coat and scarf and woolen hat on the coat rack near the front door, and was running her hands through her long black hair, made unruly by the slightest dampness and now totally out of control, or so she thought, ruing her vanity and her obsessive hair issues.

"You're right, but Nick and I are getting out of it, too," the detective replied.

"Why? You know Matt?"

"Every homicide and major crimes guy in the city knows Matt."

"The women too."

"What women?"

"The woman detectives, Bob. You left them out."

"You know what I mean."

"So what's your conflict?"

"I was the first officer," Davila said, "at Matt's first murder trial."

"The honor killing?"

"That's the one."

"You were around then?"

"I was a rookie, twenty-years-old. I was in the Operation Impact program. You never heard the story?"

"No. Tell me."

"I was riding with Jack McCann. He was teaching me the ropes. Supposedly. I was driving. Jack passed out on the way to the scene. He drank on the job then."

"Christ."

"Exactly. Anyway, the neighborhood's very bad. Dope dealers, gangbangers all over the place. I lock Jack in the car and rush in. The perp is in the basement trying to shove his dead sister's body through this one-foot opening in this old fashioned incinerator. I didn't know they even existed any more. He's covered with blood. I know backup is coming and I don't want them to see Jack. I wrestle the kid to the ground and cuff him. Now I'm covered with blood, too. The kid's telling me his sister's a whore. He's glad he killed her, shit like that. His eyes are on fire with hate — of me — but cold and calm at the same time. A bad kid. I rush him outside. There's people looking in on Jack. I back them off. The backup comes, I tell them about the body. I tell them Jack had a heart attack. It turns out they know Jack so we all cover for him."

"I never heard this, Bob."

"True. The thing is, I never gave the perp his Miranda warnings, so what he says to me — the sister is a whore, she deserves it — all that gets thrown out. I fucked up, my first day out."

"But Matt won anyway."

"Yeah. He told me not to worry and he was right. My career's been OK."

"Did he know McCann back then?"

"Yeah, and Goode. They knocked around."

Jade looked at Davila. The sly smile that she was used to seeing on his face, missing while he was telling his story, had returned.

"How bad is this, Bob?"

"It's bad," Davila replied, "and it's gotten worse. The girl's father is a big shot in Lebanon, one of the one's on our side. Healy called our C.O. and asked him to go over the case with him. He wants no holes, no fuck ups."

"What do you have?"

"The doorman says no one else came in or out, fingerprints, angry e-mails. How am I doing so far?"

Jade couldn't help smiling. Davila, a bantamweight with a chip on his shoulder because of his size, was not without his charms. One of them was his sense of humor, dry and sly.

"What's the charge?" she asked.

"One-two-five, two-seven. Murder one."

"No way!"

Jade blurted this out. Murder one—for cop killers, multiple killings and murder committed while committing certain felonies—carried the death sentence.

"We think she was raped," Davila said, his voice matter-of-fact. "They're doing the autopsy tomorrow morning."

Jade shook her head. She had left Legal Aid and opened her own office only a week ago. She had taken two shoplifting cases yesterday. Today, it's murder one, her client the son of a high profile prosecutor and an ex-lover to boot.

"Based on what?" she asked. "They were dating."

"Bruises. You'll see the pictures."

"Anything else?" Somehow she knew there was more to come. Their drinks arrived before Davila could answer. He drank half of his down, then said, "You won't believe it. The murder weapon, found in the kid's room."

"That's crazy."

"Yes it is."

"It goes against premeditation, at least."

"If you say so."

"If he had thought the whole thing out he would have disposed of the gun."

"You would think so."

"Something's wrong, Bobby, don't you think?"

Jade was fishing. She did not know if something was wrong. She had only met Michael DeMarco once, briefly, when he was seventeen. He had barely acknowledged her. For all she knew he was capable of rape and murder in a fit of rage.

Davila knocked back the rest of his whiskey and then looked around the room for a second before answering. "Maybe," the detective said, "but I'm not being paid to think, not in this case. Tomorrow it goes to Manhattan Homicide."

"What about a security video?"

"We've asked for it."

"Do me a favor," Jade said.

"What? Hold it," Davila said. "Let's have another drink." He had caught the waitress's eye. When she came over, he ordered another round. Jade watched him, knowing he was calculating the risk-reward factor of doing something for this tall half-breed who he had once dreamed of having a torrid affair with, perhaps renewing those hopes.

"I don't want the kid to spend the night in the Tombs," she said.

"So? What?"

"Keep him at the precinct. Take him downtown around seven AM. I know the head court clerk. She's a friend of my mother's. She can get him booked quickly, and arraigned at nine sharp."

"That's only one night," Davila said. "He'll be there till Monday."

"I'm going to try to get him his own cell."

"Good luck with that."

Jade watched as Davila again looked around, thinking over her request.

"I can do it," he said, finally. "But it won't be as easy as you think. And you'll owe me."

"Bob," Jade said. "You know what Robert DeNiro said in *The Godfather*, don't you?"

"No, what?"

"*I don't forget*," she answered, putting her right index finger to her temple and smiling.

"Good, I don't either," said Davila, smiling back.

The drinks came, but before they could sip, Davila's cell phone rang. Jade listened carefully to his end of the conversation:

"*Is that you, Jack?... OK... I'm at Delaney's... He's lawyered up, by the way... Jade Lee... Of course I remember.*"

"Was he reminding you that you're a happily married man?" Jade asked when he hung up.

"As a matter of fact, he was," Davila replied, picking up his double whisky and drinking it in one gulp.

"I guess we're going?" Jade said.

"Yes, they're on the Westside Highway."

"I'll get this," said Jade, placing a twenty-dollar bill on the table, noticing that the detective had not reached for his wallet. *That's your payback,* she said to herself. *We're even.*

3.

"You've grown up, Michael," Jade said.

"I don't remember you."

"We met once about five years ago at one of your soccer games."

They were in a windowless ten-foot by ten-foot interview room on the second floor of the 20th Precinct's modern brick and concrete building on 82nd Street, sitting on metal chairs, facing each other across a dented metal table. Michael's hands, resting on his lap, were cuffed. Bob Davila stood in the hallway outside, within calling distance, doing his job.

"Is it *Jade*? Or *Miss Lee*? Or *Ms. Lee*? Whatever you want me to call you, get me out of here."

"Has anybody interrogated you?"

"Are you listening to me? Get me the fuck out of here."

Jade, startled by Michael DeMarco's ferocity, leaned back in her chair, her features composed. She decided to give him the benefit of the doubt. His girlfriend was dead. Perhaps he had killed her.

"Michael," she said, her voice neutral, "in a few hours you're going downtown to be booked. The place is a dungeon. That's why it's called the Tombs. Scumbags all over the place. Just follow directions and keep your mouth shut. I'll meet you in the courtroom at nine o'clock."

"Is that when I get out?"

"No, you're charged with murder. You'll be remanded to custody without bail."

"What does that mean?"

"You'll be in the Tombs until Monday. Then you'll be transferred to Rikers. Have you heard of it?"

"Of course. It's a shit hole."

"Correct."

"And then what?"

"You have to be indicted by a grand jury within five days of your arrest. Then you'll go before a judge who will set bail."

"Is that when I get out?"

"The bail will be high, but if you can make it, or your family can, yes."

"Where's my father."

"Your father's on his way here, but you won't be able to see him."

"He'll get me out."

"No, he won't. That's why I'm telling you this. To prepare you. The Tombs and Rikers are nasty places. Get ready for a rough couple of days."

"I thought my father was a big shot prosecutor?"

"The president of the United States couldn't get you bailed until Wednesday."

Jade, noticing the flash of light in Michael's eyes, wondered for a second whether he was going to make another sarcastic remark, perhaps about the new president, but he remained silent. Michael's eyes, she could not fail to notice, were the same as his father's, dark and wildly beautiful. How far otherwise the fruit had fallen from the tree she did not know, but it seemed pretty far.

"Is she really dead?" Michael said.

Jade looked at her watch. She was wondering when he was going to ask about his dead girlfriend. Ten minutes had passed. *Not a good sign.*

"She's dead, Michael, shot twice in the back of the head and twice in the back of the neck, at close range."

"Aren't you going to ask me if I did it?"

"You were there today."

"That doesn't prove anything. It was someone else, obviously."

"They say she was raped too. Did you have sex with her?"

Jade watched as Michael absorbed this, his eyes narrowing, his wheels spinning, trying to get traction.

"We made love," he said.

"Were you arguing?"

"Yes."

"They think it was rape."

"It wasn't." His denial was forceful, but Jade did not miss the shadow that fell across Michael DeMarco's eyes as he spoke, the first crack in his armor of arrogance, always thin, especially in the young.

"And then there's the gun they found in your room in Pound Ridge," she said. "They're pretty sure the bullets will be a match."

"It's not mine. I told them that at the house."

"Your Arab friends must have planted it, don't you think?"

Jade watched as Michael paused. *This must have occurred to him,* she thought. *He's not stupid.*

"Who else could it have been?" she said, when Michael did not answer. "You think your father put it there?"

"No, I don't."

"You're sure it wasn't yours?"

"Of course. I hate guns."

"Michael, listen to me," Jade said. "Right now, I'm not interested in whether you did this crime or not. Only in figuring out defenses. If you didn't do it, the way I see it, the gun had to be planted by your so-called buddies. Do you agree with me?" *And if you did do it, ditto,* she said to herself, planning ahead, thinking of reasonable doubt.

"Yes."

"O.K. We don't have long," she continued. "You need to tell me about them. What are their full names? Where do they live?"

Michael raised his cuffed hands to his face and rubbed his eyes, then returned them quickly to his lap, shaking his head, sitting more upright. "I don't know their last names," he said. "Adnan's is F-something. *Farouk* maybe. They work sometimes for Basil, my stepfather. That's how I met them."

"When?"

"When they came to New York, a few months ago."

"Where are they from? What nationality?"

"They're Lebanese."

"Did Yasmine meet them?"

"Yes."

"How do I find them?"

"They live on Long Island, in Locust Valley. They're house sitting some rich guy's house. Basil got them the gig."

"What rich guy? What's his name?"

"I don't know.

"Have you been to the house?"

"Yes, a few times."

"What's the address?"

"I don't know, but it's huge. It's got a fountain in front with statues of dolphins in the middle. There's a golf course across the street."

"Who else knows them?"

"Who else?"

"Yes, other friends, people you hang out with."

Michael's handsome features were grim now. *These two had really fucked him.* That was Jade's educated guess as to what he was thinking. Good old Adnan and Ali.

"Just Yasmine," Michael answered finally. "The three of us just hung out."

"Doing what?"

"Getting stoned sometimes, listening to music, sometimes we went to a club."

"What club?"

"A place called Lucky's, in Queens."

"Did anyone know them there?"

"Not that I know of."

"Bartenders, bouncers, anyone?"

"One bartender did seem to know them. Another Arab guy."

"But you don't know his name."

"I do. Because it's so weird. *Rex.*"

"Rex. Where in Queens?"

"Near the Whitestone Bridge. I think it's on Linden Place."

"O.K.," Jade said, looking at her watch again. Davila had given her 20 minutes. "A couple of things. Were you questioned when you got here?"

"No. I was fingerprinted, then handcuffed to a desk."

"Did they do a gunshot residue test, or talk about one? Do you know what that is?"

"No."

"It's a chemical test to tell if you've fired a gun. It has to be done within 48 hours."

"It hasn't happened."

"You would have no problem with it?"

"I didn't fire a gun."

"Did you handle it?"

"No."

"Then I'll get it done. We have until four P.M. Sunday. I'll get someone to come to the Tombs."

Jade had been making notes on a yellow legal pad. She put the pad back in her briefcase and rose from her chair. Her height seemed to startle Michael. She had been sitting waiting for him when he was brought into the interrogation room. He looked tired, but otherwise not the worse for the wear of the events of the evening, and the afternoon, if he in fact had killed Yasmine Hayek.

"How tall are you?" he asked.

"Five-ten."

"I do remember you. When you were dating my father." Jade nodded.

"What happened there?" Michael asked.

"I'm leaving," she said, ignoring this question. "I'll see you in court tomorrow. Is there anybody you want me to call, or talk to?"

"My mother."

"Your father called her."

"I did too, but she didn't pick up. I left a message for her to call my father."

"When did you call her?"

"They let me make a call when I got here."

"One last thing, Michael."

"What?"

"Don't talk to any inmates at the Tombs or at Rikers about your case. Especially Rikers. They're all looking to make deals."

"Sure. Of course. So what happened between you and my father?"

Michael had been looking at her with great interest, the way most men did. Though her sweater was not form fitting and her jeans were just jeans, her body had a way of announcing itself.

"Do you want me to represent you, Michael?" Jade replied, moving to the door and pushing the buzzer on the wall to signal that her visit was over.

"Sure."

"Then don't ask me any more personal questions. One more and you'll have to get a new lawyer. I'll see you tomorrow."

4.

Manhattan, Saturday, January 31, 2009, 3:00AM

Matt, lucky to get a taxi to stop in a snowstorm, had had to bribe the cabbie with a twenty-dollar bill to get him to take him across town to his apartment on Columbus Avenue. Could he sleep? He didn't think so. He had a habit of putting his leftover morning coffee into an old glass milk bottle and refrigerating it for future use. Pouring some into a pan, adding milk and sugar, he stirred himself a poor man's cappuccino, turning off the flame just as the mixture was starting to boil. They had not let him see Michael at the Precinct. He was in a holding pen in the basement, Matt was told, and would be taken downtown any minute. Bobby Davila had gone off duty. No use waiting. Despite Jade Lee's admonition not to, he had called Jon Healy, and gotten through. Sipping his coffee in the apartment's small but comfortable living room, he recalled their conversation.

"Even if I could get bail set," Healy had said, *"where would you get the money? It would have to be cash."*

"Let me worry about that."

"Forget it. He's remanded."

"What's the charge?"

"125-27."

"You're kidding."

"She was raped."

"Raped? They were going out."

"This is a tough one, Matt. I'm sorry. Come in to see me on Monday morning."

"I'm in the middle of a trial."

"I know. That's one of the things we have to discuss."

On Monday he would have to sum up in *Morales,* also a rape/murder, also 125.27 of the Penal Laws, murder one, the death sentence on the table. *That's one of the things we have to discuss?* What did *that* mean? The ringing of his cell phone startled him. He looked at the screen. It was Debra.

"Hello."

"Matt? It's Debra."

"I know."

"What's going on? My phone was off. It was the middle of the night when you called."

"Michael's been arrested."

"There's a message from him too. I called but his phone must be off. Arrested for what?"

Matt remained silent, his heart heavy, for the first time in fifteen years feeling sympathy for his ex-wife.

"For *what*, Matt," Debra said. "What's going on?"

"They say he killed Yasmine," Matt said.

Debra said nothing. Seconds passed in which the line was so quiet Matt thought they had been disconnected.

"Debra?" he said. "Are you there?"

Nothing.

"Debra?"

More nothing.

Then finally he heard her say, softly, as if she were speaking to herself, "I'm coming home."

"That's a good idea."

"Where is Michael now?" she asked.

"He's being booked downtown. He'll go to Rikers on Monday."

"Are you representing him?"

"You know I can't do that. I got him a lawyer."

"Who?"

"Jade Lee. You don't know her."

"Yes I do. You went out with her."

"That's not relevant right now."

"I'm coming home," Debra said, her voice back to normal, or close to it. Normal for her meaning authoritarian, decisive, but, for the moment, without the tinge of disdain for lower creatures that had crept into it since her marriage.

"I'll call you when I know the flight details."

Click. She hung up.

Matt fell asleep on his couch. His last thought was of Debra. It's not every day you hear your son's been charged with murder. What had she been thinking in that long silence?

5.

Matt spotted Jade Lee as she came around the corner of the subway entrance. Her long wool overcoat was flared at the bottom and unbuttoned, revealing a stylish navy blue suit and those long graceful legs. A scarlet silk scarf mingled at her collar with her lustrous black hair. Her body was long and regal as she walked toward him across Union Square Park. He rose from his bench and waved as she came nearer. Her face looked grim, but nothing, he thought, surprising himself, could detract from her beauty. The grim set of her features, indeed, only added to it, made it more interesting. A quick smile crossed her face when she saw him, her high cheekbones widening for a split second, accentuating the exotic slant of her eyes, her teeth even and pretty. As beautiful as everything else about her was, it was the sight of these teeth that penetrated his being without warning, turning his heart a few degrees on its axis. The smiles they had exchanged when they ran into each other over the past five years had been fake. This one, brief as it was, was real, and, as a result, it brought back memories he thought he had successfully repressed. Such a small thing, a real smile.

She sat next to him on the slatted park bench, her briefcase on her lap, her breath steaming in the cold gray winter air.

"Hi," she said.

"Hi," Matt answered.

"How long has it been?" Jade asked.

"Judge Harris' retirement dinner."

"Two years."

"You look great," Matt said.

"Thank you. Matt..."

"You look like you've got bad news."

"I do. Or maybe it's not. I've been fired."

Matt paused for a second before speaking. "By Michael, or by his mother?"

"By both, I guess. I just got back from the Tombs. I wanted to hear it from Michael."

Matt was expecting this. Debra and Basil had returned from Europe on Saturday afternoon. Debra called him while the plane was taxiing at JFK. He told her what he knew about the case. He had visited Michael at the Tombs that morning, just missing Jade, who had been there an hour earlier to handle the arraignment, an open-court affair where Matt decided it was best if he didn't show his face. He went again this morning, Sunday. On the way out he saw Debra and Basil and a distinguished-looking, gray-haired man in an expensive overcoat, carrying a briefcase, getting out of a limousine in front of 100 Center Street. He called Jade but he got her voice mail. When she returned his call at noon, she told him to meet her at Union Square Park, an old meeting place of theirs, at one.

"What happened?" he asked.

"I got a call from Everett Stryker last night," Jade said.

"The Wall Street guy."

"Yes. The white collar guy."

"That must have been him I saw going into the Tombs this morning."

"He told me I was discharged. He was going to the appellate division this morning and the Court of Appeals if necessary. And then federal court."

"If necessary," Matt said.

"Right, he was preparing a writ," Jade replied, "while I was at my son's basketball game."

"That's where you were yesterday?"

"And then dinner. He was suspended from the team. It was his first game back."

"How'd he do?"

"In the game?"

"Yes."

"He scored five off the bench."

"Foul trouble?"

Jade smiled at this. Another real smile. When he and Jade were dating, she had gone with Matt to one of Michael's soccer games, and he had gone with her to one of Antonio's CYO basketball games. Antonio, a gangly six-foot-three twelve-year-old, arms and legs going in four different directions, determined but rudderless, had gotten quickly into foul trouble, once sending three kids—all five-four or less—sprawling to the floor while trying to force his way through a pick.

"Three in ten minutes," she said.

Matt smiled too, remembering his high school playing days. He had been a bit of a hacker himself. More than a bit. But not like Antonio, whose motives were pure, but technique bad. Scoring on the sixteen-year-old Matt DeMarco was unthinkable, and so he fouled.

"It's not good news," Matt said, returning to the present, turning to face Jade, looking into her eyes and then down at her hands clasping her briefcase. "Stryker represents stock swindlers. I doubt he's ever tried a murder case."

"I should have pushed for bail, like he's doing."

"It's a waste of time, all for show—and money—he probably had ten kids working all night on the papers. The grand jury will indict tomorrow or Tuesday and Michael will be out on bail the next day."

"I'm sorry."

"Don't be sorry. He'll soon be back in his mother's arms."

"One more thing," Jade said, "and I'll let you go."

"What?"

"I got a call this morning from Ken Leyner. He was supposed to go to the Tombs today to do the GSR. He said Stryker called him and cancelled it."

Matt thought this over. Though Stryker was not known as a street crime guy, he was smart and he had brilliant associates who would thoroughly analyze every issue. He would not lose the chance to do the gunshot residue test unless he did not want to know the results.

"Michael must have handled the Beretta," he said.

"He told me he didn't."

"He must have. There's no other reason why Stryker would cancel the test."

Matt caught Jade's eye again as he said this, tacitly confirming to her that, yes, he believed his son was a liar. He thought back to Friday night, the unbelievably loud volume of Michael's music that lasted about five minutes. Maybe Ali, the short one with the hooked nose, had gotten Michael to fire the gun out the window while Adnan was in the bathroom. *This will be fun, Michael. Come on, try it, there's nothing but woods out there.* The ultimate set up.

"Manhattan Homicide hasn't done one," Jade said, "if that's any consolation, and I hear there were no prints."

"I figured Adnan or Ali wiped the gun down," Matt replied. "And the GSR is a pain in the ass. I've never liked it. You've seen it. *Two elements, three elements. Inadvertent transfer. Were the hands bagged? Why not?* Blah, blah. It's red meat for defense lawyers. They probably think they have enough and don't want to complicate things with an inconclusive test."

"I agree, but I think Michael was telling me the truth."

Matt shook his head. He hadn't known his son to be a liar. If anything he seemed to enjoy hurting people—strike that, hurting Matt—with jabs of honesty that stung all the more because they were so dispassionately delivered. An asshole, but not a liar. Until now.

"Matt?" Jade said.

"Yes?"

"He's angry."

Matt nodded. No shit, he thought.

"I don't think it's completely at you."

"Jade..."

"I have a son, too. There's something..."

"Something what?"

"Something torturing him."

"Like what?" Just like his mother, Matt thought, making excuses for him, the man-child. It must be a female thing.

"I don't know," Jade replied. "I saw the boy in him at the arraignment. He didn't do this crime."

"That I agree with."

"I'm sorry to be butting in like this."

"You're not butting in. You're trying to help." Who else would do that? Try to help? Matt thought, suddenly very near, uncomfortably near, to a truth about himself, his life, that he had been avoiding for a long time. He looked into Jade's eyes for a second, thanking her with his own, softened now by this truth, and then down at her beautifully sculpted hands, ivory-yellow, the nails a deep brilliant crimson, resting on the briefcase on her lap.

"I owe you for your time," he said, looking up. "Send me a bill."

"No, Matt. I really appreciate that you thought of me. It was only a few hours."

"Are you sure?"

"Positive."

"I'll buy you dinner."

"No, I'll buy *you* dinner."

"We'll go Dutch."

"Sure, call me."

While they were talking, a flock of pigeons, a hundred or so strong, had gathered on the asphalt walkway nearby. After Jade left, Matt sat and watched an old black guy feed them peanuts from a five-gallon spackle container on the bench next to him. In the man's lap was a faded paperback copy of Marcus

Aurelius' *Meditations*, with the same yellow cover as the one Matt had on a shelf in his apartment. Matt sat, mesmerized, watching. As he had been mesmerized by Jade's hands.

Basil al-Hassan, swiftly crossing the Atlantic in his private jet, had come to the rescue. Everett Stryker, the super lawyer with a firm of three hundred attorneys at his beck and call, had been hired, and was issuing orders; his retainer probably 500K. He had only been half joking when he told Jade that Michael would soon be back in his mother's arms. They were too close, those two. And they had defeated him. When Michael was a boy, Matt, recently separated from Debra, had lived close to Union Square, on 17th Street. He had a dog, a mutt with a mangled eye, named Popeye, that he and Michael took to the dog run in the park, which Matt could see from where he sat. Popeye got old and sick, and Matt had to put him down. Michael was sixteen at the time and barely noticed. Michael.

Matt rose to leave, and as he did he saw the black man raise his right hand, index finger extended, pointing at him. It was a slow but surprisingly commanding gesture: stop, it said, hold on a second.

"Yes?" Matt said, staring into a pair of tired, yellowed eyes.

"Have you read Marcus Aurelius?" the man asked.

Matt noticed for the first time that the man's wrinkled brown hands, his pant legs, and his battered work shoes were covered with white paint or, more precisely, white paste—spackle. He had been working and was finished for the day, or taking a lunch break.

"Yes, I have," Matt answered.

"You should read him again. You don't want your anger to turn to despair, or self-pity." The old man nodded, dismissing Matt, and reached into his bucket, coming out with a handful of peanuts. These he flung at the pigeons, watching passively as they scrambled for them, many of them devouring them shells and all.

6.

Locust Valley, Wednesday, February 25, 2009, 1:00AM

Bob Davila and Nick Loh sat in their unmarked car looking at the shadowy outline of the mansion located at 211 Piping Rock Road in Locust Valley. From their vantage point, a knoll on the grounds of the Piping Rock Country Club golf course across the street, they had an unobstructed view of the large house's winding driveway leading on a graceful curved incline to its front entrance on the left and a detached five-car garage on the right. The fountain in the middle of the rolling, snow-covered front lawn, with three dolphins suspended in mid-jump above it, was not spewing water. It was the dead of a late February night, and 20 degrees Fahrenheit.

On the console between them were two large empty thermoses that, three hours ago, were filled with hot coffee. Taped to the dashboard were three-by-five color photographs of two young Arab men, one bald with heavy-lidded eyes, the other with a thick head of wiry hair and a hooked nose. *Suspect 1* was written across the bottom of the first picture in black marking ink, and *Suspect 2* on the second. In the detectives' jacket pockets, clipped to their NYPD ID cards, were light-blue plastic cards, with photos, that identified them as UNIIIC Special Investigators.

Shielded by a stand of tall pine trees, they could not be

seen from the house, although the dark night was their best cover. In an hour they would be relieved. In the passenger seat Loh held a pair of expensive digital night vision binoculars in his gloved hands. The Cantonese-American detective had just scanned the house and grounds.

"You love playing with those things," Davila said.

"They're very cool," Loh replied.

"I know. Too bad there's never anything to see." The house was completely dark, as it had been since midnight.

"We're committed, Bob."

"Right, we'll be promoted. I'm having my doubts."

It was Davila who had been offered the assignment and who had talked their commanding officer into offering it to Loh as well, and Loh into accepting it. Now, after three weeks of stakeouts as part of an eight-person rotating team, he was sorry he had. Suspect 1 and Suspect 2 had not left the house, not even to take out the garbage. They *were* in there because occasionally someone would get lucky and spot one or the other of them in a window with the binoculars. Groceries were delivered, but not the mail.

"*Observe and communicate.* What kind of bullshit is that?" Davila continued.

"It must be a Dutch thing," Loh replied, "or U.N. speak."

"We never should have got involved with the U.N."

"You mean this assignment, or back in 1947?" Loh said.

"1947. They hate us."

"The world loves us now, Bob. All we had to do was elect a handsome young black guy as president."

"Fuckin' U.N."

"You're working for the U.N. right now."

"No I'm not, I'm working for the NYPD, on special assignment to the U.N."

Smiling, Loh picked up the binoculars and scanned the house and grounds.

"It sounds glamorous, doesn't it?" he said, returning the glasses to his lap. "Too bad they won't tell us what we're working on."

"Right. What the fuck is *Monteverde*? Fuck-nuts mentioned it a couple of times yesterday, like it was the Vatican or the Holy Grail." *Fuck-nuts* was how Davila referred to U.N. Deputy Director of Investigations, the Dutchman Ehrhard Fuchs.

"You're very Christian-centered, Bob."

"What the fuck are *you*? I thought you were a Catholic."

"I am, but there are other religions, other holy places."

"Not for me," Davila said, looking at his watch, thinking, *45 minutes*. After these ten-to-two shifts he usually stopped by The Roost, a bar on Glen Cove Avenue where a waitress he knew was getting off work.

"So that means you'll be coming to the church on Sunday," Loh said.

"No way, Nicky, I'm sleeping in. What time at the house?"

"Noon. We're having a brunch."

"That I won't miss."

Davila had stood godfather for Loh's first son, Nicholas Robert, three years ago. His second boy, Vincent, was being baptized on Sunday. It would be the detectives' first Sunday off in three weeks.

"What's that?" Loh said, putting the binoculars swiftly to his eyes.

"A car," Davila said. "Can you get the plates?"

"Hold on," Loh said, adjusting the focus ring on the glasses. "No, they're covered."

Davila had pulled a small spiral notebook and pencil out of his coat pocket. By the time he put them away, the car was stopped on the circular driveway parallel to the front door.

"Two guys," said Loh.

The lights came on in the house.

"Suspect 2 is at the door," Loh continued. "Fuck!"

"What?"

"He shot him. Let's go."

"What about *observe and communicate*?"

"Come on, Bobby. Let's block their car in. Then we'll call for backup."

Davila was more than happy to comply. He had been about to call Fuchs. Instead he shoved his radio into his coat pocket, turned the car on, and swung past the pine trees toward the club's side entrance.

"They went in," Loh said, the binoculars still to his eyes, his voice urgent but calm. "Go, Bobby. Nice and easy."

"Are there just the two?" Davila asked.

"I can't tell," Loh replied, "the car windows are smoked."

Davila, driving cautiously, his headlights off, crossed the quiet street and headed up the mansion's driveway, stopping where the asphalt pavement looped toward the house. He did a quick scan. The house's large oak front door was wide open. Suspect 2 was lying on the threshold, his legs twisted beneath his body. The visitor's car, a black Hummer, about fifty feet away, was running, smoke from its tail pipe condensing in the cold air. His unmarked Ford was blocking the bulky SUV's exit.

Then he got on the radio.

"China 1, China 1, this is Red 2 calling. Acknowledge."

Nothing.

"China 1, this is Red 2, come in. Suspect 2 has been shot. We're going in. We need backup."

"Red 2, this is China 1. I read you. Do not enter. Repeat, do not enter. Backup is on its way. Acknowledge."

"They're gonna kill the other one."

"Do not enter. Acknowledge."

Before Davila could respond, one of the two visitors, a tall, bearded man in a long black leather coat, appeared at the front door and began to drag Suspect 2 into the house. The next thing he knew, Loh was in a crouch outside the car, pointing his service revolver at the black-coated visitor.

"Stop right there," Nick yelled, his voice sharp and crystal clear in the night air. "Put your hands over your head."

Instead of complying, the man, in one deft and swift movement, reached inside his coat, pulled out a large automatic pistol and began spraying the detectives' car from driver's side to passenger's side, back and forth, twice. Davila ducked down and scrambled out of the driver's side door, crawling around the back of the car to Loh, who was flat on his back, bleeding heavily from his chest. Davila had his Glock 19 out. Shielded by the open passenger door, he fired three quick rounds at the front entrance, but when he looked quickly he saw only the body of Suspect 2. He dragged Loh closer to the side of the car, then reached in for the radio, which he had thrown on the seat.

"Officer down! Officer down!" he shouted, pushing hard on the transmit button. "I need backup. China 1, acknowledge."

"Two minutes, Red 2, two minutes. We're on Forrest Avenue. Over."

"Call EMS! Officer down..."

Davila took a quick look at the house, then crouched over Loh and tried his version of mouth-to-mouth resuscitation. His friend's body was inert.

"Nick," he said. "Nicky..."

Inside he heard shots. He grabbed Loh's Glock, still in his right hand, stuck it in his belt, and peaked around the open car door. Nothing. Suspect 2 still lying there. Then he heard the sound of the Hummer starting up. *They left someone in the car,* he thought, but before he could react, the Hummer was backing up and smashing into the front of the Ford, whose passenger door swung wildly on impact, knocking Davila onto his back. He rolled quickly to his right, rose to one knee, and fired four rounds rapidly at the Hummer as it smashed into the Ford again, knocking it another twenty feet back and leaving Nick Loh's body lying exposed in the snow.

Looking around for cover, Davila saw the first two visitors run out of the house, both firing bursts from their automatic weapons in his direction. He returned fire and one of them went down. The other one jumped into the moving Hummer, which, trampling over shrubs and knocking a small tree half-way to the ground, careened across the snow-covered lawn back to the driveway then onto the street and away. Davila found the radio in the snow and called to Fuchs, describing the Hummer. *At least two armed suspects,* he said, *I got dead bodies here.*

The detective took off his coat and laid it over his partner's body. Then, his gun pointed straight ahead, he walked over to the man he had shot; first picking up his gun, a .45 caliber Ingram machine pistol, and putting it in his coat pocket, then rolling him onto his back with a shove of his right foot. It was not the bearded one, but his clean-shaven partner, his dark eyes dilated, his face ashen. Moaning, he looked right at Davila, who quickly kicked him back over and cuffed him, noticing as he did the blood oozing from under his rib cage.

With sirens sounding in the background, Davila moved very fast, first confirming, with a hand to his carotid artery, that Suspect 2 was indeed dead, then searching him for a weapon and I.D. There was no weapon, but in his wallet he found a biometric national identification card issued by the UK, a U.S. State Department driver's license, and a Syrian Embassy photo I.D., all bearing the name and photo of a Syrian national named Ali al-Najjar. These he put in the front pocket of his jeans.

Davila had been an alter boy in Puerto Rico, traveling around his dirt-poor rural province with the parish priest as he ministered to his flock. He no longer went to mass, but the heady mix of religion and island superstition had taken a powerful hold on his imagination as a boy and never quite let go. Kneeling at Nick Loh's side, he spit on his fingers and rubbed his saliva on his friend's forehead. *"Through this holy unction and his most tender mercy may the Lord pardon thee whatever sins or faults thou hast committed, by sight, by hearing, by taste, by carnal…"* When he finished, he looked up and saw Ehrhard Fuchs standing over him shining his flashlight in Nick's face.

"Have you been inside?" Fuchs, a stocky blond man with slits for eyes and a permanently flushed face, asked.

"No," Davila said, getting to his feet.

"Why not?"

"You told us not to."

"What happened?"

Davila looked up at Fuchs, using his hand to block out the glare of the Dutchman's flashlight. No mention of Nick. Just, *have you been inside?* As if Nick had never existed. Who *were* those two scumbags in the house? The other members of the UN team had arrived and were deploying around the mansion and its grounds. One was searching the downed bearded man. More sirens could be heard approaching.

"You took too long," Davila said, "that's what happened."

"They're doing work on Forrest Avenue. We had to go around."

"That's been going on for two weeks. Who the fuck was driving?"

"We got here as fast as we could," Fuchs replied, ignoring Davila's question. "What happened?"

Before Davila could answer, two EMS techs appeared carrying a collapsible gurney. The wiry little detective got to his feet, but kept his eyes on Nick Loh, not turning away until one of the techs, kneeling, put his index and middle fingers to his dead friend's neck for a couple of seconds, then took them away and covered the body with a brown blanket.

"They shot the fat one at the door," Davila said, facing Fuchs, who had lowered his flashlight, "then went in. We waited. A few minutes later they came out, blasting away." Davila pulled the Ingram out of his coat pocket, a small cannon that could fire twenty rounds per second on fully automatic and that both he and Fuchs knew was used by terrorists and other very bad actors almost exclusively. "Nick was just sitting in the car."

"How many?"

"Three."

"Did you get a good look?"

"Yes, at the shooter."

"We wasted no time," Fuchs said.

As Fuchs said this, a man named Alec Mason, an Englishman who had joined Fuchs' team just in the last week, had appeared out of the darkness. Later Bob would try, without success, to remember if he had been standing there all along.

"I was driving," Mason said. "I've been working days. I didn't know they were doing the street work at night. I'm sorry about your friend."

"You hung us out there," Davila said, ignoring Mason and staring hard at Fuchs. "You told us not to enter while people were getting shot at inside. Fuck you and the fucking UN."

7.

Jack McCann and Clarke Goode stood over the body of Felix Diaz slumped over a Formica table in the kitchen of his tiny apartment on Clinton Street on the Lower East Side. Don Russell, the sergeant in charge of Manhattan's Crime Scene Unit, was kneeling under the table pointing out two bullet holes in the linoleum-covered floor to the photographer kneeling next to him. McCann had sent the responding patrolman to the apartment below to see if anyone was hurt or had heard anything. The rest of Russell's team was going about its business, dusting for fingerprints and shoe prints, bagging Diaz' hands, looking for entry and exit wounds other than the four they had found. This last involved lifting the body and carefully turning it so as not to disturb evidence that was not obvious. Another patrolman was going door-to-door through the rest of the sagging four-story walkup.

On the table was Diaz' wallet with nine dollars in it.

His daughter, who had found him when she returned at midnight from her job as a salesperson at the Duane Reade store on East Broadway, was on the couch in the living room, a stunned look on her face. A neighbor was sitting next to her holding her hand. While McCann helped scan the body, Goode went in to talk to Diaz' daughter. The neighbor, a stout black lady in her fifties, was crying into her free hand. The detective gave her his handkerchief, washed and pressed yesterday by his wife of thirty years.

"Please excuse us ma'am," he said, stepping back to allow her to rise and walk across the small room where she sat in a battered easy chair. He sat down next to the daughter, the springs of the old couch sagging beneath his two hundred twenty pounds.

"Your name is Carla, is that right?"

The daughter nodded.

"I have to ask you a few questions. It won't take long." Goode watched the girl nod mutely again. "How old are you Carla?" he asked.

"Twenty-one."

"And your father?"

"Forty-five."

"You found him at what time?"

"Twelve, just after. I walked home from work."

"How long does that take?"

"Five minutes."

"And you got off at twelve?"

"Yes."

"Does anybody else live here?"

"No."

"Your mother?"

"She died last year."

"Sisters, brothers?"

"No. My brother lives in a home in Jersey."

"A home?"

"He's autistic."

Goode looked into Carla Diaz' eyes. They were still dazed. Dead mother, dead father, autistic brother. Twenty-one years old.

"Where does your dad work?"

"He's a doorman uptown."

"Did he work today?"

"No, he went to Jersey to see Johnny, my brother."

"When was his last payday?"

"I don't know."

"Where did he cash his paychecks?"

"They went right in the bank. Auto deposit."

"Who would do this to him?"

"I don't know. Nobody."

"Did he carry cash around?"

Goode was loath to ask the girl if her father was a drug dealer or involved in something else illicit. He did not want to insult her thirty minutes after finding him dead. Besides, although the killing looked like an execution to him, his instincts told him it was not related to other criminal activity.

"Carry cash?" Carla asked.

Like I asked what year he got out of Harvard, Goode thought. "Yes," he replied.

"He had no cash, everything went to extras for Johnny, books, games, clothes, extra therapy."

"What building did he work at up town?"

"The Excelsior, on Central Park West. Ten-eleven."

"Who were his friends?"

"Miss Frances." Carla nodded to the black lady sitting across the room, her sobbing subsided, her face in shock.

"Anyone else?"

"My father worked and visited Johnny."

"How old is Johnny?"

"Twenty-two."

"Did your father have any enemies? Any arguments with anybody lately?"

"No."

"We may need you to come in to talk some more, Carla," Goode said, handing the girl his card. "I'll call you."

Out on the street, Goode found McCann talking to a patrolman, the breath steaming from their mouths. Two patrol cars, their overhead strobe lights flashing blue/red, blue/red, were parked at the curb. In the back seat of one he could see a haggard old woman with a woolen cap on her head and ratty earmuffs on over that. The sidewalk had been taped off, but the onlookers were few. It was too cold, and there was no body to look at. An EMS van was double parked nearby. Goode had passed its two-man crew in the hallway, smoking, waiting for the body to be released.

"What's up with the bag lady?" Goode asked as he approached his partner and the uniformed cop.

"She was in the hallway across the street," McCann replied. "She says she saw two men get out of a HumVee and go into the building about 11:30. One had on a long black leather coat. He had a beard."

"She said all that?" Goode addressed this question to the patrolman, a rookie, he could tell, from his baby face.

"Yes, sir."

"How does she know what a HumVee is?"

"That's what she said, sir. I do think she's high, sir."

"She's probably always high, functionally high. Anything else? Faces, colors, height, weight?"

"No. Just the HumVee, the coat and the beard."

Goode looked at McCann who raised his eyebrows and said, "She's all we have."

"What's her name?"

"Mighty Mary, she calls herself."

"I.D.?"

"She's got a picture of Mayor Bloomberg in her pocket. That's it."

"Christ."

"Take her to Manhattan South," McCann said. "Give her some coffee, feed her, get a composite."

"Good luck with that," Clarke Goode said, as the patrolman walked toward his car.

"Let me ask you, Jack," Goode said.

"What?"

"Bobby Davila. He and Nick Loh caught the Hayek case."

"Yes they did."

"Didn't the girl live at the Excelsior on Central Park West?"

"As I recall."

"And Davila had talked to the doorman? Name of Diaz?"

Both Goode and McCann had read the arrest and search warrants, and Davila's supporting affidavits, before heading up to Pound Ridge to arrest Michael DeMarco. That was over three weeks ago, but Goode would be a long time forgetting that night, particularly—above all else, actually—the murderous look in Matt DeMarco's eyes as they faced each other at the foot of the stairs.

"Yes," McCann answered.

"Unless I'm mistaken, that's him upstairs."

Goode saw the light come on in McCann's blue eyes.

"That's right, Jack," he said. "That's an execution upstairs. Of a witness—a prime witness—in a murder one case."

8.

"You didn't go right home last night, did you, Bob?"

"No? Where did I go?"

Bob Davila sat at a table at Henry's Diner in downtown Glen Cove, across from Bill Crow, an F.B.I. Agent who claimed he had traveled overnight from Washington just to see him. Bob had arrived early, *Newsday* under his arm, and picked a booth along the wall, where he could watch the front door and see passers-by through the luncheonette's old-fashioned plate glass windows. He lived in Glen Cove, a run down town on Long Island's north shore, as did Nick Loh. Around the corner, on School Street, was the apartment above a storefront where Fuchs had set up his command post three weeks ago. Piping Rock Road in Locust Valley was five minutes away.

"You went to the command post," Crow replied. "We have you on tape going in."

"Oh, yeah, I forgot something."

"What was that?"

"I bought my kid a flash drive across the street at Staples. I left it in the squad when we turned out."

"A flash drive?"

"He needed it for school this morning."

"I assume you have a receipt."

"I do. At home."

"The copy machine was turned on."

Crow's face was pitted and rough looking, like someone had tried without much success to sand over smallpox scars. His eyes were dark and quietly penetrating.

"I confess."

"What did you copy?"

"My time sheets. I don't trust the U.N."

"That's all?"

"Hey Bill... Can I call you Bill?"

"Sure. First name basis."

"Is something missing? Am I being charged with something?"

Davila's tone was not disrespectful. He knew that he, himself, at five-six, one-sixty, with his scrawny goatee, did not look very tough. Not like Crow, who looked like he had survived Custer's Last Stand. He was as tough as Crow, though, this he knew. *But not now,* he thought, *stay cool. What you copied last night could get you killed.*

"What happened last night?" Crow asked, ignoring Davila's question.

"The guy came out with his cannon and sprayed the car."

"How did he know you were there?"

"The guy in the Hummer must have called him, or maybe he looked out the window." *Or maybe they knew in advance we'd be there, 'observing and communicating.' That Mach .45 Ingram came out awful fast.*

"Fuchs has some questions," Crow said. "A couple of things don't line up."

"Like what?"

"Like there's no blood in the car, no other forensics. Like Loh was shot outside."

"Did you see the windshield?" Davila replied. "I got lucky, Nick didn't."

"Fuchs is on his high horse," Crow said. "But to me, what difference does it make if Loh was shot inside the car or outside?"

"We followed orders," Davila said. "The guy just came out and started blasting. No warning."

"Did he step over the dead body?" Crow asked.

"He knelt behind it."

Davila had had no qualms about lying to Fuchs last night, and none about lying to Crow. He was not going to let Nick Loh's death in the line of duty be blemished in any way. Nick did what a cop should do, try to save lives.

"When's Loh's funeral?" the agent asked.

"Saturday."

"That's a rough thing that happened."

"Let me ask you something?" Davila said.

"Sure."

"Why do you think they left the third guy in the Hummer?"

"I have no idea."

"I feel like they knew we were there, that he was a look-out." *Like they knew about 'observe and communicate.'*

Crow took a sip of his coffee, put the chipped china mug down and took a pack of Camels out of the inside pocket of his suit jacket.

"You want one?" he said to Bob, shaking a cigarette free and pointing the pack across the table. Davila was sorely tempted. He loved to smoke, but his father and older brother, heavy smokers, had both died young of lung cancer. He had quit a hundred times in the last few years, the last time only a week ago. *He knows I want one, the fuck,* Bob thought, seeing the brief flicker of light in the F.B.I. agent's eyes.

"No thanks."

Crow lit his cigarette, and took a deep drag. "You think there's a rat on the team?" he asked, exhaling a long stream of white smoke up into the air.

Davila did not answer immediately. He was ready to leave. He had not spoken to Nick's wife, Patti, and was heading to her house right after this meeting with Crow. He knew there was a security camera at the School Street building's front entrance, but if there had been one in the small apartment they had been using as a command post, he'd have been arrested by now.

"Why not?" Davila replied, finally. "The U.N. goes by quotas, doesn't it? So there has to be at least one rat on every team. By the way," he continued, after a short pause. "Did you read the paper? They're saying it was a robbery."

Crow stubbed his cigarette out and leaned closer to Davila, his hands clasped on the table in front of him. "Let me tell you why I came up here, Bob," he said. "Fuchs' operation is something we support very much. By *we* I mean the justice department, your government. An F.B.I. team has gone over your car. There was no way your buddy was shot in it. We'll keep that our secret. We don't want to hurt Loh's reputation. More important, we want you to understand that your role is over. If you start asking questions, if you stick your nose in this thing, you'll be very sorry. Your life will change in the worst possible way. Am I clear? Tell me I didn't waste a trip up here."

"You didn't," Davila said. "It's not my business. Whatever Fuchs is working on, I wish him luck."

"I know you mean that," Crow said, getting up to leave, "but you know what Ronald Reagan said. *Trust but verify.*"

Davila watched Crow walk away, take his overcoat and scarf from the line of hooks near the front door, put them on and leave, turning his collar up as he stepped out into the freezing weather. Bob had kept his brown leather jacket on while they had their talk. He reached to its inside pocket and patted the papers he had put there last night. *Trust but verify,* he thought. *That motherfucker's gonna be up my ass.*

9.

Manhattan, Wednesday, February 25, 2009, 10:00AM

Matt DeMarco sat across from Manhattan District Attorney Jonathan Healy in Healy's low key but well-appointed office on the eighth floor of One Hogan Place, the building in the downtown courthouse complex that Matt and Healy had worked out of for the past twenty-plus years. The law books that lined the room's four walls were interrupted only by three tall windows, the two on Matt's right covered by heavy velour drapes, the one behind Healy admitting the weak mid-morning sunlight. This was, Matt knew, the four-time elected D.A.'s way of forcing all supplicants to squint as they asked him, the sun king, for favors.

"How are you holding up?" Healy asked.

"Fine. I just watched Andy Siegal open to the jury in an armed robbery case."

"How'd he do?"

"He did well."

Matt had agreed that, though not bound to do so by any hard and fast ethics rule, it would be best if he stopped handling cases while Michael's case was pending. He had been trying to keep busy advising Healy's young trial attorneys, especially those, like Andy Siegal, who were transitioning from misdemeanors to felonies, where the stakes were much higher. Healy's Chief Assistant, Nancy Coyne, had worked out a plea in the Morales case — she took the death penalty off the table — and Matt had not been on his feet, as trial lawyers put it, since.

"Good," Healy replied. "Nancy's got a good bunch of young Turks."

"I see the governor passed you over," Matt said. "Was there ever a chance?"

Matt was referring to the recent naming by New York's governor of Kirsten Gillibrand, an upstate congresswoman, to fill the senate seat vacated by Hillary Clinton on her swearing in as Secretary of State. The papers had been filled with rumors that Healy was in the running.

"Just rumors," Healy replied. He smiled when he said this, and Matt could tell, having worked with him for eighteen years, that the handsome and photogenic District Attorney had other irons in the political fire. Better irons, Matt thought, not surprised.

"But you didn't ask to see me to talk politics," Healy continued.

"No," Matt answered.

"We can't talk about Michael," Healy said. "You know that."

"I'm here to talk about Felix Diaz," Matt replied, "the doorman at Yasmine Hayek's building."

"Felix Diaz?"

"Yes."

"What about him?"

"He was killed last night. Executed."

"Executed? Where'd you get that?"

Matt, his face neutral, had been watching Healy carefully since he first sat down, maintaining eye contact as much as possible with the man, only ten years his senior, who outranked him by light years and who was never shy about putting Matt — his star prosecutor and thus, in Healy's eyes, a competitor for newspaper space — in his place.

"The Post," Matt replied.

"There was nothing about an execution in any paper."

"That doesn't mean it didn't happen. Come on, Jon."

"Where did you hear it, Matt?" Healy asked again.

"I read between the lines," Matt answered.

"Bullshit. You must have talked to McCann or Goode."

"Why? Did they say it was an execution in their report?"

"You're heading for trouble, Matt," Healy said, ignoring Matt's question.

Matt did not respond immediately. He had steered clear of Healy over the last three weeks, knowing that it would not look good for the D.A. if they were seen, or worse, photographed, together. This was their first meeting of any kind since the night of Michael's arrest. The handsome Irishman had very little trial experience, but his political skills were many and diverse. Still, Matt was surprised at how much Healy knew about the murder of a lowly Mexican doorman a short ten hours ago. Unless there were politics involved. But surely Healy knew what the circumstances surrounding the Diaz murder meant for Michael. *Someone else went into Yasmine's building.* So why the bullshit?

"Not me, *you*," Matt said, finally. "You have to tell Everett Stryker about this. If you don't, I will."

"Then you'll go before the Ethics Committee."

"You will too. Michael can get the death penalty, and you're withholding exculpatory evidence."

"I'll get your friends McCann and Goode fired."

"They did what good cops do. You'll get crucified if you go after them."

"Stay out of this, Matt." Healy said, getting to his feet. "I have my reasons. If you talk to Stryker or the papers or anyone outside the office, you'll be immediately fired."

"What reasons are those, Jon?" Matt asked, also getting to his feet. "I heard that our new Secretary of State called to congratulate you on solving the Hayek case so quickly."

"Where'd you hear that?"

"Are you denying it?"

Matt stared at his former friend for a second. "Don't

bother answering," he said, looking at his watch. "It's 10:15, February 25. Mark it down. I resign. I'll confirm it in writing when I get home."

"It doesn't matter if you're working here or not," Healy said. "You still have a conflict. The people are your client, remember that. The ethics rules still apply."

Matt walked to the door, but turned and looked back before pulling it open. "What is it, Jon? Governor? Attorney General? Is that what you're selling Michael out for?"

"He raped his girlfriend and then killed her because she was breaking up with him," Healy replied, his face hot and red. "Does that sound familiar? He's *your* son."

Matt took this in. Since he had been completely cleared in the Johnny Taylor case, he had not revealed the incident to Healy when he applied for an assistant D.A. job years ago. But the politically cunning Healy had somehow found out about it, and occasionally let Matt know that he knew—whenever a veiled threat was needed to keep the wild-man Matt in his place. This would be the last time.

"Fuck you, Jon," Matt said, finally.

"Yes, the feeling's mutual."

10.

From the floor-to-ceiling window in the study of his Park Avenue penthouse, Basil al-Hassan could see down the famous boulevard to the statue of Mercury, waving his serpent-entwined wand, atop Grand Central Station. Mercury, the Roman god of commerce, whose son was thought, in the mists of history, to be one of the founders of Damascus, the longest continuously inhabited city in the world. The same Damascus that at one time, also in the mists of history, was the center of Islam, but that was now a backwater, on the verge of irrelevance. On al-Hassan's desk behind him were copies of *Newsday* and *The New York Times,* and next to them the current edition of the *Cambridge Business Report.* All three contained news of Syria, or Syrians, that was of interest to him. His valet, Mustafa, had left a whiskey and soda on a silver tray and would buzz him when his stepson, Michael, appeared.

Hassan was not sorry to see that the house at 221 Piping Rock Road in Locust Valley had been so prominently mentioned in *Newsday,* though he was certain that it would be impossible to discover the identity of its true owner, the Assad family in Syria. The Assads owned many properties around the world, all purchased by intermediaries with the help of high-priced local lawyers, reputable cutouts who were well beyond the jurisdiction or subpoena power of any western country. Also on his desk was a list of calls that Mustafa had taken for him during the day. They included Everett Stryker, Michael's lawyer, and Khalif Wahim, the Syrian diplomat who owned, on paper, 221 Piping Rock Road. Anticipating the conversations he would have with these two men, he sipped the last of his drink and watched the lights of the city blink on as dusk turned to night.

In the window he could see his reflection and was pleased that at fifty-three his angular face was unlined, and that his hazel eyes, recessed beneath light brown brows, spoke of an inner softness that did not exist, had indeed never existed. His appearance was one deceit among the many he had learned to use in the several lives he had led since his impoverished childhood in his hometown on Syria's Mediterranean coast.

Stryker first, of course, he said to himself as he heard the muted buzz of his intercom and turned to sit in his plush leather chair.

"Sit," he said, as his stepson entered, nodding toward one of the two armchairs that faced his desk.

"Basil," Michael said, after taking the seat, "you wanted to see me."

"Yes, Michael. How are you?" Al-Hassan's tone was formal, as it always was when he spoke to Michael. This was another man's son, not his. He had had a son of his own once, a son whom the world knew nothing of, a son whose death had, by the grace of Allah, been avenged.

"I'm surviving."

"Sometimes that's all one can do, like the prisoners in Guantanamo Bay." Al-Hassan winced inwardly as he said this. The terms of Michael's bail were extremely liberal. He could not leave the state of New York or the country. He had to show up for all court proceedings. That was it. He was living in a two-story wrap-around penthouse with views of Manhattan in every direction. He had the exclusive use of a new BMW and gold-plated credit cards in his wallet. And then of course there was Debra, in agony since her son's arrest, desperate to comfort him in any way possible.

"If anyone can get me out of this, it's you," Michael said.

"Did you read the paper today?" the Syrian businessman asked, thinking of the two million dollar check he had written to post bond, and the things that money could, and could not, buy.

"No, why?"

"There was a robbery in Locust Valley last night, at the house where Adnan and Ali were living. Four people were killed, one of them a police officer."

"I thought Adnan and Ali absconded."

"No names were given," Basil replied. "I called my friend, Khalif. No one else had been given the keys. They may have returned, perhaps thinking it was safe."

"Have you spoken to Everett Stryker?"

"I have a call into him."

"This is not good news," Michael said. "If they're both dead…"

"If it was them, and if they're both dead, yes, it would be very bad luck. That's why I asked you to come see me. I wanted to tell you myself."

"I don't understand how no one had any contact with them. No one knew them."

"Except you and Yasmine."

"And you."

"Yes, I'm sorry I agreed to help them."

"What about Mustafa? He sponsored them. Has he heard from them?"

"No, nothing."

"What's to be done?"

"I don't know why the identities have not been released. I assume they will be. Then, we'll at least know if they're alive or dead." Al-Hassan watched as Michael shook his head and looked past him out the window. "This is depressing news, Michael," he said. "But you understand your mother and I are doing everything we can. We *do* believe you are innocent."

"I understand," Michael replied.

"Speaking of your mother. I am not going to tell her about this situation in Locust Valley until I speak to Stryker. Perhaps it was not Adnan and Ali. I do not want her any more depressed and anxious than she is. So we'll keep this to ourselves for the time being, shall we?"

"Yes, Basil, I agree. And thank you."

"You're welcome. Please tell Mustafa that I'll be down to dinner in thirty minutes."

After dinner, Hassan and Debra sat in stuffed chairs before the fireplace in the penthouse's large formal living room and sipped vintage port. Mustafa had built the fire earlier, and was now kneeling to light it. Bearded, muscular beneath his dark brown working abaya, his face expressionless, Hassan's manservant for the past six years rose and returned the enameled box of matches to its place on the mantel. Turning, he nodded, first to Debra and then to Hassan, and said, "Will you be returning to your office, sire?"

"Yes, I have more calls to make."

Mustafa, his hands folded at his chest, nodded and left the room.

Hassan sipped his drink and watched his wife's profile for a moment or two as she gazed at the fire. After several futile attempts early in their marriage, Debra had given up trying to engage Mustafa. When she asked Hassan why his valet was so bloodless, his response—still a joke between them—was that Mustafa, a descendant of Salah ad-Din, did not want to get close to someone he might have to kill some day to protect his master. Hassan was sure that his wife was not thinking of Mustafa or her husband's sense of humor tonight, or any night for the past three weeks.

"I have some news," he said.

"Is it good or bad?" Debra replied, turning to face him. She had kicked off her high heels and curled her stockinged legs under her.

"I don't know. Everett Stryker is looking into it."

"What is it?"

"There was an robbery at the house in Locust Valley last night. Four people were killed."

Hassan, still impeccable in the navy blue blazer, flannel slacks and Italian loafers he had worn all day, watched his wife slump in her seat, then reach to the bottle of Dow 1963 on the end table next to her and refill her empty glass. This morning a package had arrived from Stryker containing police reports, photographs, forensics and other material, what the defense lawyer referred to in his cover letter as the *discovery* in Michael's case. Debra had spent the day poring over it in her room, her face ashen when she emerged for cocktails at six. Now it was more ashen.

"A robbery?" she said. "How can that be?"

"It was in the paper this morning. It's very sketchy, but it appears it was what the Americans call a home invasion."

"Are they dead, Adnan and Ali?"

"As I say, the news report is vague. Stryker has many contacts. He will get the full story. He knows how important they are to Michael's defense." Hassan had in fact spoken before dinner to Stryker, who, after a day of trying, could gather nothing further than what had been skimpily revealed in the press: four men dead by gunfire, one a cop, the local police involved, the mansion owned by Khalif Wahim, a high ranking Syrian diplomat, signs of a home invasion.

"How do we know it was them?"

"We don't, but who else would be there? I spoke to Khalif. The place was locked tight. He had authorized no one to use it."

"Four men dead…," Debra said. "What paper was it in?"

"*Newsday*. I will have Mustafa bring it to you."

"The identities have to be revealed eventually, don't they?"

"Not necessarily. According to Stryker, information concerning an ongoing investigation can be withheld."

"He's being paid a lot of money."

"We must trust him."

"Are there other ways to find out? I know you have other...other resources."

"Other resources? Debra..."

"I am not as blind as you think, Basil. You go off to secret meetings without telling me details. You take phone calls in the middle of the night. You used to tell me everything. Something has changed in your life, and between us."

"Do you think I am having an affair?"

"No, worse."

"Worse? What could be worse?"

His wife of six years, who had been staring passively at the fire this whole time, now turned to face Basil, whose heartbeat quickened when he saw the whites of her once clear and beautiful eyes shot through with webs of blood, and the puffiness and rawness in the flesh around them.

"When this is over, Basil, can we go some place alone together? You are gone so often now..."

"There is an energy crisis at home. You know that is why I travel so much, why I must talk on the phone on a moment's notice."

"No, Basil, don't."

"Don't what?"

"No more lies."

Basil stood, reached down, took his wife's hands in his and pulled her gently but firmly to her feet. Facing her, he drew her closer and put his arms around her.

"Do you love me, Basil?" Debra said, before he could speak. Taken aback by the urgency, the near desperation in her voice, he held her tighter.

"Yes, I love you, Debra," he replied. "As I always have."

"I have never interfered with your business."

"I know."

"Are you in trouble?"

"Of course not."

"I don't mean to accuse you. I apologize. I am..."

"You are what?"

"Nothing. Forgive me."

"There is nothing to forgive. When Michael is free, we will go away, just the two of us."

"Thank you, Basil."

"Debra."

"Yes?"

Hassan hesitated for a second. His wife's mental health was not good, and he did not want to make it worse. He was still holding her gently in his arms. Before he could speak Mustafa appeared at the room's arched doorway, with his right fist to his ear. *Telephone.* Over Debra's shoulder Basil nodded to his servant, and then, separating from her slightly, he extracted the silk handkerchief from the breast pocket of his blazer and handed it to his wife.

"I must take a call," he said.

"Forgive me, Basil. Michael did not do this."

"I know. You should rest."

Debra returned to her chair. Basil turned to leave the room, but then turned back and put his hand on her shoulder. He had been about to suggest that perhaps it would be a good thing if Adnan and Ali were dead. Perhaps they could prove that they were elsewhere at the time of Yasmine's murder. Feeling the trembling in her body, looking at her pressing her hand to her eyes, trying to hold back her tears, he was glad he had been interrupted by Mustafa. If Michael had indeed killed Yasmine Hayek, then he would soon enough lose his wife.

11.

After being excused by Basil, Mustafa retired to his office, a converted pantry off of the kitchen, where he listened for a few seconds to his employer's conversation with a reporter from the Cambridge Business News. An innocuous conversation. One of many involving Basil and his American wife and stepson that Mustafa had listened to since he took his current position six years ago. He disconnected his listening device, which had also recorded the call, and sat back to think. Unlike the wealthy and pampered Basil al-Hassan, he had no window in his office, nowhere to look but inward. This he did, recalling in vivid detail the dark paneled, hushed room in the Lebanese consulate on Lexington Avenue where, in November, his efforts and his patience of the past six years had begun to bear fruit.

I think it is time, Mustafa, the colonel had said, *that we bring our orphans to New York.*

Is there work to be done here, sire?

No, but we are going to have new friends in Washington. We think they may want to help us with Monteverde.

Yes, sire.

When the time is right, we will show our good faith by offering them our orphans. They acted alone, you see. They are fanatics, angry at the west, at Lebanese secularism.

The case would be solved.

Yes, Mustafa. You and our war hero can keep them occupied until the moment is right. What safer place than right here in New York.

The Middle East is a very dangerous place, sire.

Yes, Mustafa, too dangerous to keep our orphans there.

Am I to still watch him? Our war hero?

Yes, and listen. He is up to something. Deir ez-Zour is drying up. If I catch him, no one will protect him.

I have some new information.

Yes?

He ordered a grave marker today.

A grave marker?

Yes, a replacement, from a stone mason in Latakia.

His home town.

Yes.

And the name of this stone mason?

It is in the envelope, with my report.

A grave marker?

Yes.

Mustafa had slipped out of a rear servant's door at the consulate that night. On his way through an unused kitchen he had caught a glimpse of the party, the women in glittering gowns, the men in tuxedoes, the food and drink on silver platters, the lush furniture and carpeting, all softly lit from above by three massive crystal chandeliers, glowing like the planets he used to look at in the night sky from the roof of his tenement in Beirut when he was a boy. He did not see Hassan, but he saw his American wife, smiling her supremely confident smile, and her son, Michael, talking in a corner to Yasmine Hayek, the daughter of a politician in Lebanon that Mustafa knew well, a politician who was helping to destroy the country of his birth by westernizing it, a man who thought women should work and get divorced and vote. A man who allowed himself and his wife and daughter to be photographed for western newspapers.

And then there was the meeting, just a month ago, in the cold, on a bench in Battery Park, the Statute of Liberty shrouded in fog in the bay.

This is hard to believe, Mustafa.

Yes, sire.

I cannot tell Damascus. We have joined the family of peace-loving nations.

Yes, sire.

Temporarily.

Yes, sire.

I have learned our war hero's secret. Damascus will blame him.

Yes, sire.

And you have her on video?

Yes, sire.

Then yes, go ahead.

And after?

They must both be killed.

I cannot tell Damascus, the colonel had said. *Damascus will blame him.* Smiling, Mustafa rose and laid out his mat in anticipation of *Isha'*, his last prayer before bed. So, he said to himself, my colonel will act alone in this matter, without the blessing of his superiors. *Therefore so will I, and, Insha'Allah, I will have my revenge at last.*

12.

Glen Cove, Saturday, February 28, 2009, 10:00AM

The ground was snow covered but the sky a clear blue on the day of Nick Loh's funeral. In addition to the hearse and the limousines carrying the family, there were some fifty cars in the motorcade from St. Rocco's church in Glen Cove to Holy Rood Cemetery in Westbury. Included in these were the chiefs' cars from a dozen towns on Long Island and spotless NYPD SUV's carrying brass from the five boroughs. Arriving late to the funeral mass, Matt DeMarco had been lucky to find a seat at the back of the crowded church. Jade Lee sat a few pews in front of him, her raven black hair unmistakable. Next to her was a man who, even from behind, had the look and bearing of an athlete. At a slender six-five or six, he towered above the people around him when standing was required during the mass. *Her new man,* Matt thought, thinking of the Dutch dinner they were supposed to have. He couldn't remember how they had left it, but he had not called her, and now knew why she hadn't called him.

Afterward, Matt stood among a group of civilians on the crest of a low hill and watched as an honor guard consisting of five rows of blue-dress-uniformed policemen and women, about a hundred in total, lined up at attention and raised their right hands—clad in pristine white cotton dress gloves—to salute, while six others, including Bobby Davila at the right front, lifted Loh's casket, draped with the American flag, to their shoulders. At least five hundred other uniformed police officers surrounded the gravesite, their gold jacket buttons, hat braids and insignia sparkling in the late morning sun. All came to attention as the pallbearers slowly walked their burden through the grassy corridor that separated the immediate family and friends, placing it gently on a low steel trestle next to the open grave. A bagpiper in kilts came to the last mournful note of Taps as they saluted and backed away.

Matt did not know Loh's wife personally and thought better of trying to approach her through the crowd when the service was over. He had paid his respects to her the night before at the wake, where another sea of blue had washed in and around the small, overwhelmed funeral home in town. When he got to the parking lot he saw Jack McCann, his hands in his overcoat pockets, a cigarette in his mouth, standing next to his car.

"Jack," Matt said. "What's up?"

"You resign and don't call me, Matt? What the fuck?" McCann took a last drag on his cigarette after he said this, then threw the butt on the asphalt pavement, where it hissed itself out in the melting snow.

"I didn't want to get you in any more trouble than you were already in."

"I'm not in any trouble. The two cases are connected, so I reported it."

"You reported it to *me*."

"Fuck it."

"Healy's got more shit on more people, Jack," Matt said. "You know that. And he holds a grudge. He can hurt you."

"Clarke's pissed too."

Matt could see that his friend of fifteen years was not angry, just unable, or unwilling, to control his flare for the dramatic, the Irish volatility that he laid on friend and foe alike as he went through his day.

"I'll call him." Matt said.

"What did Healy say?"

"You haven't heard?"

"No."

"He thinks Diaz was coincidental," Matt said, surprised. Healy had more than the usual control over his organization, but in an office with six hundred lawyers and three times the staff, news traveled very fast. "He's not telling Stryker."

"You're kidding."

"No. I wish I were."

"Is that why you quit?"

"Yes. I'm seeing Stryker on Monday."

McCann nodded and was about to say something but was interrupted by the ringing of his cell phone. Matt watched as the detective extracted the phone from his coat pocket, flipped it open and looked at the screen. "Hold on," he said, "it's Clarke."

"Yeah," he said, putting the phone to his ear, and then listening for a few seconds.

"O.K...I'm with him right now," McCann said, closing the phone and putting it away. "Something else you can tell Stryker," he said, looking at Matt.

"What?"

"The security system in the Excelsior, the girl's building, it looks like it was tampered with in some way."

"How?"

"Technical assistance just went through it all. They're not sure, a deletion maybe, editing of some kind."

"It's legit?"

"They say it's very sophisticated, that whoever did it used software that only big players have, intelligence agencies."

"Like the CIA?"

"Yes, million dollar software. They're taking a hard look, calling people in the industry, in friendly agencies."

"And Diaz is dead. The only witness."

"There's more," McCann said. "Clarke went out to the

company that operated the system, in Jersey. That's where he was just now. They're gone, closed up. The people next door said they vanished overnight."

Matt shook his head.

"The neighbors said they were Arabs. Syrian. They had a black and red flag in the window."

"Can someone be framing Michael? Is that possible?"

"Or just covering up for the real killer," McCann said.

"Either way, Jon Healy doesn't give a shit."

"No, he wants to be governor or some other bullshit."

"Thank you, Jack," Matt said. "I really appreciate this. Stay out of it now. Don't get yourself in trouble. I'll tell Stryker. He'll know how to handle it."

"Don't try to protect me," McCann said. "I'm not staying out of it. Nick Loh was a good kid, a good cop. And your son is in a big jam."

Matt looked at his friend of fifteen years. Jack and Clarke were the only people he had ever told the Johnny Taylor story to. Not Debra, certainly not Michael. Just them. And he knew about McCann's small piece of hell as well: the wife and teenage daughter who he never saw, who had walked away from him because of his drinking, the AA meetings he made and the many he skipped.

"Sorry, Jack," Matt said.

"I think the girl was executed," said McCann, nodding slightly, acknowledging Matt's apology.

"For political reasons, you mean?" Matt replied. He knew, as did Jack, that Yasmine's father was a pro-West big shot in Lebanon, that a political assassination on U.S. soil was the last thing the new administration in Washington wanted. Hence the joy at the state department to learn that her killing was one of passion: *the jilted boyfriend did it, thank God.*

"Maybe just to frame Michael."

"Jack, the kid's an arrogant fool, but who would want to frame him for murder? What's the motive?"

"Maybe it's you, Matt," McCann answered, his face grim,

the perennial twinkle in his blue eyes gone for a second. "You've made some enemies. All D.A.'s do. Think about it."

13.

Manhattan, Saturday, February 28, 2009, 9:00PM

Hell's Kitchen was no longer Hell's Kitchen, but Rudy's, the bar on Ninth Avenue where Matt had his first legal drink, had not changed. The faux Tiffany lamps above the bar and over the leather-cushioned booths still cast their mellow light, the wood floor was as scuffed as ever, and the unpretentious crowd—balding men in khakis and women who drank beer—chatted and watched the same small television that Matt watched with his friends in 1980. On the night of Nick Loh's funeral, Matt, in jeans, a navy blue wool sweater, and Gore-Tex boots, walked the twenty blocks from his apartment to Rudy's, his gloved hands stuffed in his overcoat pockets, a thick scarf around his neck to fend off Ninth Avenue's whistling headwind. It was fifteen degrees out, but for the first time in three weeks he felt like getting out and moving around.

At the bar he ordered a shot of Jameson and a glass of draft Heineken. He had two pieces of information that were very important: the doorman at Yasmine's building had been killed in what looked like an execution, and the Excelsior's digital surveillance system had been tampered with. Someone else had entered Yasmine's apartment on the afternoon of the murder, someone who had been deleted from the building's security video, and who had coerced Felix Diaz into lying to the police. And then killed him for his trouble.

On the ride home this afternoon from Long Island, Matt had called Jane Manning, the head of T.A.R.U., the NYPD's technical assistance unit, and asked her point blank if she was willing to testify about the security system. She said she certainly would. On Monday, Matt would impart all of this to Everett Stryker. Stryker would kill Healy with this information, both in court and, worse for Healy, in the press. The case against Michael was getting weaker all the time. The scotches that Matt had been nursing in his apartment in the evenings had been medicinal—anti-depressants—but the Jameson and beer chaser were celebratory. The fact that Michael hated his guts didn't matter. He was no murderer and would soon be free of the absurd charges against him.

He was about to order another whiskey when his cell phone rang. Jade Lee's name and number were on the screen

"I saw you today," he said, after putting the phone to his ear.

"I saw you too. Where did you go?"

"I took the back way to the parking lot."

"Where are you? Are you busy?"

"I'm at Rudy's."

"Really? Are you with somebody?"

"No."

"You're drinking alone?"

"Yes."

"We need to talk. How about if I come over?"

"Fine. Are you bringing your new guy?"

"New guy?"

"The tall one next to you in church today."

"That was Antonio. I'll be right there."

Matt clicked the phone off. *Antonio? The kid must have grown a foot since I last saw him.*

"Antonio's grown up," Matt said to Jade.

They were sitting in a booth along the back wall, Rudy's

prized seats because they were dark and out of the way and private but still afforded a view of the entire one-room bar. *Summer Wind,* the Lyle Lovett version, was playing on the jukebox. Most of the men in the place had turned to stare at Jade when she came in through the glass front door and stood to look around for Matt. When she greeted him with a kiss on the cheek he felt the pride that all men feel when they are seen by other men with a beautiful woman. The booth had cost him a twenty-dollar tip to the bartender, but it was worth it. A young waitress had just placed shots of Jameson and Heineken chasers in front of them.

"He has," Jade answered.

"What's he up to, besides basketball?"

"The Jesuits are kicking his ass."

"The Jesuits?"

"He goes to Regis."

Matt smiled. He had gone, on his father's orders, to the all boys Regis High School, on East 84th Street, for three years, from 1976 to 1979, an hour-plus commute from the Bronx everyday. Though he had been kicked out for fighting—he had broken a classmate's nose during a basketball scrimmage, and then broke it again two weeks later in a confrontation on the street—and though he had hated it while he was there, he later came to feel a quiet love for the place, and had tried to get Michael to go there, but Debra had other ideas, as usual.

"No game tonight?" Matt asked.

"He's in Florida with the team. They play three games down there on their winter break."

"To Antonio," Matt said, lifting his shot of whiskey.

"I haven't done this in a while," Jade said, lifting hers.

"It's a cold winter night," Matt said. "It'll do you good."

"Here goes," Jade said. "To Michael as well." She lifted her shot glass and clinked it against Matt's. They knocked their drinks back simultaneously, then sipped their beers.

"How about you?" Matt asked, putting his beer down. "Are you O.K.?" Jade looked fine, more beautiful than ever, if that was possible, her color high from the walk in the cold, and her amazing eyes aglow as the Irish whiskey did its work. There was, though, something off about her, something slightly forced about her smile that made him ask this question. Maybe she's lonely, he thought, with her son away. Lonely like me, he added, surprising himself. *No job, no son. Drinking alone…*

"Antonio wants to visit his father in Los Angeles. He found him on the internet."

"The producer."

"Yes."

Matt knew the bare bones of the story of Jade's relationship with Antonio's father. At seventeen, young and tall and voluptuous and unbelievably beautiful, she had left Queens and gone to Los Angeles to become an actress. She returned three months later, pregnant with Antonio, the father a producer who she described succinctly as a scumbag who wore too much cologne. Her two marriages followed, both short and painful. When she moved to 45th Street after her second divorce, she went to Mass every day at St. Malachy's, the actors' chapel across the street, to remind herself, she said, of her stupidity and of the inevitable consequences of vainglory.

"Let him go," Matt said.

Jade did not answer.

"He'll go anyway."

"The guy's rich, a player in Hollywood," Jade said. "He does big budget movies now."

"You think the kid will be seduced," Matt said, wincing inwardly at his poor choice of words, watching Jade's eyes, which went vacant for a second. She did not answer.

"You can't stop him, Jade," Matt said. "The thing is, if you try, he'll only want to go more. When does he want to go?"

"Spring break, in six weeks."

"It's his father." Matt felt the full weight of the irony of this sentence as he uttered it. Antonio would be traveling three thousand miles to see a father he had never met and who had ignored him for seventeen years. Michael could not walk thirty blocks to visit Matt. The pull of blood to blood, ancient and primal, had had no effect on his own son.

Jade remained silent. Matt watched her as she took a sip of her beer and returned the traditional, curved glass to the wooden table. Her eyes rose to meet his, and in that meeting Matt saw not acceptance on Jade's part, but something else, something more akin to fear than resignation. What was she afraid of?

"What about you?" Jade said, breaking their eye contact, and her chain of thoughts, whatever they were. "How's Michael doing?"

"I'm not sure, to tell you the truth," Matt replied. "I tried to get him to come to Nick Loh's funeral with me, but he couldn't."

"Too bad," Jade said. "Five hundred cops, not to mention Healy and the Mayor, would have gotten the message."

"Yes, that was the point, but he couldn't make it."

This was a lie. Matt had not spoken to his son since he was released on bail on the Monday after Yasmine's murder. His several messages had gone unreturned. He was sure Jade would see through it. How busy could Michael be as he hung around Manhattan waiting for trial? She would understand, he knew she would, but it stung too much for him to talk about it.

"I'm here about Michael," Jade said.

"Not me?"

"You too."

"What about him?"

"I got a strange call from Bob Davila."

"What kind of a call?"

"He knows I go to St. Malachy's. He told me there was something there for me, in a missal in a back pew on the left."

"*Was* there?"

"Yes. I went to 5:30 Mass tonight. This is what I found." Jade reached into her shoulder bag on the bench seat next to her, extracted an eight-by-ten manila envelope, and handed it to Matt.

The first thing he pulled out was a three page document with *United Nations International Independent Investigation Commission* below the UN's iconic light blue, olive branch-encircled globe, at the top of each page.

"Where did he get these?" he asked, after carefully reading all three pages.

"I don't know," Jade replied.

"Do you know what they are?"

"I think so."

"Did you see the entry for January 30?"

"Yes."

"*Fifteen-ten. Suspects 1 and 2 enter apartment building at 1011 Central Park West. Fifteen-thirty, suspects exit building.*' This is a United Nations surveillance log. The investigators' identifications are coded. *China 1 and China 6.*"

"Did you see the one on the night before?" Jade asked. "They went into Lucky's in Queens."

"I see it," Matt answered after flipping the pages backward. "That's the club Michael mentioned."

Laying the surveillance log aside, Matt pulled the remaining documents from the light brown envelope: various identification cards for one Ali al-Najjar, two three-by-five color photographs, a half sheet of plain white paper with *Bill Crow, FBI???* written on it and a print-out of a magazine article by Christopher Hatch, titled *The West Selling Its Soul.* Matt read the I.D. cards, then, after staring at the photos intently, said, "Adnan and Ali. Suspect 1 and Suspect 2. Michael's friends."

"I thought so," Jade said. "There's one more thing. Davila asked me if *Monteverde* meant anything to me. I went online. There are a bunch of hotels around the world named Monteverde. One of them is closed. It's in Lebanon. It's the headquarters of the United Nations team investigating the assassination of the Lebanese Prime Minister, Rafik Hariri."

"They're looking at Syria."

"Yes. It's supposed to come to trial in March in The Hague. I also found the Hatch article. It's pretty interesting."

"What does he say?"

"He thinks the US has offered to shut down Monteverde if Syria will make peace with Israel."

"Does he have proof?"

"Who has proof of things like that?"

"The papers said Loh was working on a drug task force."

"I don't think so, Matt."

"I don't either. Not now. Do you have Davila's number?"

"Yes."

"Let's call him. We'll ask him who Bill Crow is."

"I already talked to him. I told him you'd want to talk to him."

"What did he say?"

"He's being very cautious," Jade continued, "I think he stole this report."

"Did he say that?" Matt said.

"No, but why all the cloak-and-dagger?"

Matt let his mind drift for a moment to the day he first met Davila in 1993, when he prepped him for his trial testimony in *People v. Hakimi*. Only twenty-years old, with a background similar to Matt's, the newly-minted, bantam-weight Hispanic cop had quickly acknowledged that he had created a Miranda problem for Matt, but he was proud that he had done the right thing by Jack McCann, a fellow officer, had saved his career most likely, and his pension.

"He told me the story about your honor-killing case." Jade said.

"What story?"

"The thing with McCann, the problem he created. He said you saved his ass."

"He's exaggerating."

"You're a tough guy, Matt, a stoic, but you've got a lot of friends."

Matt let this pass, thinking *not enough to keep my son from getting indicted for a murder he didn't commit.*

"He wants to meet us tonight," Jade said. "He said he'd call me at ten to fix a time and place."

Matt looked at his watch. It was nine-thirty. "We'll sip our beer," he said.

"No more whiskey."

"No. My limit is two anyway."

"Mine is one."

Their eyes met again, and Matt was suddenly reticent, a condition he had not encountered in himself in a long time. "I have to ask you," he said, finding his tongue. "*Is* there a new guy?"

"No, there's not," Jade replied. "And you? Is there a woman?"

Matt shook his head. "No," he said. He took a sip of his beer and replaced the glass on the table. He had a question to ask: *Why did you break up with me, Jade, really?* But he couldn't get it to his lips. Five years was a long time to wait to ask a question like that. All breakups are the same and all breakups are different, but theirs was a strange and surely an aberrant one. They date for a few weeks, they make love once, and then she abruptly ends it. *I can't do it, Matt,* was all she said. *I can't do it.* Stranger still was his refusal to press her, to ask her what she meant, unable to even think about swallowing his pride, to beg. Now she was here to help his idiot son, and his pride suddenly looked more like arrogance or some weird macho self-indulgence. Matt the tough guy, Matt the guy who begged no one.

"Jade...," he said, but the ringing of Jade's cell phone interrupted him.

"It's Bobby," Jade said, looking at the screen. "He's early."

14.

Behind the wheel of her BMW SUV, seated high enough to see all the cars ahead of her, Debra al-Hassan ground her third Adderall of the day with her teeth, worked up some saliva in a mouth that was of late always too dry, and swallowed it as she drove through the Midtown Tunnel. She would need two Ambiens, at least, to fall asleep tonight, but she had no choice, she needed to be alert. She had been taking Prozac and Valium surreptitiously for over a year, but had never had to double down on them as she had lately with her new pills. She seemed always to be either in a leaden fog, drowsy and half asleep, or strung way too tight, her nerves screaming, her senses receiving and painfully amplifying the slightest whim of the world around her. No in-between. No real rest.

The tunnel's lights shocked her at first with their intensity. *Calm down,* she told herself, *calm down. It's just a tunnel, and not a long one.* Five cars ahead a nondescript blue Chevrolet with diplomatic license plates was gliding through the tunnel's graceful curves at a steady fifty miles an hour. *Don't get distracted. Don't lose that car.*

Basil was en route to Syria. She was supposed to be on her way to their beach house in East Hampton. Earlier this evening, around six o'clock, she had overheard Mustafa make what she thought were arrangements to be picked up in front of her Park Avenue co-op at eight. At seven-thirty, an overnight bag on her shoulder, wearing a Mets cap, her long brown hair in a pony tail, she had retrieved her car from the parking garage around the corner and found an illegal space in a loading zone a short distance from her building's gilded entrance.

Exactly at eight Mustafa emerged and approached the blue Chevrolet, which had appeared virtually simultaneously. Instead of getting in, however, he handed something to the driver through the passenger window. She froze as her husband's sphinx-like manservant backed away from the Chevy and gazed up and down Park Avenue before turning to go back into the building. He had not seen her. Her heart pounding, her mouth drier than ever, she decided to follow the Chevrolet.

Mustafa, whose *yes madams* and *no madams* had been tinged with contempt these past six years, especially when Basil was not present, was the key. Adnan and Ali were his lap dogs. They would never have framed Michael on their own. With Basil away, her second Adderall doing its work, curled up in a blanket by the fire, pretending to be asleep or in her usual state of listlessness, she had been able to quietly track Mustafa with her half-closed eyes and fully open ears. At six he had taken a call on his cell phone while attending the fire.

When she emerged from the tunnel, relieved to have its glaring lights and suffocating, too-narrow confines behind her, the screen in her head that she could not control pulled itself down and technicolor, surround-sound scenes of her and Michael began immediately to play. This reel was one of the many that had begun playing the night she heard that her son had been charged with murder. The screen came down and the movies came on at random moments, maddeningly random moments, like now.

Mommy, where's Daddy?

He left us, Michael.
Mommy, can I sleep with you tonight?
Yes, Michael. I'm lonely too, and afraid.
Michael, do you like Mommy's new dress?
It's beautiful, like you.
Who do you love more, Mom, me or Basil?
Who do you think?
He left us, Michael. He left us.

The reels varied in content, but the last scene was always the same. Home from Boston for the holiday break, just two months ago, Michael had announced that he and Mina—*how she hated that dimunitive, that lover's nickname*—were getting married. No preliminaries, no warmth in his voice, on his way out of the Park Avenue apartment, his coat and scarf on.

"Where are you off to?"
"To see Mina. We're celebrating."
"Celebrating what?"
"We're getting married."

A simple fact. No big deal. Her heart in shock. She could feel it even now as she was forced to watch the scene play out for the hundredth time.

"You're only twenty-two, Michael. Yasmine's not even out of college yet."
"She graduates in May. We'll be married in June."
"And her parents? Do they approve?"
"She hasn't told them yet, but they'll be happy for her."
"What about school?"
"I'll finish the semester."
"Finish the semester?"
"Yes, it's paid for. But then I'm going to work for Shell or PetroCanada. In Lebanon. Yasmine wants to return home."
"Lebanon?"
"Yes. It won't be forever."
"You've spoken to Basil?"
"No, but he's said many times that when I'm ready he would place me."

"You know nothing about petro-chemistry or petro-engineering."

"There are other career paths. Marketing, public relations. The master's I'm getting is in communications. I can finish it there. B.U. has a relationship with the American University in Beirut. You seem distressed, Mother."

"I'm not distressed, but I'm against this marriage. It can wait Michael."

"No it can't. You've been running my life for too long. I'm getting married in June. I hope you'll be there."

Cut to her bedroom:

He is not my son, Basil says. I will not interfere. Talk to his father. It is for the two of you to guide him. If he asks me to find him work, I will, as I have promised.

How she had looked forward to the reception at the Lebanese consulate last fall. Her new Dior gown, a chance to wear her diamonds. Michael flying down from Boston. How handsome he looked in his tuxedo talking to the beautiful Yasmine Hayek, the center of much attention, her father, Pierre, the recently named Justice Minister in Lebanon, a women's rights advocate, an international celebrity. And what bitter fruit.

After his announcement, she could not corner Michael, who was either with Yasmine or Adnan and Ali for the rest of his semester break. Avoiding her. He'll come to his senses, she had thought, when he returns to school, but she was wrong. On the last weekend in January, back in Boston only ten days, Michael hurried home to see Yasmine. It had been her idea to lock the penthouse, not Basil's. Why let the newly betrothed—another word she hated—couple enjoy the luxury of Park Avenue? Have sex in any room they chose to? But her son had done something he hadn't done in years; he had gone to his father's in Westchester. And been arrested for raping and killing Yasmine. And now, the real killers, Adnan and Ali, were also dead.

Mustafa, she thought, you *have* to be the key.

Her skin crawled and she felt slightly nauseous—the Adderall, taken on an empty stomach, had quickly kicked in—at the thought of her husband's stocky, never-smiling servant padding, silently alert, like a panther, around her apartment, around her life, these past six years.

Debra followed the Chevrolet as it took the Glen Cove Road exit off the Long Island Expressway, staying discreetly behind as it turned into a maze-like neighborhood of narrow streets lined with small but solid, muscular looking brick homes. When it stopped in front of one of these, she drove past, turning left at the next corner. After a K turn in a dark driveway, her headlights off, she went back and parked under a street sign that said *Frost Pond Road*. As her eyes adjusted to the moonless night, she spotted a man in a long black coat emerge from the now darkened Chevrolet, which was parked at the curb in the middle of the block. She watched as he moved in a crouch toward a car in a nearby driveway and then disappeared. Into the car or under it, she could not be sure which. A few minutes passed, perhaps five or six at the most, before the man reappeared, noiselessly got back into the Chevrolet, started it and pulled away, his headlights off. Debra ducked as the car approached, but not before getting a quick glimpse of the man's inverted-spade beard and something that looked like euphoria in his gleaming, black eyes.

Matt and Jade arrived early to the rooftop of the five story-parking garage that serviced downtown Glen Cove. They had seen a few cars parked on the lower levels as they wound their way up, but the top level was empty and silent, with piles of dirty snow pushed into the four corners. Matt backed his Ford SUV against a concrete wall, facing the up ramp. As he backed up, he caught a glimpse of Main Street, its storefronts dark, its street lights standing lonely in the winter cold.

"I'll keep the car running, it's cold out there," Matt said, looking at his watch. "We're right on time."

"It's a nice night, really," Jade replied, "except for the cold of course."

They scanned the empty rooftop and the lights of the small city of Glen Cove and its suburbs, sparkling in the clear night air. Above, a nearly full moon dominated a cloudless black sky.

"You've been quiet, Matt," Jade said, breaking the silence.

Matt did not reply immediately. He *had* been quiet on the ride to Long Island. The downed security system, the Diaz murder, these things spoke loudly of reasonable doubt. And now a new development, the U.N. surveillance log. A good lawyer would find a way to use it. It was not unreasonable to start thinking that the indictment against Michael would be dismissed. Then what? Everett Stryker would be a hero. Basil al-Hassan would be a hero. And Michael would be as arrogant and as dismissive of him as ever, probably even more so. Where would that leave Matt?

"I have to ask you," Matt said, finally. "Why...did you break up with me? I mean *really* why?"

"It took you a long time to ask that question."

Matt had been looking at Jade's hands this while, which were clad in red woolen gloves with soft leather palms and finger fronts. Now he looked up.

"I did ask. You said you couldn't do it."

"Which you accepted. As if you were relieved. 'Are you sure?' you said, and that was it."

Matt said nothing, thinking of the implications of this statement.

"That hurt," Jade said. "I figured it was my two divorces."

"It wasn't. I'm sorry."

Jade looked down now, and took Matt's hands in hers. The car was steadily idling, the windows beginning to fog, but there was something in the way Jade tilted her head that drove the world away, something that heightened his senses — to the scent of her, to the touch of her fingers lightly caressing his.

"It was Michael, he was part of it," Jade said, looking up, her eyes finding Matt's in the car's darkened interior.

"Michael?"

"I thought you were punishing yourself. That you were enjoying it somehow."

Matt watched Jade's face as she said this, saw the stricken look in her eyes, and was struck himself by how hard a thing this must have been for her to say, five years ago, when she couldn't, and now, when somehow she could. He knew she was right. He had become a beggar for his son's love. Who wanted someone with no self-respect for a lover? A mate?

"Do you still feel the same way?" he asked.

"No," Jade said. "I was too harsh. I'm afraid now that Antonio will go with his father. I'm scared to death, actually, and I'm ashamed of myself."

"Ashamed of yourself?"

"Yes. For judging you so harshly."

Jade squeezed Matt's hands tightly, then took off one of her gloves to wipe at the tears that were beginning to well in her eyes. Taking her arm, Matt pulled her gently toward him.

"There's something else," Jade said. That stricken look was still in her eyes. She was still silently crying, tears running down her face.

"No, Jade," Matt said, "It doesn't matter." He was about to kiss her tears away, when an explosion in the distance lit the night sky, the large *kaboom* reaching them a split second later.

"Jesus," Jade said. "What was that?" Smoke was now trailing upwards from the tree line of a neighborhood that appeared to be about a half mile away. Matt looked at his watch again.

"He's ten minutes late," he said.

"Bobby?"

Matt did not answer. He still had his police scanner in his car, mounted on the dashboard. In his prior life he had been to dozens of crime scenes, to breathe the air, he used to say, where a murder had been done. He turned it on. After some intermittent crackling and static, they heard the staccato voices of first fire, and then police dispatches to an address on Frost Pond Road. Within only a minute or two, arrivals on the scene were relaying information to headquarters and to other responders.

"Did you hear them say *Frost Pond Road*?" Jade asked.

"Yes, and *car bomb*," Matt replied.

"That's where Bob Davila lives."

"Shit," was all Matt could say, shaking his head, hearing the multiple sirens converging on Frost Pond Road.

"Can we go over there?"

"We'll never get close," Matt answered. "Try calling Bobby."

Jade found her cell phone in her shoulder bag, and, after scrolling quickly, pushed her send button. She held the phone to her ear for ten seconds or so before snapping it shut.

"Nothing," she said. "No ringing, no message. Nothing."

"I'll try Clarke," Matt said, bringing out his cell phone. "He lives nearby." He pushed the speed dial button for Clarke Goode's cell phone, hoping his old friend would pick up, but dreading what he would find out once he made a couple of calls of his own. As he put the phone to his ear, he looked down and saw that he was holding Jade's hand in his.

"Matt, is that you?" Matt heard through his receiver.

"Clarke, yes," Matt replied.

"This can't be good."

"It's not. There was an explosion a few minutes ago on Frost Pond Road in Glen Cove. I heard it on my scanner. That's the street Bob Davila lives on."

Goode was silent for a second. Then he said, "I'll call you back."

"He'll call me back," Matt said after pushing the *end* button on his phone. In the distance they could see the billows of smoke above the explosion site lessen as the firefighters did their work. Dozens of blue and red police and fire strobes lit up the night sky. Two helicopters appeared, searchlights shooting from each as they swept the neighborhood.

"Too late," Matt murmured.

"Too late?" Jade asked.

"Whoever wired that car is long gone."

"Matt," Jade said, increasing her grip pressure, "don't leave me tonight. If Bobby's been killed..."

"I won't," Matt answered. "And by the way, you were right."

"No, Matt, I wasn't."

Before Matt could answer, his cell phone rang. He saw on its small front screen that it was Clarke Goode. He put it to his ear, knowing in his bones that the news was bad.

15.

Manhattan, Sunday, March 1, 2009, 1:00AM

Matt sat at his desk in his apartment looking down at Lincoln Center below and to his left. People were fanning out along the Center's main plaza, emerging from an event that had just ended. Bundled against the cold, the breath streamed from their mouths as they talked about what they had seen, or what time they had to get up in the morning, or the price of gold in Timbuktu. Not about the death of a beautiful young Lebanese girl, or of a second detective friend in less than ten days, or of a son falsely accused of murder. An angry son, filled with hatred for his father. How could those innocent-looking people be talking about such terrible things?

Jade Lee was asleep in his bed, the bedroom's door slightly ajar at her request. He had made her one of his faux cappuccinos, this one laced heavily with whiskey, and put her to bed. On the couch in his pre-war sunken living room was the pile of bedding he would unravel and use when he felt like sleeping. But he didn't feel like sleeping. Too much was on his mind: Nick Loh dead; Bob Davila dead; Jade, wearing one of his shirts and not much else, asleep in his bed; the look in her eyes when she told him about Antonio going off to see his father, to meet him for the first time; the tone in his own son's voice when they last spoke, over three weeks ago.

I'm glad you're out.
No answer.
How much was the bail?
Two million.
Basil put it up?
Who do you think?
We need to talk.
About what?
Your case.
My lawyer said not to talk to anyone.
That doesn't include me.
I'm fucked.
We'll beat it. It'll turn out fine.
It's all bullshit.
I want to talk about Adnan and Ali.
What about them?
They obviously planted the gun.
Mr. Stryker is looking for them.
Did you handle the gun, Michael?
You're talking to me like I'm six years old.
Did you?
I'm not supposed to talk about the case.
Let's have dinner tonight. I can help.
You want to help? You work for the office that's prosecuting me. Go look up what their case is all about.
That would be illegal.
Then what can you do? I've got a good lawyer.
Where are you now?
Park Avenue.
We have to talk. Get settled, then call me.
Pause.
Sure.
Click.

Matt went into the kitchen, found his good bourbon and poured some over ice. He returned to his desk, bringing the bottle with him. Below, the Center's concourse was now empty. One last couple, arms entwined, was hailing a cab, in tandem, with their free arms. They might have been laughing. The moonlight that had bathed the sky over Glen Cove was not quite penetrating to the streets of the city, but above the buildings the night was very clear, with stars scattered among a few wispy clouds.

Sipping his drink, Matt turned on his computer and went to the Regis High School web site. A few more clicks and he came across the one-paragraph announcement of Regis' two-point win earlier that night over Miami's Bishop Shelby High. He printed the page and, using a yellow marker, highlighted a line in the box score indicating that Antonio Lee had scored 10 points and fouled out at 2:11 of the fourth quarter. Slipping quietly into his bedroom, he put the printout on his dresser, where Jade, sleeping the sleep of the dead, had left her wallet and jewelry.

Matt had hoped that Michael would go to Regis, and play basketball. The summer after Michael graduated from eighth grade, Matt surprised him with a professional hoop, glass backboard and all, in the driveway in Pound Ridge. He had marked off and painted the lane and three point lines himself, and put a new Wilson basketball on the free-throw line. This ball, still brand new, was on a shelf in the garage. It had never been used, never even been bounced except by Matt when he was arranging the surprise.

Take the first shot, he had said to Michael.

I suck at basketball, Michael had replied, after glancing at the set-up, then heading casually toward the house, his knapsack over his shoulder. *Oh, by the way*, he had said, turning around at the front door to face Matt, *I can't sleep over tonight.*

Why not? That's three in a row.

I'm sleeping at Jake's. His father's taking us to the Yankee game tomorrow.

By the time Matt learned the rules of soccer, a game he had neither played nor watched growing up, Michael's career at Parnell — a career he seemed to take only a half-hearted interest in — was over. At graduation, Debra showed up with her new husband, who took them afterwards in a limousine to a fancy Tribeca restaurant to celebrate. Matt tried to pay, but Basil had given his credit card to the maitre'd on the way in. His son barely acknowledged him as they ate an absurdly overpriced meal and talked about the opportunities Michael would have at NYU, where he would be a communications major in the fall.

Matt, sipping his bourbon, looking down at the traffic on Columbus Avenue, remembered thinking at the time, *maybe college will be better.* But it wasn't. It just got worse. Now there was a hole in him where his relationship with his son should have been, his healthy relationship with his son. She could fill it, he thought, thinking of Jade sleeping in his bed. Would that be love, or need? There was his pride again, always stopping him. Maybe that's all he'd have left in the end, his pride. And his anger.

Leaning back, he noticed the books on the shelf above his desk. One of them was Marcus Aurelius' *Meditations*, given to him by his father the day he left for Parris Island. *You are angry,* Matteo, Sr. had said, handing the book to him as they sat in the bowels of the dank and cavernous Port Authority Bus Terminal in mid-town. *You lost your mother. I do not say much. The neighborhood is bad. You lose your temper. You fight. I do not put my hand up to stop you.*

"Tell me about the war," Matt had asked, trying to keep the pleading out of his voice, but not succeeding. "Your Navy Cross."

"I did not win it," his father had answered. "A boy named Matteo DeMarco did. He died in the war."

"Dad…"

"Here's your bus."

Somewhere along the way on that twenty hour bus ride to South Carolina, Matt had flipped through *Meditations.* He remembered now that Matteo had highlighted a few passages in yellow marker. He pulled the book from the shelf and, thinking of the spackle-covered black guy feeding the pigeons in Union Square Park, he found the one he was looking for: *How much more grievous are the consequences of anger than the causes of it.*

16.

Born and raised in Amsterdam, Erhard Fuchs was used to cold weather in winter, but not the continuous snow that seemed to fall in New York. A woolen cap on his head, his bulky coat's collar turned up, he walked next to Bill Crow on Bryant Park's perimeter path, trying to ignore the heavy wet flakes that were, according to reports, the beginning of another storm. He usually met his grisly-looking CIA contact at the Starbucks on the corner, but today they were having their chat as they walked. *I need the exercise*, Crow had said, the scarred stumps of his missing left pinky and ring fingers on display for a moment as he handed Fuchs a container of hot coffee.

"They will not be claimed," Fuchs said. The Native American with the dark eyes and the pitted face and the loping stride had just inquired after the bodies of three of the men killed in Locust Valley last week. *Like a forest creature*, Fuchs thought. *Be careful.*

"They can't stay in the morgue forever."

"I agree."

"We'll take them off your hands."

"This offer I will decline."

"You just said they wouldn't be claimed."

"I may have a use for them."

"Like what?"

"I don't know yet"

Out of the corner of his eye, Fuchs could see Crow shaking his head. They walked for a while in silence. Both Ali al-Hajjar and Adnan Farah were Syrian citizens, with documented connections to the Mukhabarat, Syria's secret police. Both, using aliases, were known to be in Beirut in early 2005. A cell phone linked to Farah had been used to detonate the explosives, equivalent to a ton of TNT, that had killed Rafik Hariri and many others as his motorcade drove past the St. George Hotel on 14 February.

Hajjar and Farah disappeared afterward, but continuous satellite and security camera sweeps of various Syrian embassies and Syrian Arab Airlines' comings and goings had them arriving in New York, on work visas, in October last, their sponsor one Mustafa al-Rahim, the servant of Syrian oil magnate, Basil al-Hassan. Fuchs, working at the Monteverde headquarters of the UN's special commission investigating the Hariri assassination, had been sent to the United States, where he hastily put together a team to follow Hajjar and Farah night and day.

"It's a dead-end," said Crow.

"I don't agree. Someone here in New York was controlling them. I am convinced of it."

"They may be taking a different tack in Washington."

So this is what he has come to *tell me,* thought Fuchs.

"I take my orders from Monteverde."

"You may be hearing from Monteverde."

"And the Hayek girl?" Fuchs said, "I can't sit on that much longer."

"They are considering their options in Washington."

"*Washington* is considering its options? This is a *UN* investigation. I am personally responsible. The DeMarco boy faces the death penalty."

"He raped her."

"He's charged with murder one."

"A deal may be worked out on the rape."

"You mean drop the murder charges?"

"Yes."

"I will wait a day or two, no more. I will not let the boy hang."

They parted at the park's Fifth Avenue exit, and Fuchs watched Crow walk uptown through the thickening snow. He did not tell the CIA agent with the rough-hewn face that early this morning he had attended a meeting with the New York City Police Commissioner, the NYPD's Homicide Bureau Chief and two veteran detectives named McCann and Goode. Nor of his conversation last night with Daniel LeClair, the independent investigator in charge of Monteverde, who, with Farah and Hajjar dead, had given him two days to tie up any loose ends and return with his team to Beirut.

Who to trust? He did not yet know. He had been closely following the international news, as he always did. There was no doubt that the wind between Washington and Damascus had been blowing differently under the new U.S. administration. Were they actually thinking of trusting Syria? Did they not know that Damascus took orders from Tehran? Senator Kerry's press release had been amateurishly revealing: *We discussed the possibility of cooperating on a number of issues.* Did the United States not know that any prize it hoped to win from such cooperation would turn out to be an illusion, a mirage in a desert? Or worse, a knife in the back?

Fuchs headed across town to the U.N., where he had an office and a small command center. He had been in New York long enough to know that there were no cabs to be had when it rained or snowed. He did not need the walk, as the chain-smoking Crow obviously did. He used the U.N.'s lavishly appointed gym and spa several times a week. Stocky but agile, his blond hair only slightly thinning, he was fit at fifty, or *fit at fitty* as the American gangster rappers might say.

Walking east on 40th Street, hunching against the wind that was now starting to blow, Fuchs' thoughts returned to his meeting at One Police Plaza this morning. The looks on the faces of the four New York policemen were grim. Worse than grim. They had lost two of their own. Both were working for Fuchs at or near the time of their violent deaths. *What was he working on? Who were his suspects?* He had been polite, respectful, humble: you must petition your State Department or your Justice Department. I am not the one to answer your questions. Was *petition* the right word? He was not sure, there being so many words for the simple verb *vraag* in English.

Fuchs had worked for MIVD, Holland's Military Intelligence and Security Service, for twenty years before taking his current job with the U.N. Childless, the death of his wife from ovarian cancer the year before had almost killed him too. Leaving his homeland, with its countless reminders of his beloved Kaat, had saved him. But not by much. He had nothing left to lose, and was therefore free to pursue his own agenda, to choose whom to trust and whom not. The faces of detectives Goode and McCann had been especially dark. Lethal, actually.

Erhard Fuchs feared the Mukhabarat, Syria's secret police. He feared Bill Crow and the CIA, who could crush him in an instant if they wished. But it was Detectives McCann and Goode that he feared the most. As he was leaving One Police Plaza this morning, the black detective, Clarke Goode, had caught up to him on the street and walked with him to his car.

"Colder than hell out here," Clarke had said. He had not replied, just kept walking. His car, parked on the perimeter of a dozen or more patrol and unmarked cars situated at various angles to the curb, was only fifty paces away.

"Do you believe in hell?" Goode had asked, as they continued walking, the wind kicking scraps of paper up around them. *"Good and evil?"* He had remained silent.

"I'll tell you why I ask," Goode had said, the car quite near now. *"We've got two cops dead who were working for you. You can't tell us what they were working on. We'll have to ask your bosses at the UN. But they won't tell us either, will they?"*

"I doubt it."

"I do too, which means you, personally, have a problem."

"I believe you want to tell me what it is."

"I do. The thing is, I really want to know what you're working on. My partner and I want to help you. I know you're a tough guy, Fuchs. I know you were in the Marines over there in Holland, the BBE, counterterrorism. All that. The thing is, if you won't let us help you, then we'll have no choice but to be against you. I'm talking about the entire NYPD. That's forty-thousand pissed off cops. Are you following me?"

"Please don't patronize me, detective. I respect you, but I am not afraid of you."

"I think you should be."

"Why? Are you threatening me?"

"No, Mr. Fuchs, I'm not." They had reached his car. *"Let's call it a warning. A fair warning."*

As he turned right onto U.N. Plaza, Fuchs felt the vibrating of his Blackberry, which he dug out of his inside coat pocket and covered with his free hand to keep the snow from hitting it. The message was from Daniel LeClair. *Two days,* it said, *then shut down NY.*

Bill Crow's scarred face was not the result of smallpox. It was acne that had done it, the result of too much alcohol and cigarettes and junk food consumed as a wild teenager on his reservation in New Mexico. When his mother died of cirrhosis he was in the midst of those wild years, seventeen and suddenly alone, his father unknown to him. The tribal council placed him with a family who took him in only for the monthly stipend that came with him. On the day of his high school graduation, he took off into the mountains, the Sangre de Christos, aflame at sunset with the dark red color that New Mexico's earliest settlers likened to the blood of Christ. He stayed through all four seasons — one year — emerging with his face scarred but no longer erupting, two fingers lost to a homemade beaver trap, and the certain knowledge that his salvation lay in isolation and total self-reliance.

He joined the army for the sole purpose of getting special forces training, which put him on the path to his present career as a contract operative for various United States government agencies, most often the CIA or the FBI or, as in the present case, both. He lived and worked—they were the same to him—in a vaguely-bounded no-man's land with no rules except his own, killing to eat, going to sleep each night fully prepared to be awoken by the grunts of a night monster he would have to grapple with at close quarters if he could not gun it down. The mountains.

Bill Crow did not have a Blackberry, but he knew, before Erhard Fuchs did, that Fuchs' operation in New York had come to an end. It ended, not on February 25, with the deaths of Adnan Farah and Ali al-Najjar, although that was convenient, but a month earlier, with the arrival of a new administration in Washington. The Syrians would be courted. *Would they make a separate peace with Israel? Would they help broker a peace between the Israelis and the Palestinians? What would they like in return? How about the closing down of the UN investigation into the assassination of Rafik Hariri? Would they like that?*

Crow had *also* talked to Daniel LeClair—a very bitter Daniel LeClair—last night. Washington, it appears, had spoken. So easy for the great white fathers to switch sides. Fuchs and his team would be returning to Lebanon. Crow's contact in the CIA, a boy of thirty with an encyclopedic knowledge of the Middle East, thought the case was closed. But Crow was not so sure. As it turned out, there was no need to kill Farah and al-Najjar. The UN investigation would have been shut down anyway, on one pretext or another. The Syrians had overplayed their hand, and in the process two New York cops had been killed. The NYPD could not be happy about that.

The second cop, Davila, had taken something from the UN commission's command post in Glen Cove and been blown to pieces for his trouble. That there was a traitor in his midst was by now obvious to Fuchs. And then there was the issue of the dead bodies. *I may have a use for them*, the Dutchman had said. *I am determined to continue.* No, the case was not over. There was prey out there, and more hunters than before.

17.

"I can't tell you much, you know, Mr. DeMarco."

"Call me Matt."

"Certainly."

Behind Everett Stryker was a wall of glass, through which Matt could see all of New York Harbor some thirty stories below. Four tugboats were nudging a barge, top-heavy with red and blue cargo containers, between Liberty and Governors Islands. To the left, people were walking along the river on a promenade in Brooklyn, enjoying the first sunny day in a couple of weeks. To Matt's right, sitting on handsome leather chairs were two young associates of Stryker's, yellow legal pads on their laps, listening to their boss as if he were giving the Sermon on the Mount.

"I've resigned from the District Attorney's office, if that makes any difference."

"It doesn't. It's a matter of my client's consent."

"My son."

"Yes."

"Or is it Mr. al-Hassan you're taking orders from?"

Stryker raised his white eyebrows at this, but did not respond immediately. Instead he picked up a crystal paper-weight in the shape of a lion's head from the top of his large and nearly empty desktop, turned it over casually once or twice and replaced it. If possible, the tall, sixtyish lawyer looked even more distinguished and elegant, in his charcoal gray suit, creamy white button-down shirt and two-hundred dollar tie, than he did the day Matt saw him going into the Tombs with Basil and Debra.

"I represent your son," Stryker said, finally, his voice neutral.

"I came here to give you information, not receive it," Matt said. "I appreciate you seeing me." When he first sat down before Stryker's throne of a desk, Matt had asked how the case was going as a matter of making preliminary conversation, small talk. Stryker's answer—blunt and unexpected—had stung. Matt regretted his sarcastic response, ruing, not for the first time in his forty-seven years on earth, his inability to keep his temper in check.

"Would you like us to call Michael. Perhaps..."

"No," Matt interrupted, "I'll speak to him later."

"Fine. I understand. What is it you came to tell me?"

"One of the D. A.'s key witnesses was killed last weekend. The doorman at Yasmine Hayek's building, Felix Diaz. Did you know that?"

"I did not."

"Shot in the back of the head, like Yasmine."

"Are there suspects?"

"I don't know."

Stryker drummed his fingers on his desk for a second or two before answering. "Jeff, Karen," he said, looking over at the two young lawyers, "please excuse us for a moment." The associates left, closing the office's large oak door quietly behind them.

"I asked them to leave to protect you, Mr. DeMarco"

"Protect me?"

"How did you come by this information?"

"It was in the Daily News. I put two and two together."

"You know the *Brady* case of course."

Matt was silent for a second. *Brady v. Maryland* was the United States Supreme Court decision that in effect obligated all federal and state prosecutors to disclose exculpatory evidence to criminal defendants. Matt knew it well and had followed its dictates on numerous occasions, once or twice even disclosing the names of "Brady cops" — policemen with a known record of lying in their official capacity.

"Yes, I know it," he answered finally.

"Then I don't have to explain my position to you."

"Yes, you do."

"Of course. I'll wait for Healy to formally notify me of this Diaz murder. If he doesn't — and he should have by now — we'll have an appealable issue."

"Appealable issue? We want an acquittal, or a dismissal, not an appealable issue."

"Yes, but I'm your son's attorney. These tactical decisions are for me to make."

"What about the GSR test?" Matt asked, his voice and demeanor neutral, under control, but not by much. "Why was that cancelled?"

"I'm not at liberty to say."

"Michael says he didn't handle the gun. He didn't know it existed until he was arrested."

"As I said . . . "

"You're not at liberty to say."

"Correct."

"Did you know that TARU thinks the building's security system was tampered with?"

"TARU?"

"The NYPD's high-tech unit."

"The report we received was silent on the issue."

"Speak to Jane Manning at TARU. I spoke to her this morning. She thinks it's edited."

"I'll make a note of it," Stryker said, but wrote nothing down.

"The security company has absconded," Matt said. "They must have something to hide."

"And you know this how?"

"Friends at the NYPD."

"You seem to have many friends in the NYPD."

Matt ignored this. It was getting easier to control his temper now that he realized that Stryker was not only a condescending prick, which he had expected, but also an adversary, which he had not. Conflict was his milieu, it was where he had had lived nearly all his life.

"Perhaps the owner of the building knows where they are," Matt said. "It's a company called Westside Properties. You represent them."

Stryker rose from his chair.

Matt stood as well.

"I do," Stryker said. "That's a matter of public record, on file with the Secretary of State's office."

"Who are the individual owners?" Matt asked. "I'd like to talk to them."

"I'll talk to them."

"That's privileged as well, I suppose."

"You suppose correctly."

Matt was taller than Stryker by several inches. He moved almost to the edge of Stryker's long sleek desk.

"One more thing," he said, looking the older attorney in the eye.

"Yes, I'm listening."

"I don't like the picture I'm getting here. And I don't mean your million-dollar view. Michael and I have issues. But he's my son, my only child. You don't want my help, that's fine. But if you sell him out, or if you fuck his case up, I won't stop until you're out of the profession. You'll have to kill me to stop me."

Stryker did not respond. Instead he pushed a button on his desk. Matt turned and headed for the door, which swung open as he approached it, revealing Stryker's elegant middle-aged assistant, Ms. Hartman, who had greeted him with a fake smile when he arrived. She stepped aside to let Matt pass, not bothering to smile this time, her eyes looking past him to Stryker, to see what the great legal god wanted of her.

18.

Latakia, Monday, March 2, 2009,
9:00PM Damascus/2:00PM New York

Basil al-Hassan sat alone on the terrace of his spacious apartment in Latakia, overlooking the Mediterranean, on which the reflection of the rising moon formed a sparkling pathway to the beach below. To the south the lights of the pyramid-shaped, multi-tiered Meridien Hotel were also reflected on the sea, and the sound of music from the hotel's terrace café occasionally drifted his way. Beyond the tourist hotels were the city center and the modern harbor built twenty years ago, small but very busy now that Beirut—a real port city—was lost. Basil, a young engineer at the time, just out of the army, had fought hard for the construction of Latakia's harbor facilities. He had had an audience with President Assad, who, prescient and succinct, had said, *yes, build it. We can trust no one in Beirut and perhaps will not be there forever.*

He had not met with the new president Assad on this trip, only the Oil and Resources Minister and several of his subordinates. Barrels per day—the statistic around which pivoted the country's economic policy—was the only topic of the meeting. That and how to reverse the grim, steadily declining numbers. Conversion to natural-gas-fired electric plants and intensified production were discussed, as was the status of exploration licenses granted to companies from China, Russia, and the U.S., none of which had borne any fruit.

At the meeting, as was required by unwritten but strictly enforced Syrian law, was a liaison to SMI, Syrian Military Intelligence. This man, Abdullah al-Haq, Basil had first heard of several years earlier via sources connected to the Mukhabarat, a murky figure who was said to actually be Iranian, and also said to have a very high body count as a free-roaming jihadist, protected by very powerful men — a human stinger missile launched by untouchable mullahs and presidents. Basil had first laid eyes on Haq at the Lebanese consulate in New York in the fall, at the same reception at which Michael DeMarco had met Yasmine Hayek. They had neither exchanged glances nor spoken that night, but Basil had remembered and taken note of this new face in a crowd that he knew from deep experience contained as many real diplomats as fake ones working clandestinely for various Syrian intelligence agencies. It was not, he realized, by coincidence that Haq appeared at the one Oil Ministry meeting in five that Basil was required to attend.

After the meeting, al-Haq had approached Basil privately.

"It is an honor to meet a war hero," he had said. "And the discoverer of Deir ez-Zour."

Basil did not reply immediately. Al-Haq was not complimenting him.

"And *your* service?" Basil said, ending his short silence. Haq was dressed in civilian clothes, a dark suit and tie, but Basil knew that all SMI operatives had military backgrounds. He also knew that to ask such a question was tantamount to an insult in the inbred and comingled Syrian military and intelligence cultures, which was his intention, his way of putting al-Haq on notice.

"Hama."

"And your rank?"

"Colonel."

"I thought you were stationed in New York?"

"I am, but I have been called back for a few days." Basil watched Haq's eyes as he said this. Yes, *colonel*, I know who you are.

"To attend this meeting?" Basil said.

"I am a last minute substitute."

"Do you have any questions?" Basil had been through this drill many times. He never said anything to SMI that he had not said on the record at a minister-level meeting.

"Is there no hope for Deir ez-Zour?" the Colonel asked.

"You mean rebuilding the plutonium facility?" *Yes, I am in that loop. Are you surprised, Colonel?*

"No, the oil field."

"None, it is played out."

"And the other fields? Are the foreigners optimistic?"

"They would not be here if they did not think they could find oil in commercial quantities. They are spending a great deal of money."

"It takes a long time I suppose."

"They are not playing in the desert."

"Yes, I understand. By the way, I attended the funeral of Yasmine Hayek last month."

"You know the family?"

"I went to pay our government's respects."

"Very sad."

"I understand that you knew Pierre, during the war."

"We served together."

"He is a Christian, no? Maronite?"

"I did not know it at the time."

"I see. And it is your wife's son who stands accused of the girl's murder. That must be difficult."

"We are managing."

"Your two young technicians, are they still with you?"

"What two technicians? Do you mean the two young men that Mustafa sponsored?" *Technician*, Basil knew, was SMI-speak for a your-wish-is-my-command terrorist, usually young, from a poor or non-existent family, a serious fanatic, brainwashed into committing mass murder for the *jihad. So,* he thought, *they are thinking of trying to pin the Hayek murder on me.*

"Who is Mustafa?" Haq asked.

"My servant." *The person I saw you talking to at the Lebanese reception last fall as I was passing a room with its door slightly ajar, looking for a quiet place to make a phone call.*

"We understand they have disappeared, the two young men."

"That looks to be the case," Basil replied, "but you are mistaken. I have no technicians, as you call them, no employees in New York." *Were Adnan and Ali Haq's men? That would cast a different light on things.*

An Oil Ministry limousine had carried Basil the two hundred-plus miles from Damascus to Latakia, to his old house in the hills, cared for year-round by a family retainer and his wife. On the old winding road that descended into the city from the foothills in the east, Basil instructed the driver, a childhood friend who still lived in Latakia, to stop at a small stand of ancient cedars. Exiting the limousine, he made the short walk to the burial ground laid out in a small clearing beyond the tree line. Once there he tore a palm stalk from a nearby tree and placed it on the grave of his first wife and son, the only child he would ever have. Kneeling, he placed both hands on the freshly raked soil and then pressed them to his face. Rising, he faced Mecca and recited the Muslim prayers for the dead child and the dead adult.

The brown earth was still on his face when he returned to the limousine. The driver, Gamal, a short hawk-faced man in a white shirt and black tie, stood stiffly while he opened the car's rear door to let Basil in, saying nothing, not making eye contact, as if they were being watched, which was doubtful since no one had followed them and there were no cars or people on the hillside as far as the eye could see. But of course anything was possible in Syria, a Stalinist state as repressive as any in the Middle East.

In 1980, the Muslim Brotherhood, angry at what it saw as Syria's secular ways, attempted to assassinate Syrian President

Hafez al-Assad at a state reception in Damascus. Two hours later, two thousand Muslim Brotherhood prisoners were massacred at Tadmor Prison. Two years later, the city of Hama, the center of Muslim Brotherhood opposition to Assad and his BAATH Party, was destroyed, over a period of three weeks, from the air, by artillery, and by ground troops going from house to house. The outside press reported twenty thousand dead, but the number was closer to thirty thousand, many of them women and children who were unable to get out in time. This is where Abdullah al-Haq, sent to today's meeting to give him a warning, had seen "combat," probably doing much of the door-to-door killing of innocents.

Below, the row of palm trees along the beach was silhouetted by the light of the now risen moon. As Basil watched them swaying, their fronds like the hair of young girls blown gently by the cool night breeze, his thoughts returned to the framed photograph that he had placed on the dresser in his bedroom some thirty years ago, and that he had taken a long look at while washing and changing when he first arrived. In black and white, it was of Basil and Pierre Hayek in dust-covered and sweat-stained fatigues, their arms around each other, sitting on top of a tank in full sunlight in Beirut's Karantina slum. Both were smiling broadly, as if to say that the heat and the dust and the sweat and the war itself were trifles compared to their friendship. Taken in early 1976 when Basil was twenty and Pierre nineteen, it seemed to Basil to not only capture him and his former friend at the height of their youthful beauty, but at the last moment of their human innocence. The next day the shelling began.

We are even now, Pierre, he thought, on the verge of sleep. *So be it.*

The vibrating of his cell phone in his shirt pocket interrupted Basil from his thoughts. He fished it out and looked at the screen. *Mustafa.* He pushed the off button, and returned the phone to his pocket. He would call Mustafa later or tomorrow. His instincts, honed over long years of looking out for danger, told him the call had something to do with Colonel Haq. And Adnan and Ali. Surely Haq knew they were dead. And that they had killed Yasmine Hayek. One looks out for danger in Syria, no matter what one's status, and Basil's status had plummeted in recent years along with the failing yield of Dier ez-Zour. The fallen hero.

In the morning, Gamal would arrive early to carry him to the airport in Damascus. Early enough to sit and sip thick espresso and chat with Gamal and three other childhood friends, who would arrive by foot before dawn. One of them, Mahmoud, was a technocrat who would scan the small house for bugs, so that they could talk freely. Quietly but freely.

19.

Debra al-Hassan, the former Debra DeMarco of Manhattan and Pound Ridge, and before that Debra Rusillo of Arthur Avenue, the Bronx, had not always been a prisoner in her own palatial homes. In the beginning of her marriage she was free and even courageous, courageous enough to have Mustafa watched by a private detective agency. But what she learned, that his only deviation, if you could even call it that, from duty, was an occasional trip to an upstate prison, could not compare to a car-bomb killing of a New York detective. Not that he wasn't capable of it, or wasn't devious, an enemy inside her own house, but an overt killing? Of an NYPD cop? Why? In her room since Sunday morning, when she read about Detective Davila's death in the Times, she had been feeling groggy and depressed for three days, unable to focus, not hungry, sleeping too much. Could she walk, could she drive? She did not know. *Fresh air*, she thought, putting on a robe and slippers.

Outside her room, on a hand-carved Louis Quatorze tray trolley she had purchased in Paris, was her breakfast — juice and coffee — and a beaten-silver pill case containing her anti-depressant medication. She would take it later. The apartment had balconies and terraces on three sides, the widest facing the East River, where she used to like to look, on clear days, down to the harbor and the Verrazano Narrows Bridge shimmering at the horizon. Cutting through the kitchen, she noticed her reflection in one of the glass cabinets and stopped. Old, she thought, puffy, tired, haggard, dazed. *Fuck.* Before turning away, she noticed a prescription vial on the bottom shelf—had been staring at it, actually, while looking at her face. She had never even seen the bottle, content to let Basil control her medication schedule, and Mustafa the doling out of her daily pills.

Curious, she opened the cabinet door and spun the vial until she could read it. "Debra al-Hassan-1 per day." Yes, these were the blue tablets she had been swallowing, but Mustafa had been giving her two each morning and two again at night, along with her sleeping pills, telling her it was on Basil's orders. Shaking her head, she shut the glass door. *Had* he said that? She could not remember.

On the terrace, she was shocked at how cold and clear and bright the day was. She pulled her robe tight against the chill. Below, the city was in full stride. Basil had arrived home last night and had briefly stopped in her room. He had said he would be home all day today. She would tell him. But should she? Mustafa was a devoted servant, and perhaps more. Perhaps it was better to wait. If she could clear her head, she could spy on Mustafa, as she had done on Saturday, perhaps learn something...

Behind her she heard a curtain rustle, and turned to look. Mustafa was standing in the open doorway, his arms folded against his chest, staring at her.

"Mustafa," Debra said. "What? What is it? You frightened me."

"It is cold, madam. You need to take your pills."

"How long were you standing there?"

Mustafa remained silent. She leaned against the railing behind her. The drop down was thirty stories.

"I will bring you your pills, madam," he said finally. "And an overcoat."

20.

Erhard Fuchs stood at the long and high window of his office on the twentieth floor of the United Nations Headquarters, looking at the lights of the city reflecting on the black surface of the East River. The UN's promenade along the river, lit by a row of gracefully curved lanterns on stainless steel poles, was empty, as it was on most nights, especially in winter. To his left the Queensboro Bridge stretched over the south end of Roosevelt Island as it reached for the river's far side before inserting itself there like a probe into the heart of the tumultuous and very un-Manhattan-like outer boroughs. To his right he could see the lights of the three other East River bridges, the traffic on them never-ending. The beauty and the vulnerability of these bridges, the majestic Brooklyn Bridge in particular, never ceased to amaze him, and to make his heart ache.

After twenty-five years in his home country's military intelligence and counterterrorism services, he was among the relatively few people on the planet who knew of the thousands of acts of terrorism, successful and unsuccessful, perpetrated every year for the past thirty years around the world, the vast majority by Muslims bent on violent *jihad*. And this did not include the Middle East, where the numbers and the success rate were much higher, staggeringly higher, and where the ratio of Muslim-to-non-Muslim perpetrators was 100-to-zero. *And* where ninety-nine percent of the victims were also Muslim. Irony, he had long ago learned, not being in the Koran, was not in Islam's lexicon.

Behind Fuchs, a door opened and closed. He waited a few seconds, then turned and saw Alec Mason, the newest member of his team, an Englishman with a murky relationship to MI6, Britain's covert intelligence service, taking his coat off and draping it over one of the conference table's high-backed, cushioned chairs.

"Where is everyone?" Mason asked, still standing, facing Fuchs.

"Have a seat," the Dutchman said.

"Sure." Mason, extremely thin, in his forties, his three-days' growth of beard an affectation—of what exactly Fuchs was not sure, hip youth perhaps—sat. "Where is everybody?" he said. "Am I early?"

"No, you're on time," Fuchs replied. "I've been meeting with people one by one."

"Why?"

"We are to disband on Wednesday. I am giving people the option of leaving early, taking a couple of days leave."

"Yes, I understand," Mason said, nodding slightly. The reasons for disbanding—the death of Farah and al-Najjar—would be obvious to him, Fuchs knew.

"I need your help with one last item," Fuchs said.

Mason, in his choice of clothes—jeans, a black suede sport coat and expensive loafers tonight—as well as his scruffy face and long hair, also affected a studied casualness, as if to say he had other things to do besides bring down the Syrian government for the killing of Rafik Hariri. "What is it?" he said. "I'll do my best."

"Our young bomb maker, Farah, is alive."

"Alive?"

"Yes."

"I can't believe it."

"It's true."

"Where is he?"

"In a safe house."

"How did you pull this off?"

Fuchs studied Mason's face before answering. No tells, as was the case last Wednesday night when he took the long way to the Piping Rock Road house, giving the so-called home invaders time to kill both men inside, or so he believed until now.

"We thought he was dead from his wounds. He woke up on the way to the hospital."

"Where is the safe house?"

"If I told you and you were tortured, we would lose Farah."

"Tortured?"

"Yes. There is a mole on the team."

"A mole? Working for whom?"

"I don't know, but not a friend. The Syrians probably."

"What is it you want me to do?"

"I would like you to close the Glen Cove command post, gather up our equipment and paperwork. Bring everything here tomorrow morning. I am meeting here with two NYPD detectives."

"NYPD? Why?"

"I am transferring Farah to them."

"Is this related to the two dead detectives?"

"Yes, they want to know who gave Farah his orders as much as we do. And the Hayek murder occurred here in Manhattan."

"Has Farah talked?"

"Not yet, but he will."

"You have NYPD's cooperation?"

"Yes, they will charge Adnan here with killing Yasmine Hayek. They will interrogate him themselves, and then protect him until he can be transferred to The Hague, to testify."

"Why are you doing this, involving an outside agency?"

"Because no one will try to kill Farah while he is in the custody of the New York police. The Syrians will be checkmated."

"Why me? Anyone could do this."

"I would have asked Sylvana, but she's in Los Angeles, as you know. Her nephew is very sick. The others all seemed anxious to leave. They have not been home in four months. You just came on board."

"And the others, do they know?"

"No. The less that know, the better. I mistrust everyone. The NYPD will bring Farah to The Hague. You will accompany them as Monteverde's representative."

"I'll do it of course."

"Thank you."

When Mason left, Fuchs went back to the window and stood there for several minutes looking down at the river. A couple, their arms entwined, was walking on the promenade. Thick clouds now obliterated the stars and the moon, but New York at night created so much light that the celestial torches were not needed, indeed they were rarely noticed even on cloudless nights. Turning away, the Dutch cop found his cell phone on his desk, flipped it open and pushed a speed dial number.

"Hello," he said. "It's me."

"Hello," Sylvana Dalessio said.

"How are you?"

"Fine. *Bene.*"

"And our young man?"

"He needs a shower."

"What does Johannes say?"

"We can start if you wish."

"And the boys?"

"They are fine."

"You must start tonight. We are ordered to shut down on Wednesday."

"Wednesday? Why?"

"It makes sense. Farah and Najjar are supposed to be dead. It was to follow them that we were sent here. Why continue? Why waste resources?"

"Does LeClair know? About Farah?"

"No."

"The die is cast."

"Yes."

"Did you talk to Mason?"

"He just left."

"What will happen?"

"He will tell his contact that Farah is alive and talking. The Syrians will of course want to kill him before we give him to the NYPD."

"Are we really transferring him?"

"I don't know. I haven't asked them yet."

"What will happen?"

"I have asked our colleague at the NYPD for help. Detective Goode. His counterterrorism people will follow Mason. We must hope that Mason leads us to his contact so that we can be pro-active."

"And if he doesn't?"

Fuchs paused before answering, thinking of his conversation with Sylvana of two days ago, in which they concocted the story of her sick nephew in California. Of the danger she was in.

"They won't find you," he said. "I am in the open. They will come to me."

Silence. They were both in danger. It was the business they were in.

"*Bene.* And what does Detective Goode want in return?"

"The killers of Loh and Davila, and of Yasmine Hayek."

"And you agreed?"

"No, but when they take custody of Farah, I will give them what I have."

"Good. As to Mason, I would like the honor. I will gut him like a fish."

"Fine, but first things first. Our young assassin."

"Of course," said Sylvana. "I will let him shower, and then I will talk to him. He likes me, as I am the good cop so far."

"You know what to do when you're done?"

"Yes, of course. *Ciao.*"

"*Ciao.*"

21.

Manhattan, Monday, March 2, 2009, 7:00PM

Nick Loh buried and Bob Davila killed on the same day, Jade thought, walking home after work on Monday through midtown Manhattan's slushy streets, carrying the steaks and salad things for the dinner she would make later for her and Matt. Antonio in Florida, talking on the phone yesterday about his dad, not the ten points he scored the night before. Her past on her mind, her secret, praying about it at Mass yesterday and again this morning. One small thing had brightened her day. A new client had walked in at lunch time, while she was eating yogurt at her desk. The five thousand dollar cash retainer he had given her felt like an infusion of hope, she didn't know why.

As she was turning onto her block, she noticed a man in a dark overcoat crossing Eighth Avenue. He was wearing a woolen cap, pulled down low, but she could see that his face was deeply pockmarked, like her new client, who also had two fingers missing on his left hand. This man was wearing gloves and was quickly lost in the crowd of streaming pedestrians when he reached the opposite corner. Was that him, Charles Hall, who had said he thought he was about to be arrested for stealing from his business partner and wanted to retain her in advance? Maybe, maybe not, but it didn't matter; she had other things on her mind.

• • •

"So you didn't tell him about the surveillance log."

"No," Matt answered.

"I don't blame you," Jade said. "But he's not incompetent. That can't be it. He must know something we don't, otherwise he'd be pressing hard for a dismissal, instead of talking about an appeal."

"Or have another agenda altogether."

"That's a scary thought."

Jade put down her coffee cup and looked over at Matt, who was sitting across from her at the table in the dining alcove of her apartment. After Charles Hall left her office, Jade had called Matt and invited him for dinner. She wore a suit to work, with stockings and high heels, but at home had quickly changed into jeans, a faded Regis sweatshirt, and a beat-up pair of sneakers. Her hair, frizzy again in the damp weather, she had pulled into a ponytail. They had sipped drinks and made small talk as she broiled the steaks in her small kitchen. Over coffee she had asked Matt about his meeting with Stryker.

"The log is the key, but of course it's stolen," Matt said. "And it implicates us and Davila."

"And the UN has diplomatic immunity."

"Right."

"What about Jack and Clarke?" Jade asked.

"I spoke to Jack this afternoon," Matt replied. "He's calling me later tonight. We'll meet someplace."

"Did you tell him about the log?"

"No, I'll give him a copy when I see him."

"Did you tell him I want to come?"

"No. Are you sure you want to?"

"Yes, I'm sure. Bobby was killed because of the stuff he gave me."

"That's another thing," Matt replied.

"What?"

"That points a finger at the UN team. Did they kill Bobby? Could that be?"

"Anything's possible," Jade replied, "but that would be hard to believe. Hold on." She rose and went over to a desk she had set up in a corner of her small living room, returning quickly with a yellow legal pad. "I made some notes," she said, when she was seated again. "So we don't miss anything when we talk to Jack and Clarke."

"O.K.," Matt said. "Let's hear it."

"*One*," Jade said, looking at her notes and then at Matt. "We have Adnan and Ali, Michael's supposed friends."

Matt nodded.

"They killed Yasmine Hayek," Jade said.

"Yes," said Matt.

"And planted the murder weapon in Michael's room."

"And probably got Michael to fire it or at least handle it."

"Yes. *Two*," Jade continued, "we have the UN. They're looking into the assassination of Rafik Hariri. They think the Syrian government was involved. They have a team in New York who've been following Adnan and Ali. We have their surveillance log. The UN team knows they were in Yasmine's building at the time of her murder."

"Correct."

"They do not inform the NYPD of this fact."

"Correct. They don't want Adnan and Ali arrested."

"*Three*, Loh and Davila join the UN team. While staking out Adnan and Ali, Loh is killed. As are, presumably, Adnan and Ali—although we don't know this for sure—and a fourth man. Except for Loh, no identities are released by the local police."

"Yes."

"Three nights later," Jade continued, "Davila is killed in a car bomb."

"Yes."

"It was Davila who stole the surveillance log and gave it to me."

"Yes."

"*Four*, the doorman at Yasmine's building, who said he saw only Michael go in—an obvious lie—is killed."

Matt nodded again.

"*Five*, the surveillance system at Yasmine's building appears to have been tampered with in a very sophisticated way. The security company leaves for parts unknown."

"Anything else?"

"I think that's it," Jade replied.

"There's one more thing," Matt said.

"What?"

"Adnan and Ali worked for Basil al-Hassan, Michael's step-father. Basil got them the job house sitting in Locust Valley."

"And it was the lawyer hired by Basil who cancelled the gun residue test," Jade said, "and who refuses to challenge Healy on the Diaz murder."

Before Matt could respond, a phone rang somewhere in the apartment. Jade went to answer it.

"Who was it? Antonio?" Matt asked when Jade returned and was settled back in her chair.

"No. I spoke to him yesterday. It was Angelo, ex-husband number one. I asked him to do a search on Westside Properties."

"And?"

"He needs more time."

"What's he doing now?"

"He's with the State Police. He's in a fraud squad."

"Are you guys friends?" Matt asked.

"I haven't spoken to him in nine years," Jade replied.

"What about us?" Matt said.

"Us?"

"Are we friends?"

Jade got to her feet, picked up her dinner plate and Matt's and brought them into the kitchen. She had not been prepared for Matt's last question. But she should have been. Its answer was why she had invited him to dinner, why she had scrubbed off her makeup and dressed down the way she had. Why she had avoided eye contact. She returned with a bottle of Cognac and two snifters, pouring out two inches for each of them.

"I have something to tell you," she said, lifting her glass, "but I need a drink first."

"Something to tell me?"

"Yes." *Look straight at him, Jade, she said to herself.* And she did.

"About us being friends?"

"I appreciate you sleeping on your couch the other night."

Matt said nothing. It was obvious he didn't know where this was going. She did though, or thought she did.

"I wanted you to come into the bedroom, but it's better that you didn't."

"Why?"

"Because of what I have to tell you."

Again Matt said nothing.

"It's about Antonio's father. And me."

"The producer?"

"Yes, Gerry DiNardo."

"What about him?"

"He made porn movies," Jade said. "I was in two."

"Jade..."

"Do you still want to be my friend?"

Now Matt knew why Jade had been so stand-offish. Why she had tried to make herself look unattractive. Why he had felt guilty staring at her unbelievable rear end as she bent over to take the steaks out of the broiler; at the shape of her high and heavy and voluptuous breasts as she brought the plates to the table. No sweatshirt, no matter how loose fitting, could hide those breasts, with their promise of heaven on Earth. And no man on Earth could have looked at them, at her, and not felt his blood stirring.

"Is that why you go to Mass every day?" he asked.

"Wouldn't you?"

"Jade..."

"You might if you were a fool like me."

"Being a fool is not a sin."

"Matt..."

"Did you think I'd think less of you?"

"Yes."

"I've been watching you tonight."

"Watching me?"

"I've lost my son. No, that's wrong. I've lost the idea of having a son, the idea that I've clung to all these years. Suddenly I'm empty. Alone."

Jade did not reply. Their drinks sat on the table along with the rest of the dinner dishes. The apartment, and the city all around them, receded into deep shadow, a darkened, muted background to the pivotal moment of their lives.

"Remember when we met in Union Square Park?" Matt said.

"Yes, of course."

"I watched you walk toward me, and I thought, *I'm so fucking alone.* And then I couldn't call you, I don't know why. I was too proud, I guess. You had broken up with me. And you didn't call *me.*"

"Now you know why."

"The porn films? Jade, that's nothing. You were a girl with a dream, who was taken advantage of."

"I haven't enjoyed sex since. I've held back. I'm a mess."

Jade was crying now. Matt pulled his chair close to hers and took her face in his hands. "Yes, I want to be your friend," he said. "And your lover, too. If you'll have me."

Then they were kissing, gently at first and then hungrily, as if they hadn't had love to eat in years, which was in fact the case. Jade had stopped crying, but her tears were all over Matt's face. She backed away suddenly, pulled off her sweatshirt and used it to wipe them away. Then she reached around and unhooked her bra, and her breasts, large, light amber in color, with perfect brown nipples and light-brown aereoli, were there before him, and he entered heaven.

22.

Sylvana Dalessio was born and raised in Rome. She had read Laura Ingalls Wilder's *Little House* series of children's books as a girl and thought that as a result she was familiar with American farming and farmhouses. But the ancient stone and timber house where she was helping keep Adnan Farah prisoner surprised her when she first saw it looming up out of a foggy night, and kept surprising her thereafter. On the kitchen wall, above an ancient claw-footed stove, hung ten cast iron frying pans with the years 1960 through 1969 painted on them in white. Today, she had finally gotten around to asking Johannes, Erhard Fuchs' brother, what they signified, and he had told her that his grandmother, Clara Fuchs, had won the local frying pan throwing competition ten years in a row. *No targets*, he had said, *just how far you could throw it.*

And then there was the room, cold and bleak, where Clara and her husband Albert had committed suicide together in 1995 by drinking beer laced with cyanide, just after calling the local funeral director to tell him to come and pick up the bodies. *It was Heineken,* Johannes had said, with a little bit more pride than Sylvana thought was warranted. A fading print of Vermeer's *Girl with a Pearl Earring* was still on the wall over the bed with a crucifix next to it. No, this wasn't *Little House on the Prairie*.

Yesterday, she had taken the one-mile walk to the Catamount Motel on Route 12 — ten rooms facing a large, graceful
pond, surrounded on three sides by an apple orchard — that
Albert and Clara had built, and then operated for forty years
before shuttering it in the early nineties and retiring to the
farmhouse. Starkly utilitarian and clean in the old Dutch way,
the large sign out front that said APPLES FREE BEWARE
OF MOUNTAIN LION had apparently kept vandals away.
Peeking through the curtained windows, she could see that
each room still contained its original bed, night table and
dresser. On the walls were cheaply framed calendar photographs of tulip fields, windmills, and boaters on canals.

Fuchs family property for close to two centuries, the house
and the motel had been rented for a few years after Albert and
Clara died and then fell empty until the fall, when Johannes
came over to "assess, patch and sell." This was the Fuchs brothers' story in any event. When Erhard and Sylvana showed up
five days ago with Adnan Farah, his wiry black hair thick with
coagulated blood, barely conscious, Johannes, who did not
seem surprised, or even concerned, meticulously cleaned the
bomb maker's scalp wound and chained him to the bed in his
grandparents' old bedroom. He then made a call to Holland,
and the next day his sons Wilem and Josef, strapping young
men both, arrived.

Since then Farah had been kept quiet by daily injections
of morphine — except for yesterday and today. He was being
watched at the moment by Josef, the dark son with the big
hands and brooding eyes. Preparing to debrief him for the
first time, Sylvana stood at the deep chipped-enamel kitchen
sink. She had just washed her hands and was waiting for the
water in the teakettle to boil. The scene through the mullioned
window above the sink was stark and pure in its near total
whiteness. Snow was starting to fall heavily — again — and
soon the stone walls that criss-crossed the property, now par-
tially exposed, would be obliterated and the gnarled branches
of the trees that grew on each side of the long rutted dirt drive

would be bending under their heavy white load. One of these icy branches had cracked during the night, causing Sylvana to wake instantly and reach for her Ingrham.

The radio on a nearby counter top had been filled with news these past five days of the so-called torture inflicted by the Americans on terrorists captured after 9/11. Before she reported to Beirut in 2006, Sylvana had spent a week at Langley—as had everyone who worked at Monteverde—undergoing these same interrogation techniques. The news reports made it seem like the Americans were sadists, "torturing" their prisoners for pleasure. The waterboarding had terrified her, but she now knew that it would not kill her. Still, she had a simple plan to kill herself with cyanide if the Syrians ever took her.

Thank God, she had lived until today—this night—when she would confront the man who had built and detonated the bomb that had killed her father and mother, riding in the car behind Rafik Hariri that day in Beirut in 2005. The severed head of their driver had been propelled like a small rocket into her father's face killing him instantly. Her mother, her body filled with nails, had lingered three days before dying.

"Sylvana," Johannes Fuchs spoke from behind her.

"Yes," she replied, still facing the window.

"Shall we begin?"

Johannes was a retired policeman, five years older than Erhard, and had cooked them dinner every night on the claw-footed stove. On the first night he told Sylvana, as they ate pea soup loaded with potatoes and chunks of bacon, of the event in 1977 that had changed his and Erhard's life. They had just buried their father, Fredrik, after a dreadful and depressing battle with pancreatic cancer, and Erhard, nineteen, was on a train with their mother, Hellen, and thirteen year-old sister, Margret, heading to the university town of Groningen, where Erhard was to resume his studies and Hellen and Margret were planning a visit with relatives. The train was taken over by terrorists, and, after a two-week standoff, attacked by Dutch marines. The passengers had been lying on the floor, face down. Erhard had watched as the terrorist leader blew their mother and sister's brains out with an AK-47 rifle as the attack began. A week later he enlisted in the Marines and Johannes left his job as a dockworker in Harlingen to begin the process of joining the KLPD — the Dutch national police.

Sylvana turned to face Johannes.

"How's our young man?" she said.

"He's showered, fed, quiet."

A pitcher of water, a small towel, a pair of latex gloves, a very sharp barber's razor and a small, hi-tech digital video camera in a black leather case sat on a lacquered tray on the plank-topped kitchen table.

"This will not take long," Sylvana said. "He will talk or die."

23.

Manhattan, Monday, March 2, 2009, 9:00PM

"I know the guy who's the head of the UN team," said Jack McCann. "We met with him this morning. He blew us off, and then he calls and asks me for a favor."

"What kind of favor?" Matt asked.

"To follow a guy, an Englishman named Alec Mason."

"Why?"

"It's connected to Loh and Davila. They were specially assigned to him."

"What were they working on?" Jade asked.

"He wouldn't say."

"What's his name?" asked Matt.

"Erhard Fuchs. He's a Dutchman, former military intelligence."

"Is that where Clarke is?"

"Yes."

McCann, Matt and Jade were sitting in a back booth in The Square Diner, which wasn't square but in the shape of a railroad car. The place was busy at just past midnight, its proximity to City Hall, the Criminal Courts building and One Police Plaza making it a popular hangout for the law enforcement and political types who worked downtown. Over coffee, Matt and Jade had shown McCann the contents of Bob Davila's manila envelope, filling him in on the Hariri investigation and its connection, via Michael's two so-called friends, to Yasmine's murder and Michael's arrest.

"Fuchs gave you nothing?" said Matt.

"He said he couldn't, that we should talk to the Justice Department."

"Did you?"

"The Commissioner said he would call," McCann replied. "I'm out of that loop."

"What about Bill Crow?" Matt asked. "Can you find out if he works for the FBI? Where he's assigned?"

"I have an Army buddy who's an agent," McCann answered. "He's pretty high up. I'll give him a call." Then, looking at Jade: "What else did Davila say?"

"Just if *Monteverde* meant anything to me."

"That's it?"

"That's it."

"Does it?" McCann said. "Mean anything to you?"

"No, but I looked it up. It's an old hotel the Hariri investigation team is working out of in Beirut."

"Something weird went down in Locust Valley," McCann said, shaking his head.

"Something to make Bobby mistrust the UN," said Jade. "And the FBI to contact him."

"How did Michael know these two guys?" McCann asked, pointing to the pictures of Adnan and Ali on the table.

"They worked for his stepfather," Matt replied.

"The rich Syrian."

Matt nodded.

"What kind of work?"

"I don't know. Odd jobs, Michael said. I only met them the one time. Hassan got them the house sitting job in Locust Valley."

"What does Hassan do?" McCann asked.

"He's a big shot in Syrian oil," Matt replied. "Very rich. That's all I know."

"He put up Michael's bail, correct?" McCann asked. "Two mil?"

"Correct."

"And he's paying Michael's lawyer?"

"Correct."

"What about Nassau County?" said Jade.

"Zero," the detective replied. "They told us to contact the FBI. Now I know why."

"Why?" Jade asked.

"Because the UN and the Justice Department must have strong-armed them," said McCann. "There must be details about the crime they don't want made public. That's probably why this guy Crow contacted Bobby."

"Like the identities of the victims," said Matt. "Except for Nick."

"That they couldn't hide."

"No."

"So Bobby wanted me to know," said Jade, pointing to the photographs, "that these two were the ones who killed Yasmine Hayek."

"And he gets killed for his trouble," said McCann.

"By whom?" said Matt. "Not the UN."

"I doubt it," Jack replied. "But who the fuck knows? The world is crazy now."

"Did you run a search on the Locust Valley house?" Jade asked.

"Yes," McCann answered. "It's owned by a Syrian national named Wahim, a diplomat of some kind. We can't get in touch with him."

"Who pays the taxes?"

"His lawyer," the detective answered. "Everett Stryker."

"You're kidding," Matt said.

"Nope."

"He also represents Westside Properties," said Matt, "the owner of Yasmine's building."

"We know," McCann said. "The company officers are all lawyers in Stryker's firm. We're trying to get the names of the shareholders."

"This might be our answer," said Jade. Her cell phone had rung and she was looking at its screen.

"Angelo," she said, after putting the phone to her ear. Then, after listening for about thirty seconds, she said, "Thank you," and clicked off.

Matt and Jack remained silent.

"Westside Properties has one shareholder," Jade said. "A person named Rex al-Salah, of Queens, New York."

"Did you get an address?" Matt asked.

"2344 Linden Place."

"I think that's right near the bridge," said McCann.

Jade put her cell phone, an iPhone, on the Formica table, and, after surfing for a few seconds, turned it to face McCann. She had zoomed in on the satellite image of 2344 Linden Place. McCann and Matt leaned in. Across the front of the two-story building, crowded in among small warehouses and tenements, they could clearly see the words *Lucky's* above the entrance in bright red neon script.

"Michael told me he and Adnan and Ali hung out at a place called Lucky's in Queens," Jade said, "and that Adnan and Ali were friendly with a bartender there named Rex."

"A *bartender* owns a ten story apartment building on Central Park West?" McCann said.

"Unless there are two Rex's at that address," said Matt.

"Let's pay him a visit," McCann said, "and find out."

At the cash register, waiting for change, McCann's cell phone rang. Matt, who had tried to pay but was firmly nudged aside by McCann, watched as his detective friend put the phone to his ear and listened intently, his eyes narrowing.

"How did you get here?" he said to Matt after clicking his phone off.

"My car."

"That was Clarke," McCann said. "They put Mason to bed, but guess where he made a stop tonight."

"Where?" Matt replied.

"Lucky's in Queens. I'll pick up Clarke. We'll meet you there."

24.

Lucky's had a bar along the wall on the left when you walked in, backlit in blue. A series of portraits hung from a valance above the bar, with hidden spotlights on each one. The features of each face were distorted and misplaced—one was all lips and teeth with three small eyes, another had two noses in profile, another the snout and whiskers of a billy goat—the worst, it might be said, of Cubism cum Andy Warhol. At the far end three young men in their mid-twenties were sitting in front of shot glasses and beer backers, talking quietly, watching a basketball game without the sound on a flat screen television. The rest of the barstools were empty, about twenty altogether, except the two directly in the middle occupied by Jack McCann and Clarke Goode.

The place was dimly lit, the tables at the back wall, at one of which sat Matt and Jade, in deep shadow. In the middle of the room stood a platform for a DJ, empty tonight. Some kind of repetitive club music was coming from speakers hidden somewhere on the dark walls. The only light came from small fake candles on the tables and the green-visored lamp above a pool table behind the DJ station, where a man in jeans and a hooded sweatshirt was racking and hitting balls.

"I don't recognize any of these people," Jack McCann said to the bartender, pointing up at the valance.

"They're just people," the bartender said. "Nobody famous."

"Whose the artist?" Clarke Goode asked.

"I am," the bartender said.

"They're very good," McCann said, "very interesting."

"Thank you."

"You wouldn't be Rex al-Salah, would you?" Goode asked.

The bartender, a very slight man of about thirty with a beaky nose, a scruff of beard, and small black eyes, had served McCann and Goode beers and was rearranging glasses on a shelf below the bar as they talked. He had on a shiny black shirt buttoned to the top. He stopped what he was doing when he heard this question.

"Who's asking?" he said.

"I'm Detective McCann," Jack said, pulling his gold shield out of an inside pocket of his corduroy sport jacket. "NYPD. This is Detective Goode." Clarke also displayed his shield.

The bartender, a wine glass in each hand, said nothing. He looked over at the front door, where a muscular bouncer with long blond hair was sitting on a stool talking to a waitress. The glasses sparkled as they caught the blue light from the fixtures above.

"I'm Rex," he said, turning back to the detectives.

"Pleased to meet you," Goode said, extending his right hand. Rex was slow to get the point, but finally he put down one of the wine glasses and extended his own right hand to briefly shake Goode's.

"We're here to talk about the Excelsior," McCann said, "the building you own on Central Park West. One of your tenants was killed there last month."

Rex again remained silent, the other wine glass still in his left hand.

"Your security people have skipped town," Goode said.

"You'll have to talk to my lawyer," Rex said.

"Why can't we talk to you?" Goode asked, his smile gone.

"I don't own any building on Central Park West."

"No, a company called Westside Properties does," said McCann. "You own all the stock."

"Give me your cards," Rex said. "I'll have my lawyer call you."

"What's his name?" Goode asked. "We'll call him."

"Or her," said McCann. "In case it's a woman. Women can practice law in the United States."

Before Rex could respond, two men came out of a room in the back, a slice of bright light appearing and disappearing, like a semaphore at sea, as the door they used opened and quickly closed. They took seats between the group of young men watching basketball and the detectives.

"I have to wait on those guys," Rex said.

"Sure," McCann said. "We'll wait."

"We wouldn't want him to lose his job," Jack said when Rex had moved away.

"Right," said Goode, "with real estate prices so depressed in Manhattan, he probably needs every nickel he can lay his hands on."

"He might even have to sell his fucked up art."

As they talked both Goode and McCann were glancing sideways at the men Rex was serving. Both were swarthy, both in jeans and leather jackets. One had a dark vee-shaped beard, but the bar was too dimly lit to see much else beyond that. Rex served them drinks in rocks glasses, then walked back to McCann and Goode.

"I have to go off duty soon," he said. "Why don't you just give me your cards? My lawyer will call you."

"Sure," said McCann, taking a card out of his wallet and handing it to Rex. "One more thing," the detective continued, sliding three photographs he had laid on the bar towards Rex. "Take a look at these. We were told these two hang out here, and that this one was actually in here tonight."

Rex glanced at the pictures of Adnan and Ali stolen from the UN by Bob Davila, and of Alec Mason, e-mailed by Erhard Fuchs earlier in the evening to the NYPD's Counterterrorism Bureau. "I never saw them before," he said.

McCann pointed at Adnan and Ali and said, "We think these two killed your tenant."

"I don't have a tenant," Rex replied.

"This one was seen right here in Lucky's earlier tonight," said Goode. "You probably weren't on duty when he came in."

"Maybe you were taking a piss," said McCann.

"Or having a smoke," said Goode.

"We were told he went in the back room for a few minutes," said McCann. "Who'd he meet back there?"

"I don't know what you're talking about."

"Then you're completely in the clear," said Goode.

"Which is a good thing for you," said McCann. "Being connected to a murder can get you in a lot of trouble. It's frowned upon here in New York, but you probably know that, you being such a big property owner and all."

Matt and Jade watched from their table along the back wall, shrouded in darkness, as Jack and Clarke left Lucky's. They had agreed beforehand to leave five minutes after the detectives and then be in phone contact. They watched as the man in the hoody put down his cue stick and walked to the door that led to the back room. When he swung it open there was a young man standing, silhouetted, in the light spilling from the interior: Michael. Hoody went in and the door was quickly shut, but almost immediately it swung open again and an older, stocky man, in a dark suit with a white shirt and no tie, wearing a full, neatly trimmed beard, emerged: Mustafa, Basil Hassan's servant.

They watched as Mustafa spoke briefly to the two men at the bar and then returned to the back room.

"Was that...?" said Jade.

"Yes," Matt replied, "Michael. And the stocky guy was Basil Hassan's servant, Mustafa."

They were silent for a moment, absorbing this.

"What now?" Jade said, finally.

"You go with Jack and Clarke. I want to talk to my son."

"Matt..."

"Don't tell them we saw Michael. I want to find out what's going on first."

"Matt..."

"Tell them I ran into an old friend. Tell them any lie you want. But get them out of here."

Jade was silent, putting her scarf on. They had kept their overcoats on, unbuttoned, as they had their drinks. She rose, then bent to kiss Matt, whispering as she did, "I'll tell them you saw Mustafa, that you wanted to talk to him about Michael. Be careful. I don't like this place."

25.

Back-to-back snowstorms had nearly paralyzed garbage pickup in the outer boroughs, which made it easy for Matt to find and hide behind a six-foot pile of overstuffed black utility bags across the street from the entrance to Lucky's. He did not smoke, and, though he was short on patience, generally, he was long on perseverance. As it turned out neither was needed. After only ten minutes, Michael emerged and turned right, his hands in his overcoat pockets, a wool cap pulled down over his ears and nearly covering his eyes.

"Hold up," Matt said. He had let Michael go about twenty steps before crossing the street and shouting out to him. He was about to add, *it's me, your father*, when Michael took off with a start, like a scared rabbit. Matt gave chase. On the next block, Michael, running full out, slipped and slid hip first into a pile of slush at the foot of a light pole. As he was scrambling to his feet, Matt was on him, pulling him up and spinning him around to face him.

"Michael," he said, "it's me, your father." Matt was not wearing a hat. It was cold, perhaps 15 degrees Fahrenheit. His son's face was flushed, his breath steaming as he gasped for air, his eyes—Matt's eyes—flashing beneath the edge of his cap.

What was that he saw in them for a split second? A nakedness, the arrogance gone without a trace.

"Dad?"

"Yes."

"What are you doing here?"

Matt ignored this question. "Talk to me, Micheal," he said. "What are you doing out past your curfew? You'll get locked up. I saw Mustafa in there."

"You were in Lucky's?"

"Yes."

"It's Mom."

"Your mother?"

"Mustafa's drugging her. I followed him."

"Drugging her? How? Why?"

"I don't know, but something's wrong. They want me to plead guilty."

"Plead guilty? Who does?"

"Stryker, Basil."

Matt took this in. His breathing was returning to normal. The cold air still burning in his lungs felt good, cleansing. The light on the pole Michael had careened into was broken. A young black woman in a short red leather jacket, a skin-tight black and white striped skirt and blocky high-heels was standing on the landing of the stoop of a scarred old brownstone, smoking, looking down at them, her pretty face expressionless in the dim porch light.

"Where's your car?" Matt asked.

"Back there."

"Leave it. I'll drive you home. We need to talk."

26.

"They are brave men, Gamal."

"They are all prepared to die."

"But not to be tortured."

"They have their pills. Their families are safe."

"Or dead."

"Yes."

"Like yours."

Basil waited for his friend to reply, but he remained silent, concentrating on the dusty highway, looking, Basil knew, for the obscure turn-off to the even dustier, unnamed road that would take them to the village of Kawkab: godforsaken Kawkab, twelve miles south of Damascus, on what was, two thousand years ago, the Jerusalem Road, its ancient footprint obliterated by sand and wind and time. Gamal had made this trip many times, but he always paid strict attention at this point, leaving Basil to marvel at the orange glow of the hills to the east, and Mount Hermon, the old man, the Sheik, rearing its snow-capped head to the north.

The Oil Ministry's Mercedes limousine was out of place here, a gleaming black ship on wheels gliding on a sea of sand. Gamal, handling it expertly, effortlessly, turned toward

Kawkab, and a short time later stopped next to one of the twelve arches that circled their destination: the church of St. Paul the Messenger. It was a simple stone building, but to Basil's eye it was always mirage-like, shimmering with the energy left over, two thousand years later, from the vision of Jesus that felled St. Paul on this spot, blinding him, converting him, saving his soul, and, so Christians believed—and who could deny it?—changing history.

"Our friend," Gamal said. He was talking about the old man in the red-and-white checked kafiyah sitting on the church's front steps, smiling the same crooked, near-toothless smile he always greeted them with. If he wasn't there, Gamal would have driven on, not even slowing. "I will not be long."

Basil watched his friend of nearly fifty years—they had met on the first day of grammar school in Latakia in 1961—exit the limousine, walk past the old man without acknowledging him, and enter the church. Inside he would say his confession to Father Phillip, the Eastern Orthodox priest who had been running the small, impoverished parish since the church was rebuilt in 1965, rebuilt on ruins that dated back to the first century. Basil reflected on 1961, when the insanity of Sharia was just a whisper and not a drumbeat as it was now, drowning out the voices of reason in a Middle East gone mad. Was he equally mad, to think he could do something to put an end to the fundamentalists and their corruption of Islam? To have undergone such a stark conversion? Paul, on his way to Damascus to hunt down and kill Christians when he was knocked off his mule, must have asked himself the same question. Look what he accomplished.

Gamal returned a few minutes later and they drove off. Basil watched as the old man on the church steps clapped his hands above his head as a sign of Godspeed. The locals, Gamal had informed him when they first visited, clapped this way as a symbol of Paul's experience, knocked to the hard desert ground by the hand of God. *Paul, why dost thou persecute me?*

"How did it go?" Basil asked when they were out of the village.

"The shipment arrived."

"When is the next delivery?"

"They are expecting new altar stones by Palm Sunday."

"When is that?"

"April fifth."

"How many cases will that make?"

"Forty-two."

"How many more can he store?"

"Perhaps another forty."

"It is slow, Gamal."

"Yes, Basil, it is slow. But steady. We will be ready."

27.

"Did he cooperate?" asked Erhard Fuchs.

"Yes," Sylvana Dalessio answered.

"Who is it?"

"A Syrian named Mustafa al-Rahim. He is a servant, an assistant if you will. He works for Basil al-Hassan, the SPC hero."

"One of the ninety-nine names of God," said Fuchs.

"What?"

"al-Rahim is one of the ninety-names of God in the Koran. When they become jihadists they often take one of these names."

"I see. Farah referred to him with great reverence as The Servant. His eyes were shining, like Rahim *was* God, in fact, or at his right hand."

"He did not implicate Hassan?"

"He says that Hassan is an unknowing front, that he is being used."

"By whom? Who does Rahim take his orders from?"

"That was the hard part."

"Who?"

"An SMI colonel. Adullah al-Haq."

"What about the Four Horsemen?"

"He says they are a distraction."

The Four Horsemen were Fuchs' and Sylvana's shorthand for the four Lebanese generals who were being held in a Beirut jail, accused by LeClair of organizing the assassination of Rafik Hariri inside Lebanon.

"How would he know?" Fuchs asked.

"He and al-Hajjar were Haq's boys. He saved them from the rubble of Hama. He trained them personally, taught them how to make bombs. He brought them to New York, through the Servant."

"*Brought* them?"

"Yes, he is stationed here."

"And the others, the MP's?"

"Yes, he and Ali killed all eleven on orders from Haq via Rahim."

"If the Four Horsemen were not involved, then who? There had to be Lebanese help."

"Hezbollah. They brought him to a facility in Beirut where he had his pick of weapons, bomb material, and cell phones."

"For all of the killings?"

"Yes, each one first cleared by Haq, each one set up by Hezbollah people who were trusted in government circles."

"Why was he brought to New York?"

"He does not know."

"Does he know who tried to kill him in Locust Valley?"

"He acknowledges it could be Rahim on Haq's orders."

"To silence him."

"Yes."

"What about The New York detectives who were killed? Did Farah say?"

"Of that he knows nothing," the Italian replied, "except of course he assumes Haq gave the orders for the second one, Davila, the car bomb."

"So Mason was Haq's man," the Dutchman replied, saying this more to himself than to the Italian policewoman.

"*Was* Haq's man?"

"Yes, he's dead."

Silence.

"Too bad," Dalessio said, finally, then: "Erhard?"

"Yes."

"I spoke to Johannes. He said the terrorists who killed your mother and sister were Indonesian."

"One was Persian."

"Oh…"

"The one who killed them. He was the leader."

"I see."

"He was released five years later."

"By your government?"

"Yes, it was all classified, but I had sources."

Fuchs paused, waiting for Dalessio to ask another question. When she didn't, he went on: "I saw his picture in *De Telegraaf* the day I buried Kaat. He was standing behind Assad, who was greeting Ahmadinajad in Damascus."

"Was he identified?"

"In the paper, no. But I ran a search."

"Who is he?"

"Abdullah al-Haq."

Again the Italian agent was silent.

"He's come a long way," she said, finally.

"Yes," the Dutchman replied. "Born in Iran, sent on missions all over the world, now planted in the midst of Syrian intelligence."

"Why was an Iranian leading those Indonesians?"

"They were Muslims. He was one of Khomeini's fanatics. His name was Massoud Karimi then. He trained them, the whole raid was Khomeini's idea."

"Directed from Paris."

"Yes, while the French elite fed him escargot and caviar."

"And the reign of terror continues."

"Yes it does."

"And our plan remains the same?"

"Yes."

"I will send the boys."

"Sylvana, one last thing."

"Yes."

"Yasmine Hayek."

"They did it."

"As a message to Pierre and his anti-Syrian friends?"

"No, on that score Farah said something strange."

"Is it on the tape?"

"Yes."

"It can wait. I am meeting Goode and his partner. I see them parking their car."

"OK, *ciao*. Good luck."

Fuchs hung up. He was sitting in the Square Diner, a cup of horrible black coffee in front of him. The NYPD detectives were right outside his window, their coat collars turned up against the cold, the white one, McCann, taking a drag on an unfiltered cigarette and then flipping it into the gutter. The black had sounded strange on the phone. Something must have happened. *They could waterboard me*, he thought. *Would I talk?*

28.

Did you think they were sincere, our friends in Damascus?
    Silence.
    Does this change anything?
    I'll get back to you.
    This was the conversation Bill Crow had with his young
CIA contact right after the murder of Yasmine Hayek. The
contact, known to him only via a voice ID code on his cell
phone screen, had later confirmed that nothing had changed.
His mission was the same.
    But things were different now. Two NYPD detectives were
dead, one in a piece of bad luck, the second assassinated. The
Locust Valley and Glen Cove police had been muzzled. Threats
of criminal action, of charges of violation of national security
laws had had to be made in order to accomplish this. Still, the
mayor, the governor, both New York senators — all members
of the same political party as the new president — were asking
questions. But that wasn't the problem. They could be backed
off, they were politicians. It was the NYPD and the boyfriend's
father that were the problem. They didn't care about politics,
or somebody in Washington getting the Nobel Peace Prize.
    This morning he had spoken to his contact in Langley again.
The clockmaker is alive. The cat lover is holding him.

Alive?

Yes, and talking, I'm sure.

Without doubt.

He thinks the client will try to reach him.

Would they dare?

It depends on what's at stake.

If it goes wrong...

He's also talking about freeing the DeMarco boy.

That's not good.

Do you want me to take care of it?

Yes.

There will be a fee.

How much?

One million.

In the same account?

Yes. And I will need information.

Go ahead.

Sylvana Dalessio. Who is she? Does she have relatives in Los Angeles? If so, is one of them sick? A nephew?

Anything else?

Erhard Fuchs. Who are his friends in the U.S.? And I need his family history.

That's it?

Yes.

I'll get back to you.

Bill Crow looked up and down 23rd Street before step-ping away from the Chelsea Hotel's stump of a portico and heading toward Ninth Avenue. It could be, he thought, that he was wrong, that his CIA contact was not so young after all, that he just had a youthful sounding voice. How else to explain the immediate grant of authority to *take care of it*, a euphemism for *kill Adnan Farah and anyone who tries to stop you*? Of course with the administration so new and so naïve, his contact could actually *be* a thirty-year-old Yale graduate in a cubicle someplace who had been told to take care of Syria's Monteverde problem, and been left to his own devices.

Did Bill Crow care one way or the other? No. All of his fees went to a numbered account in Switzerland from one of the thousands of slush funds controlled by the CIA but untraceable to it. The only time he ever used a phone was when he talked to his contacts, who could listen to any phone conversation in the world if they wanted to, and whose own phones were interception-proof. Like the terrorists were now doing, Bill Crow otherwise communicated exclusively via simple signals or cryptic, coded messages, not unlike the way the old mountain and plains Indians did. Smoke; rocks arranged a certain way; a hatchet mark in bark. Ephemeral, they soon vanished, as did Crow when a job was done.

It was no use telling his contact who posed the greatest threat to his mission. He wouldn't care. Or he'd get nervous, even though he had total deniability, not because of the juvenile code he insisted on using, but because their conversations never existed. Such was the high level of the agency's technology, not to mention the supreme immunity from oversight it had enjoyed since it's inception in the chaotic aftermath of World War II.

Fuchs had stonewalled the NYPD, as he was obliged to do. He *had* threatened to reveal the true killers of Yasmine Hayek, but that was obviously a bluff. He planned on using the bomb maker as bait, and would not want the NYPD barging in, as they surely would if they sensed he was holding something back. They wanted Farah's bosses as much as Fuchs did. The killing of the second New York detective had been a mistake, an overplay that only a mad man would do. But then again, all *jihadis* were mad man, were they not?

If the great half-black, half-white father thought he could bring peace to the Middle East, who was Bill Crow to argue with him, to tell him that Islam permitted—obligated might be the better word—its followers to lie to infidels, to tell him that the only way to deal with Islam was to reduce it to a handful of defeated stragglers on reservations, perhaps eventually let them build casinos.

Bill Crow smiled at this thought, a rare thing for him. Tomorrow Fuchs' team would depart. On his own, or perhaps with the help of the Italian, the Dutchman would be defenseless. Crow would find out where Adnan Farah was being held and kill him, along with Fuchs and Dalessio if necessary. He would also, with the help of another person blinded by hate, take out some insurance, like any good businessman would do.

29.

"Mason is dead," said Erhard Fuchs. "He fell from his hotel room's balcony."

"Fell or was pushed?" Jack McCann asked.

"Pushed of course."

"You told us to sit on him at his hotel," said Clarke Goode. "No wonder he never came out."

"He did," Fuchs replied. "Off the balcony."

"Are there surveillance tapes?" Goode asked.

"Yes, we'll have them soon."

"Our CB people have images of the Mason surveillance," the black detective said. "They're vetting them. Do you want copies?"

"Of course."

"How many floors?" McCann asked.

"Twenty-one."

"When did this happen?" Goode asked.

"Nine-thirty."

"So who was he?"

They were sitting in a booth at the back of the Square Diner, McCann and Goode on one side, Fuchs on the other.

"A mole on my team."

"Working for whom?"

"Iran, Syria. Probably both. He was their pipeline into what we were doing."

"You were hoping he would lead you to his contact."

"Yes."

"We were in Lucky's ourselves tonight," Goode said.

"Doing what?"

"Our job. We got two cops dead, remember?"

"What led you there?"

Clarke Goode looked at his partner and raised his thick, salt and pepper eyebrows.

"You asked for this meeting," McCann said.

"I apologize. I was just being a cop myself."

"You mentioned needing our help. Again."

"I know who killed Loh and Davila."

"Who?" McCann and Goode said this at the same time, with the same deadly quiet tone in their voices. The Dutchman was suddenly very glad to have these men as allies.

"A Colonel Abdullah al-Haq of Syrian Military Intelligence, and his field operative, a man named Mustafa al-Rahim. They are trying to derail my investigation into a series of assassinations in Lebanon, starting with Rafik Hariri in 2005."

"Who's he?" McCann asked.

"He was the president of Lebanon. Very popular, very anti-Syria."

"And the others?"

"Members of parliament. All anti-Syria."

"Why our guys?" McCann asked.

"Loh was an accident. He was supposed to stay in his car until backup arrived. It appears the killers knew this, through Mason. It was supposed to be easy for them to get in and out, especially with Mason causing a delay in our response. When Loh tried to stop them, they killed him."

"And Davila?"

"He took something, I don't know what, from my command post after the shooting in Locust Valley. Whatever it was he was killed for it."

"Mason again."

"Yes. He must have passed it on."

"What went down in Locust Valley?"

"Two assassins working for Rahim were holed up there. We were watching the house."

"So Rahim is here in New York?" Goode asked.

"Yes, he works for a man named Basil al-Hassan, a rich Syrian businessman."

"That's Debra DeMarco's husband," McCann said.

"Yes."

"And he's legit?"

"Legit?"

"Not one of the bad guys."

"It seems so."

"So they're both dead now, the killers?" Goode asked.

"No, we let it out that the two men who lived in the house were killed, but one actually survived."

"Who? Where is he?" McCann asked.

"He is a bomb maker, a Syrian named Adnan al-Farah. We have him in a safe house."

"Why do you need *us*?"

"I need you to take custody of Farah. The Syrians have killed several witnesses so far. They will surely try to kill him as well."

"What about your people?"

"I have not told them about Farah."

"Why not?"

"I believe they are compromised."

"By whom?"

"Your government. I believe the U.S. has promised Syria that it will get the UN to back off on pursuing them for the Hariri assassination."

"Why?"

"Stupidity."

"So the FBI wouldn't take him either."

"No."

"Speaking of the FBI," said Goode. "Do you know an agent named Bill Crow? Is he connected with this?"

Fuchs, despite himself, was taken aback, and he knew, unfortunately, that his surprise was revealed for a split second on his otherwise professionally non-expressive face.

"We checked him out," McCann said. "He's not listed as an FBI agent."

"Where did you get his name?" Fuchs asked.

"Out of a hat," McCann answered.

"From Bob Davila," said Goode.

"He's a contract op, I think CIA, but I'm not sure," Fuchs said. "He talked to Davila?"

"It looks that way," Goode replied. "Why? Is that good or bad?"

"I don't know," the Dutchman replied.

"You don't know?" McCann said. "Whose side is the CIA on?"

Fuchs did not answer. *I don't know,* he said to himself, *I thought ours.*

"Are you saying," Goode asked, "that the U.S. government, the FBI, the CIA, *whatever*, would let the DeMarco kid go down for this?"

"They would probably quietly intervene to make some kind of a deal."

"Loh and Davila were killed on Long Island," Goode said, shaking his head, his brown, grizzled face grim. "Let's say we want to help you. We don't have jurisdiction."

"Farah and his dead partner, Ali Najjar, killed Yasmine Hayek. He has confessed to that as well. That killing occurred here in New York."

"Yes," McCann said. "We already knew that. We were waiting for you to come clean. We have your surveillance log."

"I see," Fuchs replied. "Is that what Davila stole? Our surveillance reports?"

"Yes."

"It got him killed."

"Why did Haq want the girl dead?" McCann asked.

"Her father is the Justice Minister in Lebanon. He's openly anti-Syria."

The Dutchman watched as the two NYPD detectives

shook their heads and looked at him like he had just emerged from the primordial slime covered in mud and shiny scales.

"It's the Mideast," he said.

"Did Mason know about Farah?" Goode asked.

"Yes, I told him tonight. I'm sure he passed it on, probably to somebody at Lucky's. I am anxious to see the CB pictures."

"How secure is Farah?" McCann asked.

"He is in an untraceable location, guarded by four professionals."

"You left the DeMarco kid hanging out to dry for three weeks," Goode said, "knowing he didn't kill the girl. His father's a good friend. He won't be happy."

"You can give him a copy of Farah's confession."

"And that's supposed to make everything hunky-dory?" McCann said.

"Hunky-dory?"

"All square with you and DeMarco, even-steven."

"I see. Talk to your justice department. I believe they knew."

"Fuck."

"Yes, fuck. That word I understand."

"We want to be able to use your surveillance log," said Goode.

"Of course," the Dutchman replied.

"We can't make this decision ourselves," said Goode.

"I understand. I will wait. Not long, I hope. Farah needs medical attention, and there is always the chance his location will be discovered."

"Give us twenty-four hours."

"Yes, of course."

30.

"Are you awake?" Matt asked.

Jade woke with a start, saw Matt, sitting in shadow on the edge of the couch, and placed the tips of her fingers to her eyes to rub the sleep from them.

"Yes," she said.

"You are *now*, you mean."

"Yes."

"I'm sorry to wake you."

"I was praying, then the next thing I knew, you were sitting there."

Matt remained silent.

"You're sitting on one of the four corners," Jade said.

"The four corners?"

"*Four corners to my bed, four angels there aspread.*"

Silence again from Matt.

Jade shook her head and lowered her eyes. "I say it every night," she said. "*Now I lay me down to sleep.* It's an old habit, from when I was a girl."

"Tell me the whole thing."

> "*Now I lay me down to sleep,*
> *I pray the Lord my soul to keep.*

Four corners to my bed,
Four angels there aspread:
Two to foot and two to head,
And four to carry me when I'm dead.
If any danger come to me,
Sweet Jesus Christ deliver me.
And if I die before I wake,
I pray the Lord my soul to take."

Jade had dimmed the lamp on a nearby end table to its lowest setting and then settled down to wait for Matt. She decided to say her nightly prayer, not because she was ready to sleep, but because Lucky's had creeped her out. The scrawny bartender, the darkness, the people going in and out of that back room. She had replaced *me* with *Matt* when she came to the *If any danger* part, saying the prayer like the mantra it was meant to be. Once, twice, three times, the next thing she knew Matt was sitting there.

Matt's overcoat and scarf were still wrapped over his right arm. Turning sideways, he threw them across the room to an easy chair, then turned back to face Jade, who pulled her knees up to give him more room, pulling up the blanket she was using as well. The lamp's pale yellow light did nothing to soften the wildness in Matt's face. His beautiful dark eyes met hers for a second, and in them she saw something new. Something had happened.

"What is it, Matt?" she said.

"Michael says they want him to plead guilty to rape," Matt said. "He'll do five-to-ten, with only a hard five."

"Drop the murder charge?"

"Yes."

"Who's *they*?"

"Stryker, Basil."

"Matt, that can't be. He has a perfect consent defense. And what's Healy thinking? Two shots to the head, two to the back of the neck. He's willing to bury that? He's lost his mind."

"There's something else," Matt said. "Michael and Yasmine made love, but she didn't want to at first. He was angry. He pinned her on the couch."

"Did he rape her?"

"No. He says no, and I believe him. He says she was kissing him at the end, that they were both crying. But he was *there*, Yasmine was breaking up with him, there are the emails. And only Michael's DNA was found in Yasmine."

"Those bruises, Matt, I saw the pictures."

"I told him about the bruises."

"What did he say?"

"He says he couldn't have caused them."

"But he's not taking the deal."

Matt remained silent.

"What's going on, Matt?"

"Michael was at Lucky's tonight because he wanted to confront Mustafa. He says Mustafa's been drugging Debra, giving her double and triple doses of her medication. Tranquilizers mostly."

"Why?"

"He's not sure. He says she's a mess, that it's not just the drugs."

"Did he? Confront Mustafa?"

"Yes. Mustafa said he's recorded everything that's gone on in that apartment for the past six years. All the rooms, video and audio. That was his answer."

Jade was silent. She clutched the old cardigan sweater she was wearing to her neck, thinking of the glimpse she had gotten of Mustafa as he came out of the back room of Lucky's, something about the way he carried himself, with the confidence of a fanatic, a zealot, a superior being: *I can do as I wish, I am higher than God, higher than Lucifer. I can videotape people in their private lives, and use it against them as I wish.* She realized with an inner start that Antonio's father, the man who had corrupted her when she was seventeen, did not hold a candle to the likes of Mustafa, that perhaps it had been self-pity that had ruined her life since then, and not her producer boyfriend; that he too must have his demons.

She had been right to pray for Matt, for somebody besides herself for a change, herself and Antonio.

"Do you want something?" she said. "Hot chocolate? A drink? You look like you could use a drink." She was too shocked to mention, for the moment, Matt's revelation of the constant secret videotaping of people's private lives. Shocked by such a thing, and also by the revelation she had just had about how she had been looking at her life these many years.

"No, I just need to sleep. If I can."

"Where's Michael now?"

"I dropped him off at Park Avenue."

Matt was looking down at his hands, which were laid out palm-down, one on each of his thighs, pressing against the fabric of the brown corduroy slacks he was wearing.

"Matt."

"Yes."

"Videos?"

"I think Michael sometimes slept with Debra."

Matt looked directly at her as he said this, as if not to was somehow to his mind cowardly. More silence. A river of pain to be crossed, for both of them, Jade thought, like the conversation she would have to have with Antonio when he got home. That would be a crossing. For both of them.

"Did he tell you that?" Jade asked, finally.

"No, but he did when he was a boy—sleep in her bed, I mean—for too long. I've wondered about it...He says he might take the deal."

"To keep these videos from coming out? Do you think there's one of him and Debra?"

"I think so. Why else would he do this plea bargain?"

"To protect his mother."

"Yes."

"Who's behind this?" Jade asked. "Who wants this murder covered up so bad?"

"Mustafa works for Basil al-Hassan."

"Basil? Why? What's his deal?"

"I don't know, but I'll find out."

Jade held out her hand and Matt took it.

"What about Antonio?" he said. "When does he come home?"

"He has games tomorrow night and Thursday night. They fly home on Friday morning early."

"Have you decided?"

"I have to let him go."

Matt's response was to press her hand in his.

"I'll tell him first," she said.

Matt brought Jade's hand to his lips, kissed it, and said, "Let's get some sleep."

"What will you do?"

"I'll go see Debra tomorrow. She can stop this plea deal."

"Maybe Jack and Clarke got somewhere with Fuchs. Clarke called. He said to call him when you got in."

"They talked to Fuchs?"

"He called when they were getting in their car."

"What did he say about me staying behind?"

"They were worried, but they had to get downtown to see Fuchs."

"Did *you* go?"

"No, they dropped me off. Jack has the surveillance report. Maybe he talked Fuchs into releasing it."

"Maybe," Matt replied, "but I doubt it. There's something I can't fathom going on with Fuchs. His two suspects are dead. He knows they killed Yasmine, yet he won't reveal what he knows. It's been a month now."

"At least Michael talked to you. How was he?"

"He was scared. Very frightened. He sees his choices as either going to jail for a crime he didn't commit or revealing this dark secret about his mother. He can't understand why Mustafa would be drugging Debra, though. He can't go to Basil because Mustafa is Basil's man. It could be Basil who's drugging Debra, ordering it."

"His world is falling apart."

"Yes."

"Do you think Debra will help?" Jade said. "If it means...?"

"I have to try. Michael won't last six months in prison. He'll be raped, turned into a girl. Debra will have to choose."

"Come to bed, Matt."

"I will," Matt replied, reaching for his overcoat and fishing out his cell phone. "But first I'll call Jack. I want to know what this guy Fuchs had to say about his surveillance log."

31.

"Sire," said Mustafa, "I must ask your permission to return to Syria."

"Has something happened?"

"My brother is dying. He has been sent home from hospital to die. His cancer cannot be treated."

Basil al-Hassan had had problems in Damascus. His superiors, and their superiors, could not quite believe that Yasmine Hayek had been killed by her boyfriend, *Basil's stepson.* Nor could they believe that the U.S. had really accepted Michael DeMarco as Yasmine Hayek's killer. *Could we be so lucky?* was their unasked question. *Would they actually continue to help us in thwarting Monteverde?* They had sent al-Haq to threaten him, to let him know that they suspected him. Which could only mean that they had discovered his secret, that they knew of his young wife and child buried in the hills above Latakia, and that he had a motive for orchestrating Yasmine's murder and the clever dodge of framing his own stepson. Now this.

Basil turned away from his servant to look, for a moment, out of his study window down to Park Avenue at the silent dance of cars and buses and pedestrians that went on endlessly whether he noticed it or not. He would miss New York, he thought, if it came to that.

"Do you know why I agreed to take you into my household, Mustafa?" Basil asked.

"No, sire."

"Karantina. You survived the bombings in the war."

"Yes, sire."

"My wife and son did not."

"Your wife and son?"

"I fought in Lebanon for four years. I met and married my first wife there."

"I did not know, sire."

"It was Pierre Hayek who led the attack on Karantina, a Muslim ghetto of no strategic value. He had secretly joined one of the Christian militias just the week before."

"Pierre Hayek?"

"Yes. He befriended me, he told me he was Shia."

"Did he know...?"

"No, Fatimah and Anwar were my secret. They were not Alewites you see, not even Syrian. Still, he killed them for no reason."

"No reason?"

"To terrorize Muslims living in a Christian neighborhood," Basil replied. "You were there, were you not?"

"Yes, sire. I was."

"I did not know you had a brother."

"He emigrated to Syria with me in 1976."

"And where is he living now?"

"Dera."

"The Assad family vouched for you. They told me of your bravery at Hama, of your loyalty to your adopted country."

"Thank you, sire."

"It is ironic, is it not, Mustafa?"

"Sire?"

"That Adnan and Ali have avenged my wife and child by killing Pierre's daughter, that Allah has done this for me without my asking."

"Yes, sire."

"Of course they suspect me in Damascus. That is the

irony. Do you know a man named al-Haq, Mustafa? A Colonel Abdullah al-Haq."

"No, sire."

"He threatened me yesterday."

"I do not know him, sire."

"You may of course go to your dying brother."

"Thank you, sire. Will you stay in New York, sire?"

"No."

"Where will you be?"

"I will let you know."

"Yes, sire. One last item."

"Yes?"

"Michael's father has called Debra. He wants to meet her for lunch to discuss Michael."

"How do you know this?"

"He left a message on the 2122 line."

"Where are they meeting? Did he name a place?"

"At the Garden Restaurant at the Kitano."

"Just a few doors away."

"Yes. Shall I observe?"

"No. She will hold herself together in the presence of her ex-husband. Where is she now?"

"In the shower."

"She seems worse, does she not?"

"Yes, sire."

"Perhaps we should change her medication, or the dosage. When do you leave?"

"My flight is at six tonight."

"Leave the psychiatrist's number on my desk."

"Yes, sire."

"Her son may go to prison. She is grieving."

"Yes, sire."

"Do you have children, Mustafa? I've never asked."

"No, sire, I do not."

Basil al-Hassan had been watching his servant's face carefully during their conversation. It had been as lifeless, as appropriately subservient, as ever, until now. Did he have children? Was that why his eyes had narrowed slightly for an instant before answering?

"And Michael?" Basil asked. "Where is he?"

"In his room. Sleeping."

"You can go."

32.

"Debra," Matt said, "do you know about the deal that Stryker wants Michael to make? Five years for rape?"

"Yes, he told me."

"Who told you?"

"Michael."

Matt had been sitting at a table in the rear right corner of the restaurant, his back to the wall, and was able to watch Debra as she nodded hello to the maitre d' and walked slowly toward him — too slowly — and now he saw why. Her more or less permanent Hamptons tan was gone, replaced by a pale whitish-gray pallor that reminded him of the color of an opponent's face who he had knocked down in the ring; that stunned, bloodless look. The drugs, Matt thought, trying to find his ex-wife's once handsome features behind this white, listless mask, but not succeeding.

"Did he tell you Stryker's reasoning?"

"The murder charge...the evidence."

"How do you feel about it?"

"My son's not a rapist."

"How do you think he'll do in state prison?"

"He's not taking the deal."

"Are you sure?"

"He can't."

"Did he tell you anything about a video?"

"What kind of a video?"

"Mustafa's been videotaping everything in your Park Avenue apartment for the last six years. All the rooms."

"My God..."

"Did he?"

"Did he *what*?"

"Mention videos."

"No."

Debra was even whiter now, ashen in the way a person would be whose most craven undertakings had been put on display. *It's true*, he thought, and with that thought all of his anger at his ex-wife dissipated, melted away. After all the emotional torment he had suffered at Debra's hands, he had assumed, having grimly daydreamed for years about a moment like this, that he would be happy to see her suffer one day, to see that the tables turned. But what he felt was pity, and sadness, and not just for her, but for Michael as well. In the way it has of doing such things, the universe had worked it out so that their terrible secret had been revealed, and now the price had to be calculated and paid by both of them.

"Have you spoken to Stryker at all?" he asked, finally. He would have to rub salt in her wound now, but not for his own pleasure, or to make her feel worse. There were questions he needed answers to, regardless of how much pain they caused Debra.

"No, never."

"Does Mustafa speak to Stryker?"

"Mustafa?"

"Yes."

"I don't know. I doubt it."

"Does Basil talk to him?"

"Of course. Matt..."

"Yes?" *Do you want to tell me something? That you ruined our son?*

Debra, shaking her head, was crying. A waiter had been hovering nearby, but when he saw her face he went away. They both had sparkling water in front of them, ordered by Matt when he was seated. It was untouched.

"I have to go, Matt," Debra said, drying her eyes with her white cotton napkin.

"Debra," Matt said, "I think Basil or Mustafa, or both of them, are blackmailing Michael with one of the videos from the apartment. They'll reveal it if he doesn't take the deal."

"Why?"

"I don't know why."

"Not Basil," Debra replied. "It can't be. He's secretive. He has secret friends and he does things that he keeps from me. But he would not let Michael go to prison for no reason. He would not be involved in blackmail. It's Mustafa."

"How do you know?"

"I saw him hand something to a man in a car last week. I followed the car to Glen Cove. The man got out and put something under a car on Frost Pond Road..."

"Davila," Matt said.

"Yes."

"And you didn't come forward? You said nothing?"

"I was frightened. I still am."

"He could have been acting on Basil's orders. Basil's a billionaire, Mustafa's a servant."

"No," Debra said. "It's Mustafa acting alone. It has to be. He watches me. He listens in on my phone calls. He follows me. He's the one who brings me my pills."

"It doesn't matter right now," Matt said. "There's no time. This deal has to be stopped. Only you can stop it."

"When did you talk to Michael?"

"Last night."

"What did he say?"

"You mean what else did he say?"

"Yes."

"He wants to make the deal."

"I have to go," Debra said, reaching for her purse, which was on the chair next to her.

"*Debra.*" Matt reached across the pristinely white-clad tabletop and took hold of Debra's hand before she could pick up the bag. He meant to forcibly stop her from leaving, but he was shocked by the fragility of her flesh beneath his fingers, by the tremor he felt passing from her hand to his, as if he were holding a small, frightened bird. She looked down at their entwined hands and then back at Matt.

"You can put a stop to this, Debra," Matt said.

"I know I can," Debra replied. "And I will."

Matt let go of her hand and watched as she picked up her purse and left, taking her son's future, and the remnants of her soul, with her. Their sixteen-year, post-divorce dance of anger and hate was over.

She'll do it, he said to himself, *she loves him too much. And the price will be the loss of her son.*

33.

Manhattan, Tuesday, March 3, 2009, 2PM

Two voices echoed in Debra al-Hassan's head as she stood, key in hand, on the threshold of Mustafa's office in her Park Avenue apartment. The first was Matt DeMarco's, her first love, the handsome Marine who had fallen out of love with her and left her sixteen years ago.

Mustafa's been videotaping everything in your Park Avenue apartment for the last six years. All the rooms. Basil and Mustafa are blackmailing Michael.

You can put a stop to this, Debra.

The second was Basil al-Hassan's, the dashing millionaire whose brilliant mind had turned to other things in the last few years, secret things he would not share with her, but who she could not, would not, believe, would ever do her any harm.

I have spoken again to Stryker. He thinks he can make a deal for Michael.

Adnan and Ali cannot be found. They are likely dead.

There were no prints on the gun. No paraffin test was done. The evidence points to Michael, but is legally insufficient. His DNA—and only his—was found in Yasmine. Healy will be satisfied with a rape conviction.

Now she knew the truth. Did Basil? Did he know about the videotaping? Was he part of the blackmail? Did it have something to do with his secret friends, his secret life? Or did he accept the high-priced Everett Stryker's reasoning? Her family and friends — those she had left — were both in awe of, and sneered at, her marriage. But they did not know what she knew: that Basil loved her. She was a woman through and through, and thus she knew down to her bones that, though he hid many things from her, he loved her. Perhaps he knew about the videos and was forcing the plea bargain on Michael to protect her. No. *Mustafa,* she thought, *Mustafa* is behind all this.

She had not taken her meds for twenty-four hours and felt slightly nauseous and jumpy, but otherwise lucid. Lucid enough, thank God, to have remembered that when she and Basil and Michael first moved to Park Avenue and she thought she was in charge of the apartment and her domestic affairs, she had had duplicate keys made of all the locks, including the pantry that was converted to an office for The Silent One, as she came to think of Mustafa. She inserted one of those keys now, and let herself in.

The room was small, ten feet by ten feet, and windowless. It was dominated by a desk and a swivel chair that gave access to a computer on a shelf behind the desk and a small metal filing cabinet to the right. Basil had gone out and said he would be back in at five. Michael was sleeping, or brooding, in his room. Lying awake in her room, her senses sharp for once for lack of tranquilizers, she had heard him come in around two AM last night.

The desktop was empty except for a blotter, a silver letter opener, a note pad, a dozen pencils in a round holder, and a large black molded plastic box. This was locked. She thought of carrying it back to her room, but decided that was a bad idea. The desk drawers were all locked as well. Should she turn on the computer? No, she would need a password to access anything important. Both drawers of the filing cabinet were also locked, but there was a slight movement of the bottom drawer when she pulled on the handle, enough so that she could see the top edge of two green and white Tyvek envelopes resting inside. Using the letter opener, she pried them out. Nothing else was reachable, so she pushed the drawer in and slipped back into her room, locking the former pantry door behind her.

In the first envelope was a one-page document with the heading, *New York Division of Parole*. In a box on the upper right the word DENIED was stamped in red. She scanned the text: *the prisoner, Wael Hakimi, NYSID 42325-63, remains angry and unremorseful. His next review date will be scheduled in 2015...* In the second envelope were two DVDs, unmarked. She slipped one into her player and turned it on. Adnan and Ali were getting out of an elevator, walking along a carpeted corridor, knocking at a door, waiting and then entering an apartment, the number 1102 in a brass frame on the wall next to the door. The date and time were running digitally along the bottom of the screen: January 30, 2009, 1:18 PM, 1:19 PM... The day Yasmine was killed, the beginning of Debra's descent into hell.

She ejected the disc and was about to insert the second one, but was interrupted by a sharp knock on her door.

"Yes?" she said. She was holding the second disc, hovering it near the DVD's insert slot.

"Mom. It's me."

"Michael, I'm changing. I'll come to your room."

"I need to talk to you now. Put something on. Open up. It's important."

"Hold on."

She returned the discs to their envelope, slipped the Parole Board report in with them, grabbed a pen from her dresser and scrawled Matt's name and Pound Ridge address across the front. She grabbed a pad of stamps from her desk drawer and hastily placed a row of ten on the upper right of the envelope. Then, carrying it, she walked to the door and pulled it open.

"Put this in the mail in the lobby," she said, "then come back up. We'll talk."

34.

The phone rang in Matt's apartment, and at the same time there was a sharp rapping at his door. Ignoring the phone, he undid the latch and opened it, thinking it was Jade. But it was Michael.

"Come in," Matt said. "Close the door." Then he turned and went to the phone on a stand next to the entrance to the galley kitchen.

"Jade?"

"No, it's Jack."

"Jack."

"Matt. Do you know where Michael is?"

"He's right here." Matt looked over at his son, who had gone to look out of the window in the living room. His back was to Matt. His wavy hair fell in a sort of designed carelessness onto the collar of his stylish black leather winter coat. He was always designed, his son, but something was different about the design tonight, seen from the back like this. Standing there, not knowing Matt was looking at him, he could almost be a boy of ten again, lost in the painful divide that had opened between his parents. "Why, Jack?"

"Debra's committed suicide, Matt. Homicide North wants to talk to Michael."

Matt did not respond.

"Sorry, Matt."

"How? When?" Matt said.

"This afternoon. Pills."

"Where do they want him?"

"It's routine, Matt."

"Are you sure?"

"Yes."

"Can *you* do it?"

"I don't think so. I'll call you back."

Matt returned the phone to its holder. He had not taken his eyes off of Michael, who turned now to face him.

"That was Jack McCann," Matt said.

"About Mom?"

"Yes. You know?"

"Basil called me. I went to the hospital, then I came here."

"What happened?"

"Basil was at a meeting all afternoon. He came home and found her on the floor in her room. He said she was still breathing. I met him at Mt. Sinai. She was dead when I got there."

"Michael..."

"Dad, listen. There's something I have to tell you."

"Sit," Matt said, gesturing toward the table.

"No. Dad..."

Matt remained silent, watching his son. Later he would remember, of all the things said in this brief conversation, something not said: the haunted look in Michael's eyes at this moment, the first true inward look in those dark eyes that he could ever remember seeing.

"When we first moved to Park Avenue...when we first moved there," Michael said, "I slept with Mom a few times. Nothing happened, but..."

"But what?"

"I was sixteen, Dad. Too old."

"But what?"

"I got aroused once. Mom..."

"Mom what?"

"She was happy. I don't know. I stopped."

"Did you sleep with her after I left? When you were young?"

"Yes, it was what she wanted... Dad?"

"Michael... You were just a child."

Michael's head had been sinking as they talked, but now he raised it and looked into Matt's eyes. "There's something else," he said. "I saw it. The video of us."

"You saw it?"

"Yes. We stopped, but..."

"When did you see it?"

"This morning. Mustafa showed it to me. He must have shown it to Mom. That must be why she killed herself."

"Sit down, Michael. We need to talk. The police investigate all suicides. They want to talk to you. I want you to be ready. Plus, you're being railroaded. That has to stop now."

35.

In the first of the late winter daylight, Bill Crow put his Swarovski field binoculars to his eyes, and, with his ungloved right index finger, gently turned the ridged focus ring until the Fuchs homestead, nestled in a small clearing, surrounded on three sides by tall snow-clad pine trees, came sharply into view. A black SUV with US State Department Foreign Mission license plates was parked in front. Tire marks stretched behind it the length of the 200-foot driveway. Smoke was rising steadily straight up from a centrally located stone chimney. The lights were on in the two front rooms facing him on his hill a quarter of a mile away. Just above the horizon, the North Star—the heavens' only fixed point—was pulsing and soon would be gone. In Indian lore, a young brave had climbed the highest mountain in the world. When he found he could not get down he was turned into the North Star, to honor his feat. Forgotten lore, Crow thought, meaningless, drowned in alcohol and casino money.

In his pocket was the cryptic fax he had received a few hours ago from Langley:

> SD: no relatives in the US. Parents killed in
> the RH bombing in 2005. F: wife dead, no

children; brother and nephews, all policemen, left Amsterdam 3/1, arrived NY. No
return. Paternal grandparents, both dead,
were owners of 10 RR 12, Stone Ridge,
NY—coordinates: 41°50′45″ North, 74°9′23″
West (41.845867, -74.156494)—until 1996.
Now owned by EJJ Trust of Rotterdam.
Sources confirm EJJ beneficiaries are Erhard
and Johannes F.

When he arrived on his hilltop a half hour ago, he entered
the coordinates into the European-made, CIA-adapted 90 mm
rocket launcher that had been left for him at a safe house in
nearby Hardenburgh. He had parked his pickup, also waiting
for him at the safe house, in a stand of giant fir trees near
an abandoned fire tower about a mile away, and trudged in
through the snow and the dark, carrying the thirty pound
launcher and rocket container in a duffle bag, along with a
high powered scoped rifle that he had quickly put together and
that was now resting on a stump on his right.

In the right front window, a dark-haired woman stood
smoking a cigarette, its hot orange tip arcing as she swept her
hair back and poured coffee. *Sylvana Dalessio*—her picture in
his pocket next to the fax—along with pictures of Johannes
and his two sons. No sign of them, although a few minutes
ago lights had come on briefly and gone off in an upstairs
room. Nor of the bomb-maker, Adnan Farah. Was he in there?
Without doubt, although the forensic people would insist on
making positive IDs and combing through the rubble.

Crow set the binoculars on the stump that his rifle was
leaning against, and watched quietly, as still as a buck scenting
the forest air, as the North Star twinkled one last time and
disappeared. He then snapped the rocket container into the
back of the launcher, raised the weapon to his shoulder and
pointed it at the farmhouse. As he began to pull gently on the
trigger, a second black SUV, also with diplomatic tags, pulled

around from the back of the house to the front, edged past the parked vehicle and began lumbering along the property's long, rutted driveway.

Crow eased his index finger off the trigger and watched the car until it reached the paved road — Rural Route 12 — and turned right, heading in the direction of the New York State Thruway entrance some twenty miles to the south. Then he took aim again, and this time pulled the trigger all the way back.

After the explosion, he picked up the rifle and watched the fireball for escapees, but none appeared.

36.

Manhattan, Wednesday, March 4, 2009, 7AM

Matt DeMarco stood in the shadows of a narrow alley looking across the street through a sleeting rain at the dark green canopy that led to the entrance of the Oxford Apartments. His conversation of an hour ago with Jack McCann ran once again through his head.

"The mayor's people called the justice department, Matt," Jack had said. *"They went crazy. It's not happening."*

"I don't get it. Why?"

"Other priorities. International bullshit."

"Where does he live?"

"The mayor?"

"Fuchs."

"Matt..."

"No more fucking around, Jack. I've had enough. I could find it out on my own."

"I'll come with you."

"No."

"Yes. He'll let me in. I have to tell him our answer, anyway. I might as well do it in person."

"No. I'm doing this alone."

"You can't hurt him."

"I'll try not to."

A cab pulled up, and a moment later, a man and a woman, clutching umbrellas against the sleet, came out wheeling their luggage toward the curb. The cabbie, heavily bearded, wearing a turban and a thick sweater, hustling, loaded the luggage and they were off. *No doorman, good*, Matt thought, looking at his watch. It was seven AM. He had been up a long time, talking to Michael, to Jack and Clarke, to Jade, but was not tired. Later he could be tired. Matt crossed the street through the icy rain, his gloved hand on the butt of the Colt .45 pistol that Clarke Goode had handed him an hour earlier. *Throw it away*, he had said. *It's completely untraceable.*

The lobby was small and hushed, a brass lamp on a credenza casting a square of yellow light onto a thick, blood-red carpet. On the elevator, Matt snapped the silencer Goode had also given him onto the Colt's barrel. He found apartment 301 at the end of a long carpeted corridor as hushed and mutely lit as the lobby. He knocked and looked into the reverse peephole. No answer, no footsteps. His plan was to shoot the lock off if Fuchs wouldn't let him in. He rang the bell on the doorjamb. No answer, no footsteps, but another sound, a rustling or tapping of some kind, a steady tapping.

Stepping back, Matt aimed and fired three quick rounds into the brass-plated doorknob, and slowly pushed. When the door did not give, he stepped back again and fired three more rounds in a vertical line above the shattered doorknob. The Colt will go through any lock, Goode had said, even a deadbolt. He was right. Stepping into a small foyer, Matt swung the door shut behind him and secured it with a heavy bronze urn that was on a small table nearby. The handle on the urn's lid was in the shape of a small angel, its wings spread wide. The Colt up at his ear, Matt listened and waited. Nothing, just the tapping sound.

The apartment was dark, but there was light coming from a room in the back. Heading toward it, the gun still to his ear, Matt stumbled on something. Stepping quickly away, his skin began to crawl, although he didn't know why. When he looked down, he knew. It was a body, something he must have sensed when his foot struck it: a thick-set middle-aged blond man in flannel pajamas, lying face up on the carpeted floor, his throat cut, blood slowly oozing from the long, precision-like, ear-to-ear slit. The man's eyes — a beautiful light blue — were wide open, staring into whatever comes next.

Matt stepped over Fuchs — he was sure it was him from Clarke's description — and quickly went through the other rooms, all empty and quiet, respecting the dead, except for the kitchen, where sleet entering from an open window was steadily striking a Formica table — the tapping sound. Matt looked out of this window and saw the top of a fire escape a few feet below. At the bottom was a small courtyard and an alley leading to 50th Street. Pulling back, Matt heard a thudding sound coming from the area of the front door. He stepped quickly into the small living room and, flattening himself against the wall near the arched entrance, listened as the bronze urn fell over and someone entered the apartment.

When the intruder walked into the living room, Matt stepped behind him and hit him full strength on the back of the head with the Colt. "Who the fuck are you?" Matt said, staring down at a black-haired young man in a pea coat of no more than twenty-three or twenty-four, not expecting an answer. But the man did answer — by grabbing Matt by the ankles, flipping him to the floor like he was a sack of potatoes, then jumping to his feet. Flat on his back, Matt pointed the gun at the man's chest.

"Don't move," Matt said, getting slowly to one knee and then to his feet, keeping the Colt painted on the man's chest. "Who are you?"

The young, dark-haired man did not answer. He was staring past Matt to the living room floor.

"Who are you?" Matt asked again.

"That is my uncle," the man said, nodding toward Fuchs' body. "And that is my Aunt Kat," he continued, nodding at the overturned bronze urn and the ashes that had spilled from it covering the carpet under and around it. "I am Josef Fuchs."

"What are you doing here?"

"I am delivering something to...to Oom Erhard."

"Delivering what?"

"Who are *you*?"

"I didn't kill your uncle, if that's what you think."

"I do not think that. Who are you?"

"My son got in the way of your uncle's investigation. He's been charged with murder. Your uncle has evidence to clear him. I got here too late."

"I have your evidence."

"Where is it?'

"He's downstairs with my brother."

"*He...?*"

37.

Manhattan, Thursday, March 5, 2009, 6PM

"Mr. Crow," Matt said. "Thank you for meeting me."

"Bill."

"Bill."

"Would you like to see my ID?"

"No. The local field office described you."

"Yes," Crow nodded, his face still, his eyes flat, no hint of a smile, or of irony. "I'm one of a kind."

Matt let this pass. It wasn't banter. He looked from Crow's scarred face down to his left hand resting on the varnished wood table, its pinky and ring finger missing completely, not even the trace of any stumps, just smooth reddish-brown skin at the base. The thumb and remaining fingers, all blunt-tipped and looking hard-used, formed a claw that the alleged FBI agent had used to pick up his beer glass, sip and put it down.

"They must have told you why I called," said Matt. They were sitting in Rudy's at the same booth Matt and Jade sat in the night Bob Davila was killed.

"Why don't you tell me?" Crow said.

"Sure. You know about my son?"

"Yes, I do."

"I understand the U.S. government knows he's innocent, that they're protecting the real killers."

"Who might they be?"

"The Syrian government."

"That's very far-fetched. How did you come by this theory?"

"A man named Fuchs, who's now dead."

"How did he die?"

"His throat was slit."

"Who killed him?"

"I'm guessing the Syrians."

"He was on their trail?"

"Yes."

"Who was he?"

"A UN investigator. He was in New York working on the Rafik Hariri assassination."

"How did you come to meet Mr. Fuchs?"

"That's not important."

"It could be."

"It's not," Matt said. *Steady now,* he thought, the jabbing's over, this is where the real fight begins. "The thing is," he continued, "the guys who killed Hariri also killed Yasmine. Fuchs' people saw them go into her building just before she was killed. The Syrians tried to kill these guys, two of them, to shut them up. They got one in Locust Valley a couple of weeks ago. The other one, a guy named Farah, was holed up in a house upstate. There was an explosion there yesterday."

"What kind of explosion?"

"The local police say it was a gas line, but it wasn't."

"What was it?"

"An RPG," Matt replied, "launched from a hill nearby. Whoever did it left something behind in the snow. We're trying to figure out who it belongs to."

"Who's *we?*" Crow asked.

"Nobody official," Matt replied. "Just some friends."

"Have you told the local police?"

"No, but we may."

"What do you want from me?"

"Farah wasn't in the house," Matt continued. "They didn't get their man. Very sloppy."

Silence from Crow.

"I can give you Farah," Matt continued. "I also have his confession on videotape. Hariri, other political assassinations—I think eleven in all—his Syrian contact, his Hezbollah contact, Yasmine Hayek, the whole ball of wax."

"What makes you think I want Farah?"

"Bob Davila told me about you," Matt replied, lying easily, thinking of tough little Bobby and of what he tried to do to help him, getting killed for it in front of his own house. "He said you threatened him, tried to shut him up. The next day he was dead."

Crow did not answer immediately. He tapped the two fingers of his left hand on the table. His eyes were still flat, but different, a gleam of something somewhere in their depths. *Admiration?* Matt thought, *is that it?*

"And in return?" Crow said, finally.

"I'd want all the charges against my son dropped, and a public statement that he was wrongfully arrested and charged."

"Where's Farah?"

"Do you want him?"

"I guess you think you're a tough guy, DeMarco," Crow said, "because you got away with killing your DI at Parris Island, then you were a boxing champion."

"What about you," Matt replied. "What's your story?"

"My story?"

"Yes, your story. You're a caricature of something, I don't know what. The strong, silent killer, the scarred anti-hero. Something like that."

"I haven't been insulted to my face in a long time."

"Since you were a teenager on a reservation someplace?"

Crow's face contorted into what Matt realized after a second or two was a smile, grim but not without a certain brutal charm.

"I get it," the contract op said. "You're trying to provoke me, to get me to do something stupid. Like in the movies."

"Do you want Farah?" Matt said.

"What if I don't?"

"Do you know a journalist named Christopher Hatch? The one dying of cancer? He's been following the Hariri case, writing about it. I'll give him access to Farah, the video. He'll die knowing he broke the biggest story of the twenty-first century. The United States sucking up to the Syrians, arranging it so they get away with murder. I'll put you in the middle of it, too. You know, the diversity angle, the rainbow coalition."

Crow smiled that crooked smile again. "I guess you think you've got all the bases covered," he said.

"Do you have a son, Bill?"

"No."

"Any kids?"

"No. But *your* son might be in danger. You missed one of the bases."

"How?" Matt replied, not skipping a beat, not revealing by tone of voice or cast of eye the deep grinding of gears that had just taken place in his head. If this had been a fight, either on the street or in the ring, either he or Crow would be dead in the next ten minutes.

"If he's dead, the New York DA can close his file, not pursue anyone else."

"There's still Farah," Matt said.

"He's a dead man," Crow replied.

"Are you sure you're an American, Crow?" said Matt.

"I try to think like the bad guys."

"Who are they?"

"Not redneck drill instructors, not amateur boxers. I hope you're following me."

"Do you want Farah?"

"I'll let you know."

"Good. Here's my number." Matt slid a scrap of paper across the table. "How do I reach *you*?" he said.

Crow glanced at the number on the paper Matt had flicked toward him, tore it in half, then took a pen from his jacket pocket, scribbled a number on the clean half, and pushed it back to Matt.

"OK," Matt said, glancing at the number. "One more thing."

"I'm listening," Crow said.

"The NYPD has lost two detectives in all this," Matt said. "They want to help."

"Anybody in particular?" Crow asked.

"No," replied Matt. "All of them."

"I don't need their help."

"You don't have a choice. From now on forty thousand New York cops will have your back. You'll be watched over by a lot of good friends."

"So?" Jack McCann said.

"He'll let me know."

"You gave him the number?"

"Yes. And he gave me his."

"Don't answer your other phone if he calls on it," Jack said.

"Or if you don't recognize the caller," said Clarke Goode.

"Was my buddy right?" Jack asked. McCann had called his Army friend, who had made his way pretty high in the FBI, to get information about Crow. The yield was skimpy, as it would be with all covert freelancers, and there had been no warranty of accuracy that was delivered with it.

"Yes," Matt answered.

"Did it help?" Jack asked.

Matt nodded. "I think so," he said. "He's a hardass with a hardass life behind him."

They were sitting across from Matt on the bench seat Bill Crow had just vacated. McCann had been at the bar, Goode at a booth toward the rear.

"Is that his glass?" Goode asked, pointing at Crow's still half-full beer glass.

"Yes," Matt answered, "but he wiped it down just before he left."

McCann nodded, in silent acknowledgment of Crow's craft. "I'll take it anyway," he said. A paper napkin in his hand, he picked up Crow's glass at its base and put it gingerly into a baggie he pulled from his jacket pocket. McCann and Goode were wearing the same off-the-rack sports jackets and low-key ties—the classic *do not stand out* detective's uniform—they had worn the night they appeared in Pound Ridge to arrest Michael. Matt had on the thick navy sweater and jeans that were his steady winter garb, except sometimes he would switch to a black sweater.

"What now?" Matt asked.

"We drink," McCann said. "And wait for Crow to call."

"I thought you quit," Goode said.

"I started again."

"Why?"

"The caribou theory."

"The what?" Matt asked. Goode was rolling his eyes.

"I'm culling weak brain cells to make the rest stronger."

"If you say so."

"The way wolves will cull the stragglers in a herd of caribou. It strengthens the herd."

"So it's the caribou theory of drinking?" said Matt. "The alcohol kills the weak brain cells. You'll get smarter, your memory will sharpen."

"Exactly." McCann knocked back the Jameson straight that the waitress had put in front of him, then nodded to her for another.

"The caribou *rationalization*," said Goode.

"Tell us about Crow," McCann said, ignoring his partner.

"You saw him," Matt replied. "Sand paper. Two fingers missing on his left hand."

"That's interesting," McCann said. "Did you ask him about that? How it happened?"

"No."

"You should have."

"Why?"

"Get under his skin, get him to reveal something."

Matt shrugged. Jack, he thought, *CJ*, Crazy Jack they used to call him when he was really drinking. He didn't like the name now, too many reminders. He was a good cop though. He would have gotten under Crow's skin but stayed cool, observing, registering. He and Goode and the two detectives from the NYPD's Counterterrorism Bureau who had volunteered to tail Crow were risking their careers to help Matt. The orders to stay away — far away — from the Adnan Farah "situation" had emanated not just from the Justice Department but, they had been warned, from "inside the White House."

"Did he give anything up?" Goode asked.

"No," Matt replied. "He's a tight ass. I'm pretty sure he wanted to kill me."

"What about Hatch?" McCann asked.

"He just smiled."

"Too bad he won't return our calls," Jack said.

"He's dying, Jack," said Goode.

"That's no excuse."

"What about Stone Ridge, the RPG?" Goode asked.

"His eyes got a little brighter. He wanted to know who was helping me."

"Did he ask you what was found at the scene?" Goode said.

"No."

"Did you push *any* buttons?" McCann asked.

"I called him a caricature."

"A what?"

"A caricature."

"You know, Jack, a grotesque exaggeration," Goode said.

"I know what it means," Jack said. "I'm Irish, therefore literary and smart, though I try to hide it because I disdain pretension of any kind."

"And?" Goode said to Matt, rolling his eyes again and shaking his head.

"Like I said," Matt replied, remembering the rush of adrenalin he felt when Crow said that the bad guys might want to kill Michael, deciding—he did not know exactly why, just that he should—not to tell Jack and Clarke about it, "he wants to kill me."

"But he wants Farah?" McCann asked.

"Yes, I believe he does," Matt replied. "And he's worried about Stone Ridge. I could see it in his eyes."

38.

The Bronx, Thursday, March 5, 2009, 8PM

The first person Matt saw at the funeral home was his ex-brother-in-law, Tommy Rusillo. He was standing in the entry foyer talking to the doorman, a fat guy in a black suit who Matt vaguely remembered as one of Tommy's gambling buddies. Matt shook his hand and said he was sorry, not responding to or acknowledging the *what are you doing here?* look on Tommy's face.

The large, windowless room that held Debra's body in an imposing bronze open casket surrounded by extravagant stands of flowers, many with inscriptions like *Dearest Daughter* and *Loving Sister*, was as crowded as he expected it to be. Italian clans, Matt knew, though they may fight among themselves, stuck together when things got rough, and there was not much rougher than a daughter, sister, niece, taking her own life.

As he joined the line of people to the right who were waiting to kneel and say a prayer at the casket, the buzz in the room subsided as Debra's family and friends turned to stare at him. One of them was Michael, who left his post to the left of the casket and headed over to him.

"Thank you for coming," Michael said, joining his father in the line. Matt had watched Michael approach him from across the room, the low-key light from the sconces on the walls softening his features, which were somber, his mouth grim, his dark eyes more thoughtful than sad. "She's your mother," he answered.

"You're not too popular here," Michael said.

Matt shrugged. He was wearing one of his charcoal gray trial suits, the first time he'd been in a suit and tie since the morning he quit the Manhattan DA's office. He surveyed the crowd, the old faces, remembering, with a surprising stab of emotion, the girl he had fallen in love with on his last leave home from the Marines and the whirlwind, disastrous marriage that followed.

"They'll get used to it. I'm coming to the funeral, too."

"Thanks, Dad."

"Is Basil here?"

"He's here someplace. He doesn't think it's his place to greet people."

They both looked over to the line of chairs to the left of the casket where Debra's mother, Lucille, her daughter, Linda and her two spinster sisters, all four in black from head to toe, were sitting and accepting condolences from the guests who had finished their prayer. The rest of the crowd had lost interest in Matt, the murmur volume going up accordingly.

"You look good," Matt said.

"The suit, you mean?"

"Yes. I've never seen you in one."

"I wore one for my First Communion and for my Confirmation." Michael smiled as he said this, his eyes brightening.

"As a grown-up," Matt said, the images of Michael in a white suit, at age six, his unruly hair combed seriously for the first time, and of him as a gawky thirteen-year-old in a blue blazer and khakis, appearing vividly in his mind, as if these events, which he had not thought of in years, had occurred yesterday.

"What's up, Dad?"

"What's up?"

"Yes, you look deep in thought," Michael replied.

"What about Mustafa?" Matt asked. "Is he here?"

"He's gone."

"Gone? Where?"

"Syria. His brother's dying."

Matt shook his head.

"What?" said Michael.

"Nothing, Michael. It's just being here."

"That's not it."

The line had come to one of its frequent full stops. No one was rushing through the rituals connected to a woman who seemed to have it all and then took her life at the age of forty six. Matt turned and looked his son fully in the eye. *Maybe this is my son after all.*

"Yes it is," he said.

"You're keyed up," Michael said. "Something's going on, I can tell."

"Okay," Matt replied, thinking *here goes.* "It looks like Mustafa ordered Adnan and Ali to kill Yasmine. That's why I need to talk to Basil."

Silence. Matt followed his son's gaze over to the open casket, to Debra, her long, dark brown hair framing her once beautiful face, now a waxy, surreal facsimile.

"Are you sure?" Michael said.

"Yes."

"How did you find this out?"

"I can't tell you, but trust me, it's true."

"He was drugging her, Dad," Michael said, finally, turning back to face Matt, "I know it."

"Why?"

"She must have known something."

Matt looked at Michael, expecting more.

"Not the videos," Michael said. "That would have been enough to keep her quiet forever."

"What then?"

"I don't know."

"We'll ask Basil."

"No," Michael replied, his voice emphatic, a voice Matt had never quite heard before.

"Why not?"

"Mustafa takes orders from Basil," Michael replied. "Why was Yasmine killed?"

"Her father is anti-Syria, anti-Hezbollah," Matt said. "He's pro-women's rights. Do you know what I'm talking about?"

Despite the change in his son since Debra's suicide, Matt reflexively prepared for the sneer that historically accompanied one of Michael's sarcastic or disdainful replies to questions like this, but it didn't appear. "I do," was his answer. "I've had a lot of time to read lately. The Syrian regime is worse than Saddam Hussein's was in Iraq. Torture, murder, no dissent is allowed. No free speech rights. In bed with Iran."

"Yes, and Hezbollah does their bidding in Lebanon."

"Basil and Yasmine's father were in the Lebanese civil war together," said Michael. "They were like brothers, then something happened."

"What?"

"I don't know. Yasmine told me this. She didn't know either."

"Did they become enemies?"

"I think so."

Matt nodded. "I'll be careful with Basil."

"I'll talk to him with you."

"No, Michael. Meet me at home later. Clarke and Jack have some pictures they want me to look at. Some of them were taken at Lucky's. You may recognize someone."

As he made his way out of the viewing room through its arched, open doorway, Matt saw Basil shaking hands with Everett Stryker, bidding him goodbye in the funeral home's entry foyer. When Stryker was gone, Matt approached Hassan.

"Basil," he said, when he reached him, "I'm sorry about this, about Debra."

"Matt — may I call you Matt? — thank you."

"We haven't talked much."

"No."

"Can we talk now for a few minutes?"

"Now?"

"Yes."

"Of course. There's a small alcove just there, if you like." Basil nodded toward the end of the long, wide hallway that ran along the front of the mortuary's three viewing rooms.

"That's fine."

In the alcove, quiet and thickly carpeted, they settled into plush armchairs facing each other across a small inlaid coffee table. The only light was from sconces on the walls behind each chair, casting mellow halos over their heads.

"How can I help you?" said Basil, crossing his legs and brushing a manicured hand along the expensively clad thigh of the leg on top.

"I know this isn't a good time," Matt replied, "but it's about Michael. It's important."

"Go ahead."

"Do you know a man named Haq, Basil? A Syrian colonel?"

Matt had been watching Hassan's face carefully. Jack and Clarke had told him that it was Mustafa who ordered Yasmine's killing, that Hassan was an unwitting front, a cover for Mustafa and his boss, a Syrian colonel named Haq. There had been no light in Basil's eyes. They were lifeless, inward-looking, just like any husband who had suddenly lost a wife he loved. Until now, at the mention of Colonel Haq.

"Yes," Hassan said, "I do. What about him?"

"I believe your servant, Mustafa, is working for him," Matt replied. "I believe Haq ordered Mustafa to have Yasmine Hayek killed, and to frame Michael for it."

"You *believe* . . ."

"I have proof."

"What kind of proof?"

"I have one of the killers, Adnan Farah, in custody."

"*You* have him in custody?"

"Yes."

"*You* have him in custody?" Hassan repeated himself. "What about the authorities? Your Justice Department, the New York police?" The elegant Syrian was shaking his head, fully engaged now, which was not surprising to Matt. This was pretty potent information. *Betrayed and used by Mustafa; Adnan alive; the involvement of his government's secret services in a murder on American soil.* Plenty to make him shake his handsomely groomed and charming head.

"Yes, I'm dealing with this privately," Matt replied.

"I don't understand."

"I also have Adnan's confession, so if anything were to happen to me..."

"Yes," said Basil, "*that* I understand. What is it you want of me?"

"I saw you with Everett Stryker just now," said Matt. "Can you tell me how you came to hire him?"

"Why? I mean, why do you ask this?"

"Because I think he's sabotaging Michael's case."

"Sabotaging? In what way?"

"Is he a friend of yours?"

"No."

"Have you used him before?"

"No. He came recommended by Mustafa."

"How did Mustafa come to recommend Stryker?"

"He spoke to Syrian friends, who spoke highly of him."

"Did Stryker tell you he represents the owners of Yasmine's building?"

"No."

"That the building's security cameras were tampered with after Yasmine's murder?"

"He said there was no proof of this."

"The New York police think there is."

After saying this, Matt watched as Michael's stepfather's eyes brightened a bit more and narrowed in thought.

"You believe Stryker is involved in this frame-up?" Hassan asked. "Is that possible?"

"Michael did not handle the murder weapon," Matt answered. "The lawyer I hired, Jade Lee, ordered a gun residue test. Do you know what that is?"

"Yes."

"Stryker cancelled it, the one thing that would have immediately pointed to Michael's innocence. Did he tell you that?"

"He said it would be devastating if it were positive."

"He didn't believe Michael."

"No."

"No criminal defense lawyer would have passed up this test under these circumstances," Matt said. "Michael could have handled the gun in the room, he could have even fired it out the window at Ali or Adnan's urging, as if they were playing around. A positive result could have been explained away. A negative result would have freed Michael."

"This was not explained to me."

"Tell me about Haq?"

"He is an SMI agent—Syrian Military Intelligence. It is headed by Assad's uncle."

"Haq takes his orders from Assad's uncle?"

"It's not as simple as that. Syria is a puppet of Iran. An operation like this would have to either originate in Iran or receive their approval."

"An operation like *what*? Why kill Yasmine?"

"Her father is anti-Syria, anti-Iran, anti-Hezbollah. Very popular. Syria wants Beirut, they claim it is part of Syria, going back centuries."

Matt shook his head. *This is what Michael got himself involved in, this insanity.* "Did you know," he said, "that Mustafa was videotaping everything that went on in your Park Avenue apartment?"

"Excuse me?"

Matt nodded. He had assessed the credibility of hundreds of witnesses, both in and out of the courtroom. Listening to Hassan's answer, hearing the surprise in his voice, seeing the squint of disbelief in his eyes, he thought, either this guy's innocent or he's a highly trained actor.

"Videotape?" said Basil.

"Yes," Matt replied. "He was blackmailing Michael with a tape of him sleeping with Debra, at age sixteen — I take it you have separate bedrooms. *Had* separate bedrooms. I believe Stryker was in on it."

Silence. Matt could see the shock on Hassan's face. His wife kills herself, now this. "Blackmail?" the Syrian finally said.

"Yes," Matt replied. "Stryker was urging him to plead guilty to the rape. They were lovers, Michael and Yasmine, consent is an obvious defense."

"Why?"

"To protect his real clients: Haq, Syria, Iran, Hezbollah. They killed Yasmine."

"Did you see the pictures?" Basil asked.

"Of Yasmine, you mean?"

"Yes."

"Yes, I did. It was Adnan and Ali who raped her, violently, wearing condoms."

Basil remained silent.

"It's a defense lawyer's dream," Matt said. "The security system tampered with, the doorman killed — did you know the doorman was killed?"

"No."

"He told the police that only Michael entered the building. Then he was killed, the same way Yasmine was killed. The same weapon. I told Stryker. He refused to use it."

"Videotapes? Hidden cameras? In my apartment?"

"Yes, Basil. When you go home, check the place out."

"Have you seen the one...the one with Michael and Debra?"

"No, but Michael has. Mustafa showed it to him."

"Shall I fire Stryker?"

"Yes, re-hire Jade Lee."

"Consider it done."

"Thank you. One more thing."

"Yes."

"Mustafa was doubling and tripling Debra's drug dosages."

"Why?"

"That's one of the questions I'd like to ask him."

"He's gone," Basil said. "He went back to Syria. His brother is dying, or so he claimed."

"What can you tell me about him?"

"He is Lebanese, a Shi'ite. He was orphaned in the war and made his way to Syria, where he served in the army. I needed an assistant some years ago. He was recommended by people close to the president."

"How would an orphan, not Syrian, a regular army serviceman, have such connections?"

"I don't know."

"But you accepted him."

"In Syria, it is not wise to reject a recommendation from the President's inner circle."

"Are you in that circle?"

"I am a petrochemical engineer, from a poor family. I discovered the only commercially viable oil field in Syria. That was thirty years ago. I was a national hero. But the field is running dry. Along with any influence, or government friends, I may have had."

"Can you tell me anything else about Mustafa? How old is he?"

"He's fifty-five."

"Is he married?"

"No. That is, he's never mentioned a wife."

"What does he do for you?"

"He runs my household, answers my phone when I'm not at home, makes travel arrangements, schedules meetings, appointments."

"Have you ever had any reason to mistrust him?"

"He told me he did not know Haq, but I saw them talking once at a reception."

"Anything else?"

"I can tell you one more thing."

"Go ahead."

"After he left yesterday, I went through his office. It was

emptied out. Last night, when I was going through Debra's things, I found a dossier on Mustafa in her desk. I don't know where she got it. I think it was given to me when I was asked to hire him."

"And?"

"Two things I had forgotten, or more likely did not think remarkable at the time. Mustafa had once lived in New York, in the early nineties. And he had a different name then."

"What was it?"

"Hakimi, Mustafa al-Hakimi."

39.

Manhattan, Thursday, March 5, 2009, 9PM

You fucked up.

Do you still want him?

We'll let you know.

I earned my fee.

Not the second half.

The father will go to Hatch. It'll be all over the news. Don't take long.

Silence. Crow smiled, thinking, *killing Hatch is crossing this guy's mind.*

I can still find him and kill him.

People are asking about your prints.

What people?

Not your friends.

Do you want me to finish the job? You told me to take care of it, remember?

That can't be, I've never spoken to you before tonight. We're not even talking now.

I had help.

I don't know what you're talking about.

He said the NYPD has my back. I thought they were out of it.

They are. But we can't control everyone.

I can track you down.

Laughter. *I'm just a voice. I might just be a machine.*
I can't wait long.
You're exposed, we may have to use someone else.
I earned my fee. The money better be there.
Click.
Bill Crow pushed the red *end* button on his cell phone and settled back in his easy chair. Out of the window next to him he could see First Avenue rushing by. His new hotel's neon sign, two stories below, above the sagging canopy that marked the front entrance, shone a sick yellow-green. Some of its glare licked toward him on his third floor perch.

It was almost time for him to leave, to disappear into the mountains, but not quite. He had not earned his full fee, a first for him. And then there was, of course, the matter of Matt DeMarco and his NYPD friends. They had his lens cover, with his prints on it. This was another first: the first mistake he had made in fifteen years. His prints were not in any database, except the one with the CIA's huge wall around it. But they could easily give him up. Hand something to DeMarco or his friends through a small hole in the wall. Unless he finished the job. Then he could, he realized, smiling his crooked smile, solve this fingerprint problem, earn the second half of his Farah fee, *and* earn the bonus from Mustafa. Did Haq, the mysterious mastermind, the slaughterer of innocents, know what his servant was doing? Probably not, but did it matter? Not really. Haq would have to go. That would be a pleasure.

He didn't think he'd been followed, but Manhattan wasn't the desert or the mountains. There, he would know for sure. But not here. He would have to change rooms. The junkie at the end of the hall had a window in his room with access to a fire escape. He would be happy to swap. A hundred bucks would get him high for a day or two. One more night, perhaps two, then he could disappear for good.

These thoughts were interrupted by the buzzing sound of his phone that meant he had received the text message he was waiting for. He opened the text screen and read what was there: *Abu Dhabi dep has arvd*. He looked at his watch. Nine PM; six AM in Zurich.

He closed the screen, pushed a button, put the phone to his ear, and waited.

This is Jade Lee, he heard a female voice say. *I'm not available right now. Please leave a message.*

"Miss Lee," Crow said. "This is Charles Hall. Could you meet me at my office tomorrow morning at eight? I gave you the address. It's on the second floor of my warehouse in Queens. I received a subpoena for thousands of documents. I want to go over them with you."

Crow ended the call and dialed another number. When a male voice answered, he said, "Eight AM," and clicked off.

40.

Matt and Michael stood with Jack McCann behind Clarke Goode, who was sitting at the dinette table in Matt's apartment, working Matt's laptop. On the screen was an image labeled *Lucky's 14* from a series of fifty or so taken by the Counterterrorism unit tailing Alec Mason on the night he was killed. It was of the two men whom Rex the bartender had gone over to talk to while Jack and Clarke were questioning him. The light was bad, but they looked Arab and one had an inverted-spade beard.

"It's the same beard," said Jack McCann.

Earlier they had reviewed stills from the security camera at Mason's hotel, which revealed clear shots of a young Arab man with the same shaped beard entering the Englishman's room.

"It's dark," Goode said.

"I'm betting it's him," McCann said.

"I agree," Goode replied.

"After you left, Mustafa came out and spoke to those two," Matt said.

"He comes up soon," said Goode.

"Keep scrolling."

Goode resumed bringing up the amazingly high quality pictures one at a time, keeping each on the screen a few seconds before moving on. Rex and the doorman were in several, as were the young men watching basketball. He stopped longer at image forty-nine.

"Is that him, Dad?" Michael asked.

"I think so," Matt answered.

On the screen was a picture of Mustafa al-Rahim, aka Mustafa al-Hakimi, at the doorway to the back room at the Queens bar. His face was visible over the shoulder of a man with his back to the camera. Mustafa was holding the door open for this man, the light from the bar's valance illuminating his face.

"That's Mason going in," Goode said.

"It was sixteen years ago," Matt said, "and he didn't wear a beard then, but I think it's him. He was at the trial on the first day and the last day. When do you think you'll hear from your guy at DCS?"

"He said he'd try to get back to me tonight."

"Let's go through the rest."

"Who's that?" said Matt when an image of the man in the hooded jacket playing pool by himself appeared.

"We don't know," Clarke replied. "A guy playing pool. He went into the back room and came out a few minutes later, but the bathrooms are back there."

"Was Mason in back at the time?" Matt asked.

"Yes, he was."

"Any more pictures of him?"

"No, why?"

"He looks familiar."

"His face is in shadow, Matt."

"Can you zoom in?"

Goode zoomed in on the hooded man's face.

"Nothing," said Goode. The man was leaning forward, directly under the lone green-shaded lamp over the table, extending the cue stick as he lined up a shot. His face was in profile, the hood covering the top half, the shadow it cast covering the bottom half.

"The Grim Reaper," said Michael.

"Wait a second," said Matt, as he saw Clarke hovering the cursor over the *next* button. "Can you zoom in on his hand, the one forming the bridge?" Goode complied, sliding the cursor arrow down to the hand and closing in on it, the resolution still good, the light bright from the lamp overhead. The hand was rough hewn, like gritty sand paper. Its middle finger was resting on the smooth green felt of the pool table, the index finger on top of it. The thin end of the cue stick was nestled between the index finger and the thumb, its blue-powdered tip poised as it pointed to the white cue ball an inch away.

"Can you see the other two fingers?" Matt said. "Can you zoom in again?"

Goode zoomed closer. The middle finger was virtually laid flat on the tabletop. It seemed to extend almost back to the wrist in one straight line.

"They're not there," Matt said. "It's fucking Crow."

Goode nodded and was about to say something, but was interrupted by the ringing of his cell phone. He reached into the inside pocket of his beat up brown corduroy sport coat and fished it out.

"Goode," he said, the sharpness of his usually soft voice matching the grim, edgy vibe in the room. He listened for a few seconds, then clicked off and put the phone down on the table.

"That was the latent print unit," he said. "There's one partial match, not enough ridge minutiae."

"He must not have wiped it good enough," said Jack.

"What's that mean?" Michael asked. *"Not enough ridges."*

"It means statistically it's not admissible in court," Matt replied.

"Is there a *but?*" said Michael.

"Yes," said Jack, "when we see this as cops we know it's our guy, but we need corroboration, more proof."

The four men, two cops, an ex-prosecutor and his young son accused of murder, redirected their gazes to the image of Bill Crow—good guy, terrorist, double agent, triple agent, madman, *what?*—on the computer screen.

"Could Crow be involved in Loh and Davila?" Matt asked, breaking the silence. "Is that possible?"

"Who the fuck's he working for?" Jack said.

"It looks like Mason reported to both him and Rahim on Monday night," said Goode.

"Are there more pictures of him?" Matt asked.

"No," Goode replied. "That's the only one. In fact it's the last picture."

"Why don't I call him?" said Matt.

They were all sitting at the table by now, Michael and Matt across from Clarke and Jack, who looked sideways at each other when Matt said this.

"Why?" Jack said. "You want to go on a date?"

"He'll come," Matt said. "He hates me."

"And then what?"

"I'll kill him."

"You'll kill him?"

"Yes."

"How does that help Michael?"

"Crow threatened to kill Michael."

Silence, as all three men stared at Matt.

"What did he say exactly?" McCann asked.

"He said if Michael was dead, Healy could close his file, not have to pursue anyone else."

Goode and McCann looked at each other, silent for a long moment. In this moment, Matt glanced at Michael just as a light appeared in his son's dark eyes. What was he thinking?

"He meant the *bad guys* would kill Michael," said McCann. "Rahim."

"There's a partial match, Jack," Matt said. "Crow blew up the house in Stone Ridge. He probably killed Fuchs. He's one of the bad guys."

"What about the trade for Farah?" Goode said.

"The FBI will send someone else," Matt said. "If they want the deal, they'll call me."

"We can't trust the FBI now," Goode replied. "I mean, you called the field office and they sent Crow."

"He's right, Dad," Michael said. "Think about it. We don't know who our friends are."

Matt looked at his son. *Think about it, Dad,* he had said. Softly, no emphasis. But there it was: stop being a hot head. That was the light in Michael's eyes: recognition, insight, and something else, separation. Unlike his father, he could stay cool.

41.

Manhattan, Friday, March 6, 2009, 1AM

"So what now?" Jade asked.

"We wait," Matt replied, "for Crow to tell me if he wants to make the deal."

"Do you trust him?"

"I won't give him Farah until the indictment's dismissed."

"What about double jeopardy?"

"I'll get a representation from Healy that he won't be re-indicted."

"And Farah is unreachable?"

"Yes, Josef and Wilem have him."

"Where?"

"You don't need to know more." The less Jade knew about Farah the better. Matt had already put her in danger, simply by involving her in Michael's defense and all of the nastiness that came with it.

"How are they, those two boys?"

"Ready to kill."

"I could imagine."

"They'll do anything Jack and I and Clarke say."

Matt and Jade were drinking cognac at her dining room table. The three candles Jade had lit while Matt was pouring their drinks were reflected in their glasses, three bright yellow tear drops floating in burnt orange, tilting on the same axis as they lifted, sipped and set the fat, round snifters down. Matt had left Michael at his apartment after their picture review and walked to Ninth Avenue, where he had begun to fill Jade in on the events of the day.

"There's more," Matt said.

"What?"

"Basil's going to call you. He's firing Stryker and hiring you."

"Good, the first thing I'll do is serve the UN report. I'll worry about admissibility later. Then I'll ask for the Diaz file, I'll raise the Brady issue."

"What are you doing tomorrow?"

"I'm meeting a client early, eight o'clock."

"What's that about?"

"He's a guy about to be indicted for stealing from his partner. *Allegedly* stealing from his partner. He's been served with a subpoena for records. I'm meeting him to go over the response. What about you? Are you going to the funeral?"

Matt had never thought of who would die first, him or Debra, or, if it were Debra, if he would attend her wake and burial. He had paid his respects tonight but now realized that wasn't enough. His son's mother, whose vindictive treatment of him he now ascribed to near psychosis, had died. He had to go to the funeral. He had to see her put into the ground.

"Yes," he said.

"What time is it?"

"Ten AM."

"Call me. I'll fill you in."

"You mean about Antonio?"

"Yes. I'm picking him up at noon at the school."

"Picking him up?" Regis was not that far away from Jade's apartment and Jade did not have a car.

"We'll walk. We'll stop for lunch."

"And talk."

"Yes."

"Good luck."

"Thank you. Matt?"

"Yes?"

Matt watched as Jade put her glass down and looked at him with a blank face, a blankness that was, he quickly realized, a mask, a sort of deliberate expressionlessness—if that was a word—as if she were about to negotiate something and was looking at a screen in her head, calculating, mapping out her tactics in advance. *Something's coming.* Outside, it had started to rain and the wind had picked up and Matt could hear tapping somewhere in the apartment as the wind pushed the rain against a window, the tapping sound softening the noise of traffic on Ninth Avenue, now noticeable because of its near absence. It was not unlike the tapping he had heard in Erhard Fuchs's apartment just two days ago. A light above the stove in the kitchen was on, but the apartment was dark otherwise, the darkness covering its smallness, its sadness.

"Yes?" he said again.

"Why are you so angry?"

"I'm not angry."

Jade did not respond. Her expression, or rather lack of expression, did not change. I will see this mask again, Matt thought. I should get used to it.

"Did something happen?" Jade asked.

"You mean in my past?"

"Yes."

"I killed a guy in the Marines."

"You mean in war? In combat?"

"No. He was a monster, a drill instructor."

"How old were you?"

"Eighteen."

"And you got away with it?"

"Yes. I said it was an accident. My buddies backed me up."

Silence again. Some glimmer of something in Jade's beautiful eyes, a softness, a peek beneath the Chinese mask.

"You're always fighting monsters, aren't you?" she said. "That's why you became a prosecutor. To fight all those monsters."

"You're probably right."

"But why?"

Matt put his right thumb and index finger to his eyes and pressed, using the bone, the zygomatic arch, for leverage and then squeezing in from the sides.

"My father used to tell me that he died in the war. When I would ask him what he did, he would say that Matteo DeMarco died on Iwo Jima, that the person I saw before me was not him."

"He retreated."

"Retreated?"

"Into himself."

"Yes."

"You didn't do that to Michael, did you?"

"No."

"It's worked out OK."

"It took a while."

"A false murder charge. More monsters to slay."

Matt did not reply. He removed his fingers from his eyes. He would let Jade question him. Whatever she wanted to ask. Whatever she wanted to say. However she wanted to say it. He had thought when they made love for the first time that he had reached a turning point, but he was wrong. This was it.

"What did he do in the war, your father? Did you ever find out?"

"After I killed my DI at Parris Island, I was pulled from training for three weeks. I was given permission to use the base library, where the Pacific Theater Archives are. He was awarded the Navy Cross on Iwo."

"For what?"

"He rappelled down a mountainside with twenty grenades strapped on, then threw them into a series of caves where the Japanese were holding out, mowing people down with fifty-caliber machine guns. He was shot in the leg, then cut himself loose. He was swinging in the wind, an easy target. He landed on his shoulder on a ledge. I asked him once why he smoked cigarettes. He told me it helped the pain in his shoulder. So then I knew where it came from."

"Jesus. Did you tell your father what you did?"

"No, but he knew. He knew me. *You want to fight monsters*, he said. *That's fine. Just don't become one.*"

"What did he do? When he got home?"

"He drove a dump truck for a company on Long Island for twenty-five years."

"And your mom?"

"She drank too much. Probaby because my father was so silent, so remote. One night, when I was ten, she fell down some stairs and cracked her head and died. My father never remarried, never held anything against her, or against anybody, really. He knew life was hard."

"He told you that?"

Matt smiled. "No," he replied. "He would never say anything like that. *Life is hard*. But I could tell from looking at him that he believed it was, that it had to be endured."

"A good father is all," Jade said. "Everything else is air."

Matt shook his head, and was about to speak, to ask a question of his own, but Jade spoke first: "It's a Chinese saying."

"And yours?" he said. "Your father?"

"He was great. Antonio is named after him."

"Was?"

"He died last year."

Matt said nothing.

"My mother was the problem," Jade said. "She couldn't forgive my running away, my coming home pregnant. The loss of face."

"Is she alive?"

"Yes. The Dragon Lady of Queens. She takes in sewing, drinks tea, and argues with the neighbors."

"Is she coming around?"

"I think so, a little. Antonio and I are all she has."

Outside the rain was coming down a little harder, the tapping sound against the window was a little louder.

"You should sleep," Jade said.

"No," Matt replied. He reached across the table and took Jade's hand, laying it flat and stroking the back of it. *We're married now*, he thought with a shock, *how did that happen?*

"Bed, then?"

"Yes."

"Do you want me as much as I want you?"

"Yes."

"Do you know why?"

"Love?"

"No. Surrender."

They held each other for a few long minutes as the clock on Jade's night table ticked toward 2AM, the darkened room a welcome cocoon.

"You never told me about Crow," Jade said, her voice, though soft and whispering, pulling them back to the world. "What was he like?"

"He's weird," Matt replied, thinking of Bill Crow's twisted soul, as if he could see its terrible outline before him in the room's shadows. "He's..."

"Is that your phone?" Jade said, her face nuzzling Matt's neck. "Do you hear it?"

"Yes," Matt replied. "It's in the dining room."

He swung out of bed, naked, and was back a few minutes later.

"Clarke," Matt said.

"And?"

"Wael al-Hakimi had one visitor in 1993 at Green Haven, a person named Mustafa al-Hakimi, who listed himself as his father. Then none for ten years, then two visits a year starting in 2003. These were by Mustafa al-Rahim, who also lists himself as his father."

"Mustafa..."

Matt handed Jade his phone. On its screen was a picture of an Arab man in his mid-thirties in a beard.

"Is that him?"

"That's him in 1993, the guy who came to the first and the last day of Wael's trial."

"His son."

"Yes."

"So," Jade said. "You have your answer."

"I do," Matt said. "A son for a son."

"Matt..."

"There's something else," Matt said. "Wael's lawyer visits him regularly too. His name is Everett Stryker."

42.

The Bronx/Queens, Friday, March 6, 2009, 2PM

"Mr. DeMarco?"

"Yes."

"It's Antonio Lee."

"Antonio?"

"Yes."

"Welcome home. What can I do for you?"

"I'm at my mother's office. She's not here. She was supposed to meet me at school..."

"Did you go home?"

"Yes. She wasn't there.

"Have you called her cell?"

"Yes, nothing, voicemail."

"She told me she was meeting a client in Queens," Matt said. "She probably got delayed."

"But she didn't call me."

"Did you call her service?"

"Her service?"

"She has an answering service she sometimes uses."

"No."

"I'll call them."

"Thank you."

"Don't worry, it's nothing."

"Should I stay here?"

"Go home, I'll call you. Are you calling on your cell?"

"Yes."

"Hold on, before you go, do me a favor. Is there a folder for a Charles Hall around your mom's desk or office, or something in a Rolodex? Look around, I'll hold." Matt waited, picturing the tiny one-person office Jade had described to him that she rented on East Broadway, near Manhattan's Chinatown. Low rent, she had said, that's the big thing. *It's small,* Matt thought, *if something's there, he'll find it.*

And he did. "There's a folder here," Antonio said. "There's a card here. Mechanical Pumps Corp., 2411 137th Street, Queens, Charles Hall, President."

"Is there a telephone number?" Matt asked.

"Yes. 718-987-6654."

"Text it to me."

"Okay."

"Go home, Antonio. If your mother shows up, ask her to call me. I'll call you later."

Matt looked around for Michael, spotting him near the restaurant's foyer in a group that included Debra's mother and cousins on Debra's side. The post-burial luncheon, at one of Arthur Avenue's famed Italian restaurants, was beginning to wind down. People were saying their goodbyes. Basil Hassan, whose face and demeanor, whenever Matt caught sight of him, were quiet and contemplative, was nearby. He saw Matt and came over.

"Are you leaving, Matt?"

"Yes."

"Thank you for coming."

"Of course."

"I have put a call in to Ms. Lee."

"Thank you."

"Here, take this." Debra's widowed husband handed Matt a business card. "Please call me. I would like to discuss Mustafa with you. And Haq."

"I hope you are who you say you are, Basil," Matt replied. "For your sake."

"I may or may not be," Hassan said. "Tell me, what is it you want, ultimately?"

"I want the charges against Michael dropped, and I want a public apology."

"And how do you plan on accomplishing that?"

"I've already set the wheels in motion."

"I'm afraid you've placed yourself in very grave danger, and your son as well."

"Michael has been in grave danger, as you put it, from the moment Yasmine was killed and he was framed for the murder."

"You may have made it worse by interfering."

"He's my son. What would you have done?"

"The same. Yes, without question."

Matt looked at Basil's card, then put it in his suit coat pocket. "I'll call you."

"Dad, I think I know this building."

"You do? How?"

Matt and Michael were sitting in Matt's car, which was parked on 137th Street, across from number 2411. There was no *Mechanical Pumps, Inc.* sign to be seen, but the building was clearly industrial, the type containing a machine shop and small warehouse that can be found scattered throughout the back end of Queens, hard by the twenty-four/seven grit and noise from the major highways that in the fifties and sixties turned old ethnic neighborhoods into isolated islands of shocked despair. Sagging tenements, empty or near empty, straddled number 2411. The street was busy, with traffic flowing continuously and cars parked on both sides as far as the eye could see.

On the ride from the Bronx, Matt had called Jade's answering service and learned that they had not heard from her since the day before. On 154th Street they had passed the subway entrance for the line Jade would have taken from Manhattan. There had been nothing on the radio about a breakdown on this or any other line in the system. Matt had also called both Jade's cell, which had gone to voicemail, and Charles Hall's number, which had produced a "not in service" recorded answer.

"There's an alley around back," Michael said. "The back entrance of Lucky's is there. Adnan and Ali and I hung out in an office in this building. I'm pretty sure it's this building. Let's drive around back."

Matt swung the car onto 137th Street, turned left and then, as Michael pointed out a sign that read, *PWE-9098*, left again. The day was bright and sunny, but now, as he edged his SUV cautiously down the narrow street, an alley really, around dumpsters and piles of rusted chain-link fence and other debris long forgotten by the sanitation department, they were in shade, the sun obliterated by the tenements looming on both sides. An occasional spindly tree reached for the sky. "Stop," Michael said as they approached one of these. "Pull over."

"That's Lucky's on the right," Michael said, pointing to a sheet-metal door covered by a grate. "And that's the warehouse," he continued, nodding toward a rusting rolling door set above a suet- and grime-blackened concrete loading platform. "The office is upstairs."

"Why hang out there?" Matt asked.

"Adnan and Ali said they knew the owner. It was quiet and safe. We smoked grass and listened to music."

"Was it an active business?"

"No, it was dead in there. We cleaned up the office a bit, but the rest of the place was a mess. The thing is, Dad, there's an underground walkway that leads to Lucky's basement. We would park in the alley here, get high, then use the tunnel to go to Lucky's to have a few drinks."

"Is that how you got in?" Matt asked, pointing to a worn out but solid looking door to the right of the corrugated steel dock door.

"Yes. They had a key."

"Let's try."

"Okay."

As Matt was about to exit the car, his cell phone rang. He pulled the phone from his jacket pocket and looked at the screen: *Private Caller*. "It's not her," he said, realizing for the first time just how worried he was.

"Hello?"

"Listen carefully," a male voice said. "You will not hear this message again. I have Miss Lee. She is safe at the moment. I want to make an exchange."

"Who are you?"

"I am Mustafa al-Hakimi."

"What kind of exchange?"

"I want my son released from prison."

"The one who killed his sister."

Silence.

"Are you listening, Mr. DeMarco?"

"Go ahead."

"Put Wael on a plane to Damascus. When he arrives, I will tell you where Miss Lee is and you can collect her."

The rush of adrenalin Matt suddenly felt was not new to him. He had experienced it in street fights when he was a boy, in the ring in the Marines, in the moment just before he cracked Johnny Taylor's neck in half, in the courtroom when he felt that an adversary or a judge had insulted him. All his life he had felt this hammering in his brain and never once had he resisted it. But now he had to. Jade could die. He looked at his free hand clutching the steering wheel, a death grip he would one day apply to Mustafa al-Hakimi. But not today. Today he would control himself, shake the pounding from his head. He had no choice.

"And Mr. DeMarco," Mustafa continued, "do not doubt me. If you do not do as I ask, your woman will die, but first she will suffer. I have young men with me who are sexually active. Do you understand?"

"I'll need some time," Matt said.

"Yes, I understand. I will give you twenty-four hours. I will call you tomorrow at this time. If Wael is not on his way to Syria, your Miss Lee will die and I will disappear."

"Who was that?" Michael asked after Matt clicked off.

"Mustafa."

"Mustafa?"

"Yes."

"What did he want?"

"I'm dropping you off at Jade's apartment. Don't let him call the police."

"Dad..."

Matt's phone, still in his hand, rang again. He clicked the green receive button and put it to his ear.

"DeMarco?" his caller said.

"Yes."

"Bill Crow."

"Crow?"

"We're ready to deal."

"Ready to deal?" Matt replied. "Okay, hold on, I want to turn on my tape recorder."

"You can't stop being a wise guy, can you, DeMarco?" said Crow. "You must have a death wish."

"Okay, it's on," said Matt. "Let's be clear. You get the charges dismissed against my son, I'll give you Adnan Farah."

"Who you've kidnapped."

"You're wrong there, but I *can* deliver him. Is that the deal?"

"Yes."

"Good, I'll meet you at Jon Healy's office tomorrow morning. When the charges are dismissed, I'll turn Farah over to you."

"No," said Crow. "That's not how it's going to work."

"No? How, then?"

"I need to talk to Farah, in person."

Matt, thinking this over, did not respond.

"Take it or leave it," Crow said.

"Okay," said Matt, "but I'll need time to make arrangements."

"What kind of arrangements?"

"The same kind you'd make if you were in my position."

"How much time?"

"Twenty-four hours."

"I'll call you tomorrow morning. Have a good day."

Matt clicked off and began to pull away from the curb.

"Who was that?" Michael asked.

"Crow. He says he wants to make the deal."

"What did Mustafa want?"

"He also wants to make a deal."

"Mustafa? What's going on, Dad?"

"Does this street go through?" Matt asked.

"No," Michael said. "You have to make a K-turn. It's wider at the end." Matt inched his way along until he came to the garbage-strewn courtyard of an abandoned tenement building, where he started his three-point turn.

"What's going on, Dad?" Michael said again.

"Mustafa has Jade. He wants to trade her for his son."

"He has Jade?"

"Yes."

"His *son*? Dad..."

"Yes."

"Where are you going?" Michael asked. Matt had turned the car around and was heading out of the alley.

"I think I know how to reach Mustafa."

"How?"

"You don't need to know."

"What about Jack and Clarke? They'll help."

"I don't want them involved."

"Why not?"

"I started this, I'll finish it."

"You started it? How?"

"I put Mustafa's son in jail for life."

"What did he do?"

"He killed his sister. She was dating a boy, so he stabbed her fifteen times."

"That was your job."

"I rubbed it in, Michael. I rubbed the kid's face in it, and his father was watching. I even tried to get the death penalty, but Jon Healy wouldn't go for it."

"His father?"

"Yes, Mustafa."

"Mustafa?"

"You're repeating yourself. Yes, *Mustafa*. He had Yasmine killed just to frame you, to put *my* son in jail for life. I started this whole thing."

"No, you didn't."

"I was a tough guy, a Marine. Once a Marine..., you know the saying. I hated the kid, what he did. I rubbed it. But he was just a kid, ruled by his father, brainwashed by his fanatic father."

"Dad..."

"Just babysit Antonio. Tell him I'm looking for his mom, that I think I know where she might be."

"Do you?"

"Maybe. I'll call you."

43.

"You have three very dangerous adversaries," Basil al-Hassan said. "Haq, Crow, and Mustafa."

Hassan's spacious and beautifully appointed apartment, with its high ceilings and tall windows, had been as quiet as a church, as if Debra's death had left a pall that still lingered. This inner room, Hassan's *sanctum*, was even quieter. *It's the place where he grieves*, Matt thought. He had been drumming his fingers on the polished wooden arm of his chair, but he stopped abruptly, the sound too loud in the hushed room. Basil, outwardly calm, his face unreadable, sat across from him at his large, impeccable mahogany desk.

"You need to put your cards on the table, Basil," Matt said. "You offered to help, remember?" Basil may have been grieving, but Matt had no time to waste on sentiment or to soften his words. The point needed to be gotten to as quickly as possible.

"Debra said you were hot tempered."

"That's in the past."

"Are you sure? Because the game you are about to enter is quite dangerous. Emotion has no place in it. It gets you killed."

"What game?" Matt was not at all sure about his ability to control his temper. There was a fire in him that all his life had been impervious to his attempts to put it out. It was raging now, at the thought of Jade being gang raped and killed. The best he could do was control his outward demeanor, a skill he had learned the hard way as a boy. Hassan was rich and Middle-Eastern, and therefore likely to have resources, cultural and financial, well beyond Matt's. More than that though, there was something about the Syrian's demeanor when they were talking at the funeral luncheon that rang true, that spoke of a man who was willing to be an ally, but who, for reasons Matt could not plumb, needed one as well. It was this last, a hunch, really, a desperate one, that had driven him to accept Basil's offer, and to reveal to him the facts as he knew them that had laid down the bloody trail to his door.

"What about the New York police?" Basil asked, ignoring Matt's question. "Surely they want Farah. He killed Yasmine Hayek in Manhattan."

"They've been told by the U.S. government to stay out of the case. Fuchs offered them Farah and they turned him down, on orders from the Justice Department."

"What about your two detective friends? Are they disobeying orders?"

"Yes, they'll help me if I ask them."

"If you ask them?"

"They don't know about Jade."

"You haven't told them?"

"No."

"Why not?"

"I'm going to kill Crow and Mustafa. I don't want them to lose their careers." Matt did not have to mask his feelings as he said this. On this issue his blood was cold as well as hot. He had had enough of the Indian and the Servant. He would find a way.

"What about your career?"

"My career is to rescue Jade and free my son of the murder charge against him."

"What else did Adnan confess to?" Hassan asked.

"He and Ali assassinated Rafik Hariri."

"Hariri? On Haq's orders?"

"Yes."

"And he will testify in The Hague?"

"Yes, but for some reason my government doesn't want him to."

"How did you manage this?"

"I didn't, Fuchs did."

"I don't doubt that Crow blew up the house in Stone Ridge," Hassan said, "or that he killed Fuchs. As to whether he and Haq and Mustafa are working in concert, if demons can be said to work together at anything, I cannot say."

"You said something about a dangerous game. I don't have a lot of time. Can you help me or not?"

"Haq is an Iranian high up in the Syrian Secret police, the Mukhabarat," Basil said. "He was sent here to kill Adnan and Ali, and to keep an eye on me."

"How do you know this?"

"It is a guess, but an educated one."

"What about Yasmine Hayek? Was Haq behind that?"

"This I do not know. I did not know until now that Mustafa has his own agenda."

"Why are you telling me all this?"

"I was a hero in Syria until recently. A war hero and an oil hero. I have many friends, many contacts. Haq has more powerful friends, in Syria and in Iran. The balance has shifted in his favor. My friends can no longer protect me. I believe Haq wants me dead."

"Why?"

"I represent sanity. Syria has gone insane."

"That's it? You're sane, he's not?"

"No, there's more. I am one of the people in Syria who are hoping for a revolution. More than hoping, preparing."

"How?"

"When the riots start in Damascus and Dera and Hama, I want to be ready to help."

"How?"

"With arms—handguns, automatic rifles, missile launchers, RPGs."

Matt remained silent, taking this in. "So the oil was a cover?" he said, finally.

"No," Hassan replied. "I discovered Syria's only successful oil field. The Assads let me get rich. But the field is drying up, and Iran has grown very powerful over the past ten years or so. They give orders, Syria obeys."

"I see. How's it going? The arms business, I mean."

"Not well, except for Libya. In Syria and Iran I will need your government's help."

"It looks like they're on Syria's side right now."

"Yes. We shall see."

"What about Debra?" Matt asked. "Was she a beard?"

"A beard?"

"To give you easy access to the U.S.?"

"No. I loved her. It took a long time, but I finally loved someone again."

"But it didn't hurt to have an American wife."

"No, the Assads loved that."

"Sorry. I felt I had to ask about Debra, for my son's sake."

"My cards are now, as you requested, on the table," Basil said. "With this information you can easily have me killed."

"Or get myself killed."

"Yes."

"How can you help me?"

"If you can bring Mustafa to me, I can get him to let your woman go."

"That's a tall order. How do I reach him?"

"Perhaps Mr. Stryker can help you. I have made inquiries. He is on the Mukhabarat's payroll. This may give you leverage."

"What about Crow?" Matt asked.

"You wish to kill him too."

"Yes."

"I cannot help you with Crow."

"Okay, just asking."

"He may still be important to your government. I may need their help soon."

"What kind of help?" Matt asked.

"I may need asylum, or rather what you call witness protection. It may be the only way I can escape Haq's reach."

"Let's kill him too," said Matt.

Hassan smiled, and Matt smiled back, but he wasn't kidding.

"I've thought of that," Basil said. "It would not be easy. But first things first. Bring me Mustafa. I guarantee he will cooperate."

"Before I go," Matt said. "I assume you've swept this place clean. If not, we're dead men."

"I have," Basil replied. "People were in this afternoon."

"What did they find?"

"High-tech mini-cameras, two in every room."

"Did you talk about your arms business here?"

"No, never, not even in this country."

44.

"Put your hand on the cutting board, Everett," Jack McCann said. He was standing to the right of the seated, white-haired lawyer. In his right hand McCann held the meat cleaver that he had found, along with the two-inch thick cutting board, in Basil al-Hassan's uber-designed and exceptionally well-stocked kitchen.

"What?"

"This is crude and old-fashioned," McCann said, "but I've never seen it fail with an amateur like you."

"You're insane."

Jack looked at Clarke Goode, who was standing to the left of Stryker at the large and solidly built oak utility table in Hassan's kitchen, and nodded. Goode, whose hand was bigger than the meat cleaver, took hold of the lawyer's right wrist and pressed it to the cutting board.

"Spread your fingers," Goode said. "Unless you want to lose them all at once."

Matt DeMarco, standing next to McCann, leaned in as Stryker complied. He looked at his watch. He had no doubt that Mustafa's deadline was real. At one PM tomorrow, Jade would be dead. And sometime tomorrow morning Crow would be calling, wanting to see Farah. They had to be working together, Mustafa and Crow. He was glad he had changed his mind about involving Jack and Clarke. They had "arrested" Stryker outside his office building an hour ago. Another kidnapping. But how else to sit him down and open him up? If this turned out badly, they'd all be going to prison.

"Stryker," Matt said. "Listen to me. Syria's been on the United States' terrorist-state list longer than any other country. You've been fronting for them, setting up phony corporations, misstating the true stockholders, buying property, all illegal, all as an unregistered agent of an enemy country. Only the people in this room know this at the moment. If you don't help us, you're going to jail. If you do, you can walk out of here. I don't care how you make your money."

"Where's Hassan?" Stryker said. "Why am I here?"

"He left the country," Clarke answered. "He was working undercover for the NYPD."

"One more time," Jack McCann said, raising the heavy, professional-grade cleaver, its five-inch wide blade gleaming, "can you reach Mustafa al-Rahim?"

"Fuck him," Clarke Goode said. "Take the pinky."

"*Yes*," Stryker said before Clarke had finished his sentence. Sweat was beading on his forehead, and soaking through the collar and armpits of his thirty-count, custom made Egyptian cotton dress shirt. There was even sweat in his eyes, which were darting back and forth from McCann to Matt.

"Good," McCann said. "Let me ask you a few questions first."

"Can I wipe my face?" Stryker asked.

"Sure." McCann reached into his back pocket, pulled out a white handkerchief and handed it to the lawyer, who took it with his free hand and wiped the sweat from his eyes and brow.

"Let me," Matt said. He could see that Stryker had given up. His Ivy League education and country club existence had prepared him to betray his country for a few million dollars, but not for this. Not for Clarke Goode's big black hand flattening his wrist to a scarred cutting board with a meat cleaver hovering over his manicured fingers.

"Has he come to your office?" Matt asked Stryker.

"No, never," the lawyer answered.

"How many deals have you done with him?"

"Four, the Excelsior, the two places in Queens, and the house in Locust Valley."

"What's the other place in Queens?"

"An old factory and warehouse on 137th Street."

"The one behind Lucky's?"

"I believe so."

"Why are you visiting his son?"

"To make sure he's not being mistreated. To show the prison authorities he has some clout."

"And the money for the property purchases was all wired to your trust account?"

"Yes."

"If we trace it," Goode said, "where do think it will lead us?"

"I don't know," Stryker said, his eyes shifting from Matt to Goode. "Mustafa told me he was working for a wealthy oil man. I thought it was Hassan."

"Have you met Mustafa?" Matt asked.

"Yes, twice."

"Where?"

"In Battery Park, near my office."

"Where in Battery Park?"

"At the War Memorial."

"The concrete slabs?"

"Yes. By the eagle."

"Did he come alone?"

"Yes."

"What were those meetings about?"

"Both times it was to pass letters from his son that I smuggled out of the prison."

"Good, tell him you have another one," said Clarke.

"No," Matt said. "Tell him he has to sign papers for Wael's release, that he's getting out tomorrow. Tell him he has to agree to take custody of Wael."

"Here's your phone," Jack said. They had thoroughly searched Stryker both in their car and when they arrived at the Park Avenue apartment. "Call him. Tell him to meet you there at ten."

"What if he says no?"

"He won't," Matt said.

"What if he does?"

"He won't," Matt said. "Trust me."

"Put that thing down," Stryker said, looking at the meat cleaver.

"No," said McCann. "If you fuck around then the whole hand comes off."

"Don't miss," Goode said, edging his hand a bit north of Stryker's wrist, but continuing to apply the same pressure, if not more.

With his free hand, the white-haired—and now white-faced—lawyer took the phone from Jack McCann and began dialing.

45.

Queens, Friday, March 6, 2009, 9PM

"It's locked," said Michael. He had just returned from the men's room at Lucky's, where he had taken a moment to try the door at the end of the back hall that led down to the basement, the door that he and Adnan and Ali used to use when they took the tunnel from the building across the alley.

"Let's go," Antonio replied.

"No, we've only been here ten minutes."

"I don't want to wait."

"We have to. They know me. It won't look good."

"How long?"

"One more beer. Drink up."

"If you say so."

Michael nodded to Rex and pointed to the glasses in front of him and Antonio. Rex, smiling, began pouring two fresh beers from one of the taps arranged in the middle of the long bar. When he brought them over, Michael said, "Is Mustafa coming in? I have to talk to him."

"He's gone," the bartender answered. "Visiting his sick brother in Syria."

"When will he be back?"

"I don't know."

"Can you reach him?"

"I can try to get a message to him."

"Tell him I want to take the deal, but I want to speak to him first. He'll know what I'm talking about. Ask him to call me."

"Of course."

"What about Moe and Curley? Have they been around?"

"Moe and Curly?"

"The two guys who are always here. One has a funny beard, like the ace of spades. I think they work for Mustafa."

"What about them?"

"I'm just asking. Maybe they can reach Mustafa for me. I really need to talk to him."

"They're gone too," said Rex. He wasn't smiling now, but Michael didn't care. The whole Lucky's crew had betrayed him, starting with Adnan and Ali. Had made a fool of him, had framed him for murder.

"OK, thanks," Michael said. "I appreciate your help. I'll wait to hear from Mustafa."

"Why are we driving around Queens?" Antonio asked.

"I want to make sure we're not being followed."

Antonio remained silent. His mom kidnapped. Fuck. Could that really be?

"Keep checking your mirror," Michael said. "I'll pull over by that lot up there."

The vacant lot was surrounded by a chain link fence trampled down in two or three places, where locals had entered to strip an abandoned construction site of all moveable objects. Just a cinder block foundation, framed by rubble and strewn junk, including a muddy mattress and a twisted tricycle with no wheels. It was on a corner, meaning it had good views of cars coming from two sides.

"I should call the cops," Antonio said.

"My dad said not to."

"Why not?"

"I told you. They'll kill her."

"There's no one following us."

"OK," said Michael. He had been watching the traffic as far down both blocks as he could see. No one had stopped when they had, no one had circled the block. "One thing," he said.

"What?"

"We could get killed."

"You told me."

"I'm telling you again."

When they talked on the phone when he was in Florida, his mom had sounded funny to Antonio. A little different. After being the only man in her life for the last five years, since she divorced asshole number two, he could tell when something was different, when something was on her mind. Caught up in his own life, he had never asked her what that particular thing might be. A man? A case she was working on? Money? It was in her again last night. He should have asked her. "Tell me the plan," he said.

"We probably have to go in through a window. The tunnel has a light, but we won't turn it on."

"What kind of a tunnel? Can I stand in it?"

"It's a hallway, really. Yes you can stand. You might have to duck a little. How tall are you?"

"Six-five."

"The door to the basement opens behind an old wooden coal stall. We can check the room out and not be seen."

"What kind of a room?"

"A square room with junk in it, some shelves with junk on them. Old paint cans, shit like that."

"How big?"

"Not big, like the size of your bedroom. The ceiling's low, so you'll have to duck some more."

"Let's go," he said.

46.

Matteo, Sr. had taken Matt to the East Coast War Memorial on the day it was dedicated by President Kennedy in 1963. His father's brother Sabato, a merchant marine man lost in the North Atlantic in 1942, was one of the names inscribed on the eight stone slabs that flanked a bronze eagle on a raised semi-circular concrete platform at the north end of the park. Matt, one at the time, remembered nothing of the day. He liked to go to the dedications, Matteo, if he could. He went by himself to the dedication in 1951, by President Eisenhower, of the Marine Corps National Memorial in Washington. When Matt was ten, in 1972, his dad took him to see the Corp's Sunset Parade at the Memorial, featuring the Drum and Bugle Corps and the Silent Drill Platoon. *The flag flies every day here,* Matteo had said. *It's the only one.* In 1986 they went to the dedication of the Beirut Memorial at Camp Lejuene, where the tears fell like rain, including Matteo's. They were planning to go to the opening ceremony for the Korean War Memorial scheduled for July, 1993, when Matteo died. Matt went without him, but that was his last, until tonight. *Are you here, Pop?* he said to himself. *I hope so.*

"He's late," Matt thought. They had arrived early, he and Jack and Clarke and Stryker, in time to give the lawyer his simple instructions: *Stand there and wait, we'll do the rest,* and to post themselves as invisibly as they could. His watch now read 10:05. He was sitting on a bench under a copse of trees about fifty yards away, watching Stryker, who was standing next to the eagle, his hands in his pockets, the collar of his camel hair coat up. The eagle was lit by recessed ground lights, which formed a spotlight of sorts on Stryker. The wind off of New York Bay was up and whipping the lawyer's white hair into a froth. *A character out of Shakespeare,* Matt thought, *or a Greek tragedy, the king about to take a big fall.*

His gloved hand gripped the Ingram 19 in his coat pocket, produced nonchalantly by Jack McCann from the glove compartment of his unmarked car on the short ride down to the tip of Manhattan. *CB's got plenty of these,* Jack had said, smiling, holding his own Ingram to Stryker's ribs in the back seat. Jack and Clarke were in the trees behind the platform, also some fifty yards away. The starkly bare trees afforded little cover, but the night sky was filled with thick clouds, making the park beyond the cone of light around the eagle a dense, near-impenetrable black.

A bearded figure appeared, bulky in a short thick coat and a woolen cap, climbing the six or seven steps that swept visitors up to the memorial's promenade. He had appeared from Matt's right, seemingly out of nowhere, but then Matt realized he had been standing among the trees nearby all along, waiting in the same black cover as he and Jack and Clarke were, doing his own reconnaissance. Matt got to his feet and began walking toward the memorial. Jack and Clarke, he knew, were doing the same. He had taken only a few steps, still hidden by the night, when two other men appeared, from behind the stone slabs, and took up positions on either side of Mustafa and Stryker. Both were wearing dark leather overcoats. One was tall and thin, with a perfect V-shaped beard on his face, the other squat and full-bearded. Both had their hands in the pockets of their overcoats.

When Matt reached the steps he pulled his Ingram out

and stepped quickly onto the platform. "Hold it," he said, pointing the pistol at Mustafa and his two young soldiers. "Don't move." At almost the same moment, Jack and Clarke appeared, Jack from the right, Clarke from the left, their pistols in their hands, their arms extended. "Get down," Clarke shouted. "Down on the ground." He was about twenty steps away from the four men clustered under the bronze eagle, the ground lights on them as if they were players on a stage, frozen for a second, but waiting for a cue to perform. V-beard and his partner each drew pistols from their coat pockets, but before they could take aim, Matt began firing, as did Jack and Clarke. Mustafa pushed Stryker in front of him as this hell broke loose. In a matter of seconds, Mustafa, Stryker, V-beard and his partner were down, all shot in the chest, all dead.

"Leave your guns," said Jack. "Take theirs."

"Leave our guns?" Matt said.

"They're CB guns, Matt," said Clarke. "Untraceable."

"These two guys killed Mustafa and Stryker," Jack said, picking up a Glock 17 and placing his Ingram next to V-beard's gloved hand. "God knows why. That *is* Mustafa, isn't it?"

"Yes," Matt answered.

"Good, drop your gun next to him," said Clarke. Matt did as he was told, while Goode picked up full-beard's gun and replaced it with his own.

"Must have been a hell of a shoot out," said Jack, smiling his wicked smile.

47.

Michael and Antonio stopped at the door to Lucky's basement. They had groped the secret passage's rough stone wall in the pitch black, keeping their eyes on the rectangular line of light around the door at its far end. Standing still, trying not to breathe, they listened to the faint but unmistakable sound of rock music on the other side of the door. Turning the knob as silently as he could, Michael pushed the door open and they stepped quietly into the basement, finding themselves, as Michael had said, behind the seven-foot high wooden frame of a long abandoned coal stall. The music was louder now, coming from the opposite side of the room, which they could see was lit by an electric bulb in a wire cage hung between dirt-encrusted steel beams in the exposed ceiling. They crouched and waited for some other sound, but heard nothing.

Gesturing to Antonio to stay low, Michael stepped on the concrete foundation that held the stall and peered over the top plank. A man, about twenty, his eyes closed, his head against the wall to his right, an automatic rifle resting on his lap, was sitting on the bottom step of the open wooden staircase that led up to Lucky's back hallway. Next to him on an overturned plastic bucket was a transistor radio on which the Doors' *Light My Fire* was playing at low volume through the hiss of interspersed static. Michael scanned the room quickly, then crouched back behind the wooden wall. He mouthed *I don't see her* to Antonio, and was about to indicate that there was a man with a gun, when the teenager gripped the top of the stall and began to rise to look for himself. As he did, the top plank tore off with a loud crack. Plank in hand, Antonio ducked and froze, as did Michael. At first they heard only the music, but within a second or two came the unmistakable sound of footsteps approaching the coal bin. When they got close, Antonio sprung out and swung the plank full force, striking the guard, if that's what he was, in the side of the head, knocking him to the concrete floor and sending his rifle clattering across the room. Before the man could move, Antonio swung the plank again, this time hitting him square on the top of his head and knocking him out cold.

"He's out," Michael said. "Listen. Do you hear anything?"

They stood still for a second or two, looking down at the felled rifleman.

"No," Antonio said, finally. "Just the music."

"Is she here?" said Michael. They both looked around the room, which was filled with more junk than Michael had remembered. Dusty cases of old soda bottles were piled on the floor. Gallon paint cans, bags of grout and stacks of cracked ceramic tiles lined the shelves, a chipped sink covered with cobwebs sat in a corner. The smell of mold and must filled the air.

"What was he guarding if it wasn't her?" Antonio said.

"She has to be... *There.*" Michael pointed to a tattered blanket, army green, hanging over the space under the stairs. Antonio reached the spot in one long step, sweeping the blanket away to reveal Jade kneeling on a dirty mattress, her hands trussed behind her back to her feet, a bruise covering the whole of one side of her face, gagged, a towel tied around her eyes.

"*Mom,*" Antonio said, kneeling and taking her face in his hands. "Mom."

48.

Stoneridge, Saturday, March 7, 2009, 1PM

The Catamount Motel, with its apple orchard and pretty, oval pond, was set in a small hollow, surrounded by rocky, tree-covered outcroppings on all sides. On one of these out-croppings, behind a row of stunted mountain laurel, crouched Matt DeMarco and Basil al-Hassan. Both had field glasses to their eyes, which they had trained at the moment on the entrance of the motel's driveway on Route 12. Occasionally one or the other would swing his binoculars over to look at the door to Room 6, and then back again. The same strong wind that had riled Everett Stryker's thick white hair last night had swept away the clouds over the Hudson Valley, leaving a clear, pale blue sky through which the sun was shining brightly. The surrounding snow-clad fields and woods, the frozen pond, and the motel's low-pitched snow-covered roof were glistening with a liquid whiteness as the first warm sunlight in a month reached them.

Adnan Farah was not in Room 6. He had been there for the past three days, but was now on his way to Beirut at the request of the Dutch government. From conversations he had had with McCann and Goode, who had been summoned to the commissioner's office for a six AM meeting, Matt had learned that The Hague had not taken well the loss of the

Fuchs brothers, who had dedicated most of their lives to keeping The Netherlands safe. Apparently Josef and Wilem had been on the phone while they were holed up with Farah in Room 6 of the Catamount. The Dutch prime minister had called the Secretary-General of the UN, and persuaded him to demand that Farah, a suspect in the UN's investigation into the assassination of Rafik Hariri, be handed over to Monteverde, and that Erhard Fuchs' surveillance log be made available, as was Ehrhard's wish, to the Manhattan District Attorney. The US, officially in full support of the UN investigation, had agreed. *Bill Crow?* Jack had said, *He doesn't exist. Alec Mason? A suicide. That's a different league they play in, Matt.*

Someone high up in the US Justice Department had called Jon Healy, who had then moved, with undignified alacrity, to dismiss the charges against Michael.

Jade, who had been mistreated but not raped, was at Matt's house in Pound Ridge, resting. Michael and Antonio were there as well. Jack and Clarke had rounded up some off-duty NYPD officers to do protection duty. Many more than were needed had offered. Matt had called Crow several times, to try to lure him out, but his calls had gone to a dead phone. *Back into the woodwork*, Matt had said to himself, *with the other cockroaches.*

Which left Haq, the mastermind, the start of all the killing, the dead bodies all pointing back at him. Basil wanted him dead, and Matt, leaving Jack and Clarke out of it, had agreed to help the man who had posted Michael's bail and buried his mother, who had tried to help him rescue Jade, and who was a Muslim on the side of the angels in an Islamic world gone mad.

Early this morning a young Syrian associate of Hassan's had materialized in a beat-up van, wired the door to Room 6 with a quiet professionalism, and vanished in the space of thirty minutes. Then, Basil, through a maze of official and unofficial channels, had reached Haq, his countryman, his compatriot, and told him that he knew where Adnan Farah was and that he felt it his patriotic duty to inform him of the young technician's whereabouts. *He cannot move,* Basil had told Haq. *He is sick. He wants to talk to you, Colonel, only you. The people that were holding him have vanished. He says they told him many interesting things about the Hariri investigation, things he would like to pass along to you personally. He called me, but he won't speak to me, only to you or Mustafa, who has returned to Syria to be with his sick brother.*

Why would he believe you? Matt, who had heard Basil's end of the conversation, asked.

He thinks I am desperate, trying to curry favor, Basil had answered. *He cannot reach Mustafa. He may think his faithful servant has turned on him, that he has his own agenda.*

Freeing his son?

Yes. Adnan can expose him. I think he will come.

What if he doesn't show?

One way or another, I will need asylum.

They had taken up their position after the call to Haq. Three hours had passed. A few minutes ago, a pickup went by on Route 12, the only car they had seen all morning.

"We could just leave," said Matt. "The bomb will go off whether we're here or not."

"He may send someone else," said Basil. "I want..."

Before Basil could finish his sentence, the gleam of a car turning off Route 12 onto the Catamount's snow-covered driveway caught both of their eyes at the same time. They raised their binoculars to see a black Mercedes sedan with diplomatic plates churning slowly through the snow toward the motel, then stopping in front of Room 6. Three men got out, one from the front passenger side and the others from the back, all dressed like bankers in overcoats and wool scarves, and headed across the small concrete apron that ran along the front of the rooms. The driver stayed behind, pulling the large sedan forward into the motel's parking lot, where he began to make a sweeping U-turn in the snow. Matt followed the sedan with his binoculars for a second, then returned them to Room 6.

"Is one of them Haq?" he asked.

"Yes," Hassan replied. "The one on the right."

Matt could see that Haq was older, perhaps sixty, the other two younger, in their twenties. One of the young ones approached the door first, reached for the doorknob and began to turn it. Then all three disappeared in a ball of fire as Room 6 exploded, spewing smoke and burning debris out to a fifty-foot perimeter, some of it, still burning, landing on the hood of the sedan, which had come to a sudden stop in the middle of its U-turn. Matt and Basil watched as the Mercedes, snow spraying from the treads of its German-made tires, circled the ashen debris field, sped along the driveway and turned onto Route 12, disappearing quickly from view behind the tall pine trees that lined it.

"Let's go," Basil said, smiling, getting to his feet.

Then a shot rang out and the handsome Syrian was on the ground, a bullet hole, perfectly round, ringed with blood, in the middle of his forehead.

"Fuck," Matt said, throwing himself flat and bellying toward Hassan. "Basil?" he said, when he reached him, taking him by the arm and shaking him. Dead. "Fuck." Then another shot hit a tree behind him and another hit the small boulder he had been crouching behind. Staying on his stomach, Matt reached for his binoculars, crawled to a small opening between the boulder and the mountain laurel and took a look across the hollow, a distance of about a hundred yards. The sun was behind him, shining on the opposite rocky ledge. His eyes were drawn to a quick bright flash. Swinging the glasses toward it, he saw Bill Crow, on one knee, aiming a scoped rifle in his direction.

Looking around, Matt saw a laurel branch, narrow at the bottom but still leafed at the top, in the snow some ten feet away. He belly-crawled to it, and, reaching it, turned onto his back and pulled off his black Gore-Tex jacket. Still on his back, looking up through the trees to that pretty blue sky, he placed the leafy end of the branch inside his jacket, up near the collar. Taking hold of the other end, he raised the jacket and almost immediately a shot ripped through it above the breast pocket, where a person's heart would be. He pulled the jacket down, turned onto his belly again and elbowed his way back to the opening next to the boulder. He saw nothing, no flashes from a scope, no Crow. *No more moving,* he said to himself. *The sun's behind you, there won't be a reflection from your lens.* He reached into the back pocket of his jeans and pulled out the SIG P226 Jack had given him last night to replace the Ingram he had left at the War Memorial. *It's a present,* Jack had said, pulling the pistol from a case of un-numbered automatic and semi-automatic handguns that his friends in the Counterterrorism Bureau had given him. *You may still need it.*

Wait, he said to himself. *Wait until dark.*

But he didn't have to wait. There was Crow stepping down from his rock perch, his rifle slung over his shoulder. When he reached the pond, Matt, still fully prone, extended his arms, cradled the SIG and aimed it at Crow's feet. *It'll kick like a motherfucker,* McCann had said. *Aim low, keep it on automatic. The rounds will spray upward.* When Crow was almost to his side of the pond, Matt pulled firmly on the trigger, then watched as the Native American with the large chip on his shoulder, the chip that had killed him, pitched forward onto the ice, slid a few feet and came to a stop, his arms and legs splayed out like he was skydiving. Skydiving and bleeding at the same time, the ice around him turning a deep shimmering crimson.

Epilogue

The thumping sound from the driveway re-announced itself when Matt turned off the water after rinsing the last of the lunch dishes. Except for that, the house and the whole neighborhood was quiet, as it always was in Pound Ridge. Peaceful. The boys had devoured the potatoes and eggs and hot peppers he had made and served with thick slices of Italian bread, and then gone out and shoveled the last of the snow off the half-court he had laid out eight years ago. The court had never been used, and neither had the Wilson ball that Michael retrieved from a utility closet in the garage. The day was clear and sunny and warm, the first touch of spring in the air. Jade was out buying food for dinner.

Last night in bed, she had told him about her conversation with Antonio.

He cried, Matt. He said it wasn't right that my life was so hard. Only God can judge, he said. He said he knew that's why I went to church all the time, to ask God for something. He said he would make my life better. He promised he would.

He's a good kid, Matt had said, holding Jade close, hoping that her porn movies, a teenaged lapse of judgment that she saw as her big sin, were behind her at last. *We punish ourselves,*

Matteo used to say. *We make the stick from hard wood and pick it up and use it until God takes it from our hand.*

In his bedroom office, Matt made a fire, then sat and turned to the two weeks' worth of mail that he had pulled from his mailbox last night. He sorted it, threw away the junk stuff, then opened the bills, putting them aside for payment. From here, through the window at his desk alcove, he could see the boys playing. Michael was no match for Antonio, but he didn't seem to understand that. He kept crouching, hustling, dogging the taller and much more graceful and naturally athletic teenager, making him work for every basket. When he had the ball, Michael was equally blind to his own lack of talent. Using his elbows like pistons he somehow managed to score twice while Matt was watching, to Antonio's seven buckets. Not bad for a kid with soccer legs and no jumping ability. Antonio, for his part, was not taking Michael lightly. He scowled as much as he smiled at his much smaller opponent's tenacity. *I think they like each other.*

After the bills, there was only one item left, a padded brown envelope with Debra's Park Avenue return address in the upper left corner. *Debra, what are you sending me?* In the sixteen years they had been divorced she had never sent him so much as a note, not even a sarcastic one. Inside were two DVDs in white, unlabeled sleeves, and a note, in Debra's hand, on beautiful cream-colored paper with her initials embossed in flowing script on top. He picked up the envelope he had just torn open to look at the postmark. March 3rd, the day she killed herself. Outside, the thumping continued. He could hear Antonio laugh and say something to Michael.

He read the note first:

Matt,

> *Please tell Michael not to plead guilty to anything. The enclosed videos prove his innocence. There is another video that may come out after*

I'm gone. So be it. You don't owe me anything, not after I turned Michael against you, but I'm asking you, for his sake, to defend me. What I did was very bad, but I would have stopped Adnan and Ali. I was planning to. Blame it on my drugs. They made me more paranoid, not less, more insecure, not less. I was hallucinating, playing out a secret wish that I knew I could stop at any moment. Mustafa tricked me, and used Adnan and Ali for his own purposes. When I told him to put a stop to it, he told me they could not be reached. He said they had run away with the money. And then it happened, and I entered hell.

One more thing, tell Michael about the day we met, the person I used to be, that we loved each other once. And that I will always love him.

Debra
March 3, 2009

He slipped the first DVD into the slot on the TV on the shelf to the right of his desk and pushed the play button. After some static and a gray screen, Adnan and Ali appeared, knocking on the door to an apartment with the number 1102 on it. The date and time were running digitally along the bottom left. *January 30, 2009, 1:18 PM, 1:19 PM . . .* Yasmine Hayek let them in, and the short video came to an abrupt end. *You must have stolen this from Mustafa,* Matt said out loud, *that took some heart.*

He ejected the first DVD, inserted the second one and pushed the play button again, expecting a continuation of the first tape, perhaps Adnan and Ali coming out of Yasmine's apartment. Again the static and again the gray screen, but now there was Debra, sitting at a desk in an office somewhere, a small, feminine study. Park Avenue, most likely. Adnan and

Ali were standing across from her. And there was sound.

Sit, Debra said. She was impeccably dressed, as usual. Her long dark hair framed her handsome face, as usual. But something about her was not as usual, something that chilled Matt's heart as he sat and watched.

As you wish, Mrs. The two young killers sat on chairs with flower print cushions facing his ex-wife.

Have you considered my offer?

Yes.

Are you willing to do this for me?

Yes.

Adnan, the smart one, was doing the talking.

Here, Debra said. *There's ten thousand dollars there.* She handed a thick brown envelope across the desk. Adnan took it.

Do you know where she lives, the Excelsior, apartment 1102?

Yes, we know.

Do you have your tickets?

Yes.

I do not wish to see you again, ever.

As you wish, Mrs.

The date and time ran across the bottom of this DVD as well, January 25, 2009, 5:02 PM. 5:03PM . . .

Matt ejected the DVD and brought it with him to the window at his desk. The thumping had stopped. Michael and Antonio were sitting on the ground, back to back, against the steel post that held the backboard. Michael's face was flushed and he was laughing. Antonio was smiling and shaking his head. Jade was pulling into the driveway. The boys got up and began to help her unload the groceries.

Matt took the second DVD and the note and brought them over to the fireplace, where the fire was crackling, giving off a warmth he did not feel. *Debra,* he said, pressing the thumb and index finger of his free hand to his eyes, seeing his ex-wife's face, young and beautiful, on the day they met in 1987, and then on the day she killed herself, when he told her about Mustafa's secret taping; death, the idea of suicide, in her eyes. *Debra.*

Then he threw the note and the DVD into the fire, and watched them ignite, melt and disappear.

About the Author

James LePore is an attorney who has practiced law for more than two decades. He is also an accomplished photographer. He lives in South Salem, NY with his wife, artist Karen Chandler. He is the author of three other novels, *A World I Never Made*, *Blood of My Brother*, and *Sons and Princes*, as well as a collection of three short stories, *Anyone Can Die*. You can visit him at his website, www.jamesleporefiction.com.